TOMORROW

THERE WILL

BE SUN

TOMORROW THERE WILL BE SUN

DANA REINHARDT

Pamela Dorman Books · Viking

VIKING
An imprint of Penguin Random House LLC
1745 Broadway
New York, New York 10019
penguinrandomhouse.com

A Pamela Dorman Book/Viking

LIBRARY OF CONGRESS CATALOGING-IN-PUBLICATION DATA
Names: Reinhardt, Dana, author.
Title: Tomorrow there will be sun: a novel / Dana Reinhardt.
Description: New York, New York: Pamela Dorman Books, 2019.
Identifiers: LCCN 2018028214 (print) | LCCN 2018033006 (ebook) |
ISBN 9780525557975 (ebook) | ISBN 9780525557968 (hardback)
Subjects: LCSH: Families—Fiction. | Vacations—Fiction. | Trust—Fiction. |
Puerto Vallarta (Mexico)—Fiction. | Domestic fiction. |
BISAC: FICTION / Family Life. | FICTION / Contemporary Women. |
FICTION / Literary. | GSAFD: Humorous fiction.
Classification: LCC PS3618.E564555 (ebook) |
LCC PS3618.E564555 T66 2019 (print) | DDC 813/.6—dc23
LC record available at https://lccn.loc.gov/2018028214

Printed in the United States of America
1 3 5 7 9 10 8 6 4 2

Set in Berling LT Std
Designed by Meighan Cavanaugh

For my father

WITH PROFOUND THANKS

To Pamela Dorman, editor extraordinaire, and Jeramie Orton for asking all the right questions and for their patience while I tried to find the answers. And to Brian Tart, Andrea Schulz, Kate Stark, Lindsay Prevette, Roseanne Serra, Alison Klooster, Mary Stone, Allison Carney and the rest of the Viking/Penguin team for all of their hard work on behalf of this book.

To Douglas Stewart for his many years of guidance and friendship and for always being the very best person with whom to discuss ideas even when they are in their most inchoate form. And to Szilvia Molnar and Danielle Bukowski at Sterling Lord Literistic and Jason Richman at UTA for their support and encouragement.

To Lara Bazelon, Deborah Bishop, Deborah Goodman, Chelsea Hadley, Daniel Handler, Juliette Kayyem, Rima Lyn, Laura McNeal, Tom McNeal, Diane Merkadeau, Carmen Naranjo, Christopher Noxon, Justin Reinhardt, Janice Ricciardi, Stephanie Rubin, Ann Sokatch and Daniel Sokatch for reading early drafts of this book and offering invaluable feedback and insight.

TOMORROW

THERE WILL

BE SUN

VILLA AZUL PARAISO

Bienvenido a casa, or "welcome home," to this exquisite private villa built for comfort as well as unsurpassed luxury, situated on the sparkling blue Bay of Banderas. Since its construction in the 1960s, Villa Azul Paraiso has been Puerto Vallarta's exclusive address for lavish parties and weddings. It has housed the rich and famous, from Richard Burton to Martha Stewart, and has served as the premier vacation destination for many foreign dignitaries, including the former US president Richard M. Nixon. You might even recognize Villa Azul Paraiso from its appearance in season four of the hit reality TV show *For Love or Lust: South of the Border*.

With four levels of expansive living, five en suite bedrooms, three living rooms, a swimming pool and a rooftop Jacuzzi, there is plenty of space to spread out and come together again with your nearest and dearest. Our warm and highly dedicated staff will prepare delicious, authentic meals and see to it that your every need is met. Come, stay with us, soak up the abundant sun and leave your troubles at home.

SATURDAY

A perfectly prepared margarita (rocks, salt, subtle with the triple sec, less so with the tequila) placed in your hand when you didn't even ask, with an itty-bitty half lime floating up top, something local, grown just down the street where the patchy pavement gives way to dirt, which then surrenders to jungle, can almost take the edge off a day of truly shitty airport mishaps. Let's not recount them. Airport mishaps are dull. They're like dreams. We convince ourselves that ours are pot-boilers, cliffhangers, whodunits. They're not. And yet, despite the entirely predictable debacle that was our direct flight from LAX to PVR, in business class no less because those were the only seats left for which we could use miles and so drained our entire account, we still managed to arrive at Villa Azul Paraiso before the Solomons.

They should have been here more than an hour ago, so I'm sure they'll breeze in any minute dying to share their own travel horror stories. But if Roberto—who greeted us in a freshly pressed white zip-up coat that looks like it belongs to a doctor, not the house manager of a luxury Mexican beach rental—hands them margaritas of the same caliber as the one I am currently sipping, perhaps they'll get distracted and spare us the details.

Clementine and Peter have gone off exploring. The villa's wide whitewashed open corridors stretch out in either direction. There are two bedrooms to the right and three to the left, including the master with the rain forest shower and soaking tub carved from volcanic rock. They all have views of the ocean. Every inch of this house does. It's built tall, wide and shallow, with no walls on the ocean side save for the bedrooms, and built on a curve that matches that of the private beach below. The kitchen and dining room sit one floor down. Up a flight is a deck with a hot tub and chairs for stargazing. And on the ground floor: Ping-Pong tables—two of them in case you want to get a proper tournament going—and the swimming pool. I'm standing in the villa's main living room. It's one of three, and the only one with comfortable furniture. I know all of this because I studied the website for this place like I was studying for the GREs, which is the last time I studied for anything.

Clem comes bounding in, bikini clad, demonstrating the kind of enthusiasm I was hoping for when we first told her about this trip to celebrate her father's fiftieth. But she had quickly calculated that this trip meant she wouldn't see Sean or her friends for seven whole days, and that those seven whole days would fall on spring break, when there would be parties or hangouts that she would never recover from missing, and she didn't much care that every room has ocean views, or that every bedroom has its own bathroom, or that there would be three meals a day prepared by a full-time staff.

Except for the ocean views, this pretty much summed up her life back at home.

"The wi-fi here is sick," she says. "I sent Sean a pic of the view from my room and he texted back, like, in seconds."

"What did he say?"

She ignores my question. It was a dumb one, but I'm tired from the airline snafus and I'm sucking up the last few drops of a midday margarita, so admittedly, I'm a little off my game.

"I'm going to go lie by the pool."

The pool is only ten feet from the beach, and there's a faucet to wash the sand off your feet before you dive in so you don't clog the drain. I walk to the balcony to take a look. Yep, there it is: two floors below, shaped like a kidney, with six cushioned loungers and palapa umbrellas that won't provide the kind of UV protection my nearly albino daughter needs.

"Sunblock," I say.

"Duh," she replies and trails off down the central staircase.

Roberto returns with a pitcher. "More for you? And one for the mister?"

Why not? I let him fill my glass halfway so it'll look like I'm still nursing my first margarita when Peter returns from escorting our bags to the master bedroom. I take one for him, too, even though he's more of a bourbon guy.

"*Muchas gracias,*" I tell Roberto. He smiles, nods and disappears.

I stand at the railing and take in the vast blue of the ocean and a deep breath of the warm perfumed air. I look down at Clem who sits in a chair with her back to the beach, staring at her phone.

Peter comes up behind me, kisses my shoulder and takes the margarita from my hand. "FaceTime with Sean?"

"No doubt."

"What could they possibly have left to say to each other?"

"I can't imagine."

He takes a long sip of his drink. His shirt is soaked through with sweat. "Ahh. This is nice."

"Did you check out the volcanic tub?"

"No. That sounds unpleasant."

"You don't bathe in lava. It's volcanic rock. It's supposed to be good for the pH balance in your skin. Or something."

"Got it."

"It's in the master bath. Along with the rain forest shower."

"Oh. I didn't really look. I put our bags in the bedroom that way." He points to the right. "It has a gorgeous view."

"Every room has a gorgeous view. That's the whole thing about this house." I point to the left. "But the master is that way. Quick—let's grab it before they get here." I start to make my way toward the left-wing bedrooms even though I already know how this is going to end, and it is not going to end with me soaking in a volcanic tub.

"I thought we'd leave that one for Solly and Ingrid."

"You did?"

"Jen." He's already defensive.

I have a choice. I can point out that we are paying exactly 50 percent of the not insubstantial rent on this house. I can point out that I'm the one who found this particular villa, that Ingrid sent links to places shy a bedroom or with half-mile hikes down treacherous cliffs to unswimmable beaches. I can point out that even though Peter is six months older than his best friend and business partner, he defers to Solly like a browbeaten younger brother. I can point out that the Solomons vacation far more often than we do and never spare expense; that luxury like this is commonplace to them, and so we deserve that fucking rain forest shower and volcanic tub because it will be fucking special to us.

In short, I could choose to start an epic battle a mere fifteen minutes into our holiday.

Instead I say, "But it's *your* fiftieth birthday."

"Solly's, too," he replies.

I don't say any more. This trip is meant to celebrate both, but Solly's birthday isn't until October and Peter's is on Wednesday, and any way you cut it, it's just not the same, and we both know it.

"And besides"—he rubs my arm a little—"that side has the three bedrooms so the boys won't need to share. It makes more sense like this."

I also don't point out that Ivan, who's five years old, still sleeps with his parents. And that even though Ingrid claims he stopped breast-feeding last summer, I suspect he still sneaks in a good suck in the middle of the night when Solly's fast asleep.

I sigh. "Fine."

Peter leans in for a kiss. "You're the best."

Just as this peace is forged, the bell chimes. Once. Twice. Then Solly's thunderous voice: "Hellooooo? Anybody home?"

Roberto opens the door balancing a tray of margaritas. The taxi driver is there, too, helping with the luggage. Seven bags for the four of them. Solly peels a few bills from a large roll of pesos he has stuffed in his pocket. I read in our guidebook that it isn't customary to tip taxi drivers unless they go the extra mile, like helping you with luggage or unloading groceries, and in that case a few dollars should suffice. Though I'm still working out the exchange rate, I can tell from the driver's face as he accepts the cash that Solly didn't read about, or doesn't care about, what's customary.

Ingrid passes on the drink, but Solly takes his and downs half of it before coming straight for me, arms outstretched.

"Hello, gorgeous." He squeezes a little too hard, but that's the Solly way. His hair is expertly gelled. His light blue linen shirt is dry and crisp, like he ducked into the airport lounge for a shower and shave. He steps back, takes in the view and raises his drink before polishing off the rest of it. "Hello, beautiful house! Hello, dream vacation! Hello, second half century of life!"

Solly and Peter embrace and slap backs. Peter kisses Ingrid on both cheeks. Ivan lets me pick him up and he hands me some sort of LEGO robot for inspection before quickly snatching it back again. Ingrid's long dangly earring gets caught in my hair and it takes Solly's help to untangle us. All the while, Malcolm stands on the perimeter, fumbling through his backpack.

I haven't seen Malcolm since my last trip to New York to visit Maureen nearly two years ago. He's grown a half foot and now sports facial hair that, despite its haphazard look, is probably carefully curated. He's still got the same big, sad eyes.

"Hi, Malcolm."

He looks up from his bag and gives me a shy smile. He takes a few tentative steps toward me, and in an effort to minimize his suffering, I keep the hug quick and businesslike, trying not to give anything away about how it feels to see the little boy I used to know suddenly standing before me a full-grown man at seventeen.

Look, I have a daughter who is right now sitting by the pool filling out a bikini in the most enviable way when it was only yesterday she paired a striped Hanna Andersson tent dress with polka dot leggings. Change happens. I know it all too well.

"I want a snack."

Ingrid crouches down so she's eye level with Ivan. "Let's get settled in and then we'll get you something pronto. Okay?"

"Ding dong."

Ingrid looks from Ivan to me with an apologetic shrug. "It's something he just says sometimes. I'm not sure why."

"I want a snack now," Ivan whines. "I'm huuungry."

Roberto reappears, this time with a bowl of chips, some guacamole and a plate of sliced mango. He's with another man: younger, shorter, heavier and wearing the same white zip-up coat, only his is slightly dingy.

"Please. I will help you with the bags," the younger man says, grabbing two in each hand.

Peter points toward the bedrooms to the left. "Let's take them that-a-way."

Solly sticks out his hand. "Hi there. I'm Solly."

The man puts two of the bags down and wipes his palm on his jacket. "Enrique."

"Enrique. Nice to meet you. Thank you for your help." Solly reaches for the roll of cash again. Enrique is going to be waiting on us for the next seven days. He is part of the villa's staff. We are expected to leave a generous tip at the end of our stay, not to press pesos into his palm every time he lends a helping hand.

"Solly," I whisper. "Put the money away."

Solly shrugs and stuffs the wad into his pocket. He looks to Peter and points to the left. "This-a-way?"

"Three bedrooms," Peter says. "Plenty for everyone."

"Grand."

"Grand," Ivan mimics. His mouth is stuffed with mango, juice running down his chin.

The men, including Malcolm, take the bags toward the bedrooms, leaving Ingrid, Ivan and me standing in the living room.

"What a view. Ivan, honey, isn't this a lovely view?"

"I don't like views," he says.

We go to sit down. Ivan climbs into Ingrid's lap and wipes his sticky hands on the floral cushions.

"You wouldn't believe our day," Ingrid begins.

Ingrid and I have managed to forge something resembling a real friendship. I wasn't sure this would be possible given how close Maureen and I were, and given the fact that Ingrid is eighteen years younger than Solly, but more important, she's fifteen years younger than me. When Solly took up with her, I was forty. She was twenty-five: an entirely different species. But now she's thirty-two and she's a mother, and the vast echoing gulf between us has contracted, even if I still sometimes hold her impossibly thin limbs and perfect skin against her.

"Malcolm didn't get in from New York until two a.m. That's two o'clock in the morning!"

"Yes, Ingrid. I know what *a.m.* means." She laughs, which I'm glad about, because I was going for funny, but instead it came out bitchy.

"Maureen, in her infinite wisdom, booked his ticket on the last flight out of JFK. It was due in at one-fifteen but it was forty-five minutes late. Not that it makes such a difference at that hour. I mean, a quarter past one in the morning isn't exactly a reasonable time to collect someone from the airport to begin with. Solly went to pick him up, of course, and when they got back to the house Django started barking and then freaked out when he saw it was Malcolm, so much so that he peed all over the foyer, and the chaos woke Ivan, who isn't the best sleeper under ideal circumstances." Ivan turns around in her lap and shoots her a proud grin. She pats his head. "So Maureen got exactly what she wanted. We're all exhausted and cranky."

Ingrid typically doesn't rag on Maureen in front of me out of deference to what was once a tight allegiance, but the truth is it's hard to maintain a close friendship from clear across the country, especially when one friend is spending so much time with the other friend's ex-husband's new wife.

"Sounds hellish," I say.

"Indeed."

"You know what would help?"

"What?"

I lift up my empty margarita glass. "One of these."

"Oh, no. I can't. I'm not drinking."

When you are thirty-two, and you are a woman, and you suddenly stop drinking, it can mean only one thing.

"Are you . . . ?" I look at her belly, hidden behind Ivan, who has his thumb in his mouth and the kind of heavy-lidded blank stare kids get seconds before falling asleep.

She looks down at her midsection and then back up at me. "Oh, no. No, no, no. Not that. I have my hands full already with this one." She gives Ivan a squeeze. He snuggles deeper into her embrace, and then he's out.

Having never had a boy, I think all boys are handfuls. I'm not saying Clementine was a perfect child, but she played quietly with toys that mimicked real life—houses, buses, schools, farms and little plastic figures to inhabit these places, onto which her primary goal seemed to be imposing a sense of order. When Ivan or other boys play, they typically want to smash, crush and kill. This is a big generalization, I know, but look at that cushion. Clem never would have wiped her sticky hands on a couch cushion. She would have reached into my bag for a wet wipe or found a sink, or, more likely, she would have skipped the mango altogether because she hated few things more than having sticky hands.

"I'm on a new health regimen." Ingrid kicks off her clogs and pivots on the couch, moving Ivan with her, bringing her long legs up and stretching them out. Her toes are painted sky blue. I meant to get a pedicure before leaving, but we needed a new suitcase, and Clem needed a new bathing suit, and I had to arrange for someone to feed the cat, and also there's the matter of my book deadline that came and went two months ago. "My nutritionist has me off sugar and alcohol."

I don't understand why you'd need to hire a nutritionist to tell you to avoid sugar and alcohol. That seems like basic, entry-level stuff. "She took you off sugar and alcohol right before a vacation?"

"It's a he. And it's been a few weeks, actually."

"But . . . why?" I also don't understand why someone with Ingrid's body would consult a nutritionist in the first place.

"Oh, just general health. I've been tired. Lacking energy. A little foggy." I want to say—*Welcome to your thirties*, or *Welcome to motherhood*, or *Just wait, it only gets worse*—but after my last comment, I don't trust myself to sound appropriately jokey. "He's got me on proteins and limited complex carbohydrates," she continues. "I think it's actually working."

Whatever Ingrid is or isn't drinking, is or isn't eating, shouldn't have any impact whatsoever on my capacity to fully embrace my *fuck it I'm on vacation* attitude and fulfill my destiny of gaining five pounds in the next seven days.

"Well, that's good," I say. "At least it's working."

"And it's been great for my writing," she says, managing to braid her hair expertly while lying down beneath a sleeping child. "My word count has been off the charts since I started. Or at least off the charts for me. I know there are people who do three thousand words a day and I'll never be one of those people, but I'm hitting almost a thousand, even on the days when I have to pick up Ivan early from preschool, so for that alone it's been worth the deprivation."

It never takes Ingrid long to bring up writing. It's my cue to offer advice as the seasoned YA novelist with three books published and a fourth that's two months overdue. But I haven't written anything in ages so my word count is roughly zero, and also, I'd do anything to delay the inevitable ask of *would I con-*

sider sending the draft of her book to my agent when she's done, so I change the subject.

"Why is it that all children look like angels when they're sleeping?" I nod toward Ivan. It's true. His shaggy blond hair frames his face, his cheeks red from heat, his long dark lashes, the blue-gray tint of his eyelids. It occurs to me that I haven't seen Clem's closed eyelids in years. I no longer know what she looks like when she sleeps.

Ingrid laughs. "Because looks are deceiving."

I'M A BIG BELIEVER in unpacking. I don't care if the vacation is for only one night; I always put my clothes away in drawers, my toiletries into bathroom cabinets, and my suitcase in a hidden spot so it can't serve as a reminder that too soon it will need repacking.

Peter does not share this compulsion. He'd live out of a suitcase for months. The upshot is that I inevitably end up unpacking for him because the sight of his suitcase is just as disruptive to me as the sight of my own.

Once I have everything put away neatly and our luggage tucked under the bed, I change into my tankini and the new pink gauzy cover-up I bought when I took Clem bathing suit shopping at Nordstrom. The department where she found her suit and I found the cover-up is for "juniors," but I convinced myself I could pull it off by choosing to take Clem's silence as approval.

I put the expensive sunblock on my face and the cheap stuff on my body. My complexion tends toward olive, yet I try and model sun safety for my daughter who gets her fairness from her father. More than a few times when Clementine was younger I was mistaken for the nanny. People saw my dark hair and brown eyes and my pale golden child, and things just didn't add up. Now that she's older, and she is getting my high cheekbones, I can see the ways in which she is starting to look (just a little) like a more beautiful version of me. But Clem rejects this observation wholeheartedly.

I finish by applying the sunblock to the tops of my feet, the one place I do tend to burn, and then reach into the drawer for a hair band before remembering that although I didn't get that pedicure, I did manage to get my hair cut just short enough that I can't wear it up anymore. I told my stylist to go for something a little edgy, but instead I walked out with a full-on suburban-mom bob.

Peter is lying on the bed, reading his book, still in his clothes from the flight. His eyes look like Ivan's did just before he passed out with his thumb in his mouth.

"Aren't you going to come down to the pool?" I ask.

"Eventually."

"But everyone is headed there."

He puts his book down on his chest. He looks me up and down. "I like that thingy you're wearing."

"It's a cover-up."

"Come here." I walk closer. He takes the edge and lifts it, examining my tankini underneath. "I like the suit, too. You didn't wear the one I hate. The one with the built-in skirt that looks like something my mother would wear."

"I didn't even pack it. Happy birthday."

He smiles, takes my wrist and pulls me down onto the bed

next to him. His shirt is still damp with sweat and he smells. "Take a nap with me."

"Come to the pool with me." I try to wriggle out of his embrace, but he has me in a tight lock.

"You're a bully," he says.

"And you're lazy."

"And a little bit misanthropic. Don't forget that." He kisses me quickly with the first hint of what will be a full beard by the time our week comes to an end. Forget a five o'clock shadow— Peter grows stubble by noon, and he didn't bother to shave yesterday in anticipation of our trip. His beard will come in white, just like his thick head of hair. He went white before I met him, somewhere in his early twenties, so he long ago made his peace with it. I don't tolerate it on my own head—I packed a brown touch-up stick for my roots that looks like a lipstick and doesn't really work—but I do love *his* white hair. I always have.

"Want one?" Peter is holding out a half-eaten pack of Life Savers. Butter rum. My favorite flavor. Peter always buys a pack of Life Savers for each of us before we board a flight. It's a strange superstition he inherited from his grandmother that we have fully adopted in our family. We suck on them as the plane takes off and believe that this small act guarantees us safe passage.

I open my mouth and he pops one in.

"Hey," he whispers in my ear. "Do you think Richard Nixon did it with Pat in this bed?"

"I'm pretty sure when Richard Nixon stayed here he got the master suite with the rain forest shower and volcanic tub."

Peter gives me a little shove and I stand up. I grab my hat and sunglasses. "I'm going to go sit by the pool."

"I'll be down in a few." I know this means it'll be at least an hour, probably more. He'll nap, he'll spend an inordinately long time in the bathroom, he'll probably pick up the *New Yorker* from the desk where I left a copy and stand in the middle of the bedroom reading an article from beginning to end. It doesn't matter. This is vacation, and the whole purpose of this particular sort of vacation is that there is no corralling to do. Everyone can and should move about at his or her own pace. Except for showing up to the dinner table at the agreed-upon hour, there is nowhere anybody has to be at any particular time.

"No hurry," I say. He likes this. The vacation version of me. He takes a pillow from my side of the bed, props it under his head and goes back to his book.

CLEM IS STILL STARING at her phone, but she's not on Face-Time with Sean, she's scrolling through whatever app she's into these days. She doesn't ever email, or use Facebook, because, as she's pointed out, *"I'm not, like, a hundred years old."* I follow her on Instagram and Snapchat. There are YouTubers whose channels she subscribes to and sites she combs for deals on vintage T-shirts. She still texts with some of her friends and obviously with Sean, but I notice that she texts far less frequently than she used to. I've learned from reading about teenagers, which I do because I have one and because writing about them is my vocation, that there are new apps and sites and ways to communicate and share information that I can't see or uncover, even though, like any good parent, I try to keep a close eye on everything she does online.

Solly is the only other person down at the pool. He's sporting a straw fedora and American flag swim trunks. He has a fresh margarita and some sort of toasted sandwich on a plate with tortilla chips.

"It's a torta," he says, holding it out toward me. "And it might be the most delicious thing I've ever put in my mouth. I stopped in the kitchen. I met Luisa. She doesn't speak English and I don't speak Spanish but I was able to communicate, through the international language of gesturing to my stomach and making a pouty face, that I was nursing a monster hunger. And so she whipped this up for me and changed my life forever because, I'm telling you: She is a fucking magician. Here. Have a bite. Don't ask me what's in it because I don't know and I don't care."

"He tried to get me to taste it, too, and I was, like, *ewww*," Clem says without looking up from her phone.

I walk over to Solly and I take a bite of his sandwich. He's right. It's delicious.

"Shall I have my new best friend, Luisa, make you one?"

I look at my watch. It's 3:15. In an email exchange with the rental company we settled on dinner for our first night to be served at 6:30. I figured we'd all be tired from traveling and might want to turn in early.

"No, thanks."

I want to bug Clem to put down her phone, to make eye contact and conversation, to maybe turn her chair around to face the gorgeous private beach and calm waters of the bay, but I decide to give her a one-day pass. Good for today only. Tomorrow I will nag. I will threaten to take the phone away. I will hand her one of the three YA novels I brought along that I know she'd love if she'd only give them a try. None of them was written by me, because I know how she feels about my books, but two of the titles are by writers I know a little bit, and they are all three about teen love and angst, which she's in the thick of with Sean, so she'll relate. She's the kind of kid who wants a mirror in a book rather than a window. Assuming, of course, she wants the book at all.

"Jenna, you've outdone yourself. My hat is off to you." Solly takes his hat off, then puts it back on again. "This place is spectacular."

"Thanks, Sol." I settle into the chair next to him, across the shallow end of the kidney from Clem. "You only turn fifty once."

"Thank God for that." He lowers his lounge chair and turns his face up to the sun. "You know . . . I've been thinking . . . as I reach this midpoint in my life—"

"Midpoint? Just how long are you planning on living, Solly?"

"Don't be a buzz kill. I know that's hard for you, but try, okay?" He squeezes my knee affectionately. "As I was saying, as I reach this midpoint in my life, I realize that *these* are the moments that matter. Time with the people I love the most. In a place that is beautiful. With a sandwich that's sublime. What could possibly be better?"

"Aw, fucknuggets." Clem tosses her phone onto the towel by her feet. "The wi-fi is down."

"Clementine. Language."

"Please, Mom. Spare me. Solly just dropped an F bomb, like, thirty seconds ago."

"You're sixteen. Solly is fifty."

"Solly is still forty-nine!" He raises a toast with what's left of his margarita.

Malcolm unlatches the gate from the beach. I'd assumed he was holed up in his room, probably on a device similar to Clem's, but no, he's already been out for a walk. He's holding a starfish in his hand.

"Whatcha got there, champ?" Solly asks.

I think I see Malcolm bristle a little. After all, he's seventeen. Not five. And Solly's forced camaraderie can annoy anyone, so why shouldn't it annoy the son he sees only twice a year, the son for whom he's done little to earn that camaraderie?

Malcolm holds up the starfish. "It's for Ivan. I thought he'd like it."

"Oh, he will. Knowing him, he'll probably try throwing it like one of those Japanese star-shaped weapon things."

"A *shuriken.*"

"A what?"

I'm about to tell Malcolm to rinse his feet so the pool won't clog, but I don't need to. He's already found the faucet and he's doing it on his own.

"A *shuriken.* That's what those Japanese star-shaped weapon things are called."

"Look who's a smarty-pants."

"I take martial arts, Dad."

"Of course. Of course. I know that."

"Clem? Did you say hello to Malcolm?" I ask. "It's been a long time since you two have seen each other. You know, you used to bathe together."

"Yeah, Mom, you've only mentioned that, like, a thousand times. And I saw him earlier on his way out. Of course I said hello."

"She did," Malcolm says. "I can confirm it. And I can confirm that I said hello back. And I can also confirm that we used to bathe together, because my mom has a picture of us in the bath."

It's nice to hear that this old picture of the kids survived Maureen's move to her new apartment with her new boyfriend, Bruno, whom she has told me she will never marry because marriage is bullshit.

"I know that picture," Clem says. "We have it, too. You had an Afro."

I'm not sure it's still okay to say *Afro*, especially in the presence of someone whose mother is African American, so I shoot Clem a look.

"Why are you staring at me like that?"

"Nothing. Never mind."

"Because I said *Afro*? For your information, Mother, *Afro* is not a bad word."

Malcolm laughs and rubs his hand over his short-cropped curls. "That *was* an epic Afro."

"Yeah, but . . . I think I like your hair better now," Clem says, looking at him from behind her sunglasses. He's shirtless, with baggy khakis rolled up to his knees. He's lean, but muscled, with a tattoo on his right calf, some kind of swirling pattern in black ink that barely stands out against his light brown skin. I can't believe he got it with Maureen's approval. Can you get a tattoo without parental approval? I make a mental note to look that up.

Malcolm takes the chair next to Clem, turning it around so he's facing the ocean. She gets up and turns hers around, too.

"It's nice to see them together again," Solly says. "Feels like the old days."

EVERYONE SHOWS UP TO DINNER on time. The table is set with multicolored napkins, blue and white Talavera pottery plates and a large pitcher filled with birds-of-paradise. I wear the nicest dress I packed, the one I planned on saving for Peter's birthday on Wednesday. I bring my pashmina in case I'm not warm enough. I worried about all this openness when I studied the website. Doesn't it ever get cold? What about rain? The description said only something vague about the house being built for comfort as well as unsurpassed luxury, which I took to mean that nobody is going to freeze to death at Villa Azul Paraiso.

Roberto and Enrique stand ready to take our drink orders, freshly slicked back hair and tropical flowers pinned to the collars of their white coats.

"Please." Roberto gestures to the open balcony. "Enjoy the sunset and the appetizers before we sit down for the dinner."

I suppose I should make very clear here that this is not a level of service with which I have any sort of familiarity. At home, I prepare our dinners. Peter can step in if the need arises with an excellent three-bean Texas chili and a perfectly passable repertoire of soups. At home, nobody offers us drinks—*Passion fruit or hibiscus margarita, anyone?* At home, nobody beckons us to the balcony to enjoy the sunset while we nibble on mini shrimp tostadas. At home, nobody sets such a whimsical dinner table.

We do have someone who comes to clean our house once a week—Alice, a fortysomething cranky musician from Seattle who never figured out a plan B and resents every minute she spends folding our underwear—but that's as far as we go with the domestic staff. So while I may be enjoying this level of service, I'm not 100 percent comfortable with it.

"*Muchas, muchas,* muchas *gracias,*" I say as Enrique hands me my first margarita of the evening, which also happens to be the first hibiscus margarita of my life.

Peter stares at me. He's trying to tell me to cool it with the *muchas,* but *muchas* and *gracias* are about the only two words of Spanish I know.

I shrug. "I'm grateful. Sue me."

I appear to be the only one who thought to dress up. The men have donned short-sleeved button-downs and shorts, Malcolm paired a black T-shirt with his rolled-up khakis and Ivan is already in his pajamas. Clem is wearing spandex pants and a cropped tank top. I've stopped asking her why she goes to school dressed like she's going to the gym because she's only following a trend. When I drop her off in the mornings, she's one of a sea of girls whose labia are on full display.

And Ingrid, well, it doesn't much matter what Ingrid wears; she always looks like she just stepped out of a magazine. Not a fashion magazine, more like a home design spread, something showcasing the perfect cook's kitchen or a library with books arranged by color, and there she is stirring up a hollandaise or reading a vintage red-spined copy of *Light in August,* looking elegant in a blousy shirt, ripped jeans, bare feet.

"Roberto," Solly begins.

"Yes, sir?"

Solly moves in closer. Rests a hand on his shoulder. Lowers his voice, like he's sharing a secret, but not so quietly that we can't all hear perfectly. "Hey. I'm a Roberto, too. Robert. Robert Solomon, but everyone calls me Solly. So from one Roberto to another—drop the 'sir,' will you? 'Solly' will do just fine."

"Okay, Solly."

Solly reaches into his pocket for his iPhone. "Can you acquaint me with the sound system here?" He shuffles his feet and wriggles his hips in an embarrassing effort to demonstrate his dance moves. "There must be some way to get some tunes playing."

There's built-in surround sound with an iPhone docking system, which Solly would know if he'd bothered to read the emails I sent him. He's hard-core about his music. He'd be insufferable for seven days if he couldn't play DJ.

I look over at Clem. She's holding a drink the same color as my hibiscus margarita, talking to Ingrid and Ivan. I know she drinks sometimes. I'm not naïve. And also, I read her texts. A few weeks ago she barfed on Ariella's parents' Turkish kilim runner. She puts on a good show—I might not have even known she was wasted when she got home that night, delivered safely by a sober Sean in a Lyft. But since I can see her texts on my laptop (*WTF Clem? That rug is expensive! My parents are gonna kill me!*) I busted her, and she cried, and I made her stay in the following weekend, hardly a punishment, because we let Sean come over and they made pizzas and watched *Napoleon Dynamite* for the ten-thousandth time. Anyway, I don't think she's brazen enough to drink in front of me, but just in case, I go in for a closer look.

"It's a hibiscus spritzer, Mother," she says. "Hibiscus juice and sparkling water. Want a taste? It's kinda gross."

Ivan is walking in tight circles around Clem, faster and faster until he falls down.

"He napped for three hours," Ingrid says. "He'll never go to sleep tonight."

The sun has slipped away, leaving the sky a Rothko of pink, orange and a deep purple-blue. Solly has hooked up his playlist and the house fills with music—Cesária Évora, a Cape Verdean who sings in Portuguese, so not an entirely apt choice, but still, she fits the feel of the evening just right. When Cesária Évora died a few years ago, her obituary described her songs as infused with *sodade*, the Creole term for "nostalgic longing." It's how I feel right now, gazing at the multihued sky: a nostalgic longing, even though I've never been to Puerto Vallarta, never even been to Mexico. It makes me want to pull my husband close, forgive him the millions of things he does every day to make me hate him just a little bit. Because, like Solly said, these are the moments that matter, spending time with the ones you love most. So it could be nostalgic longing, or it could very well be that I'm kind of drunk. Either way, I look for Peter, but he's not here.

"Where's Peter?" I ask Solly, because Solly is Peter's *other* other half.

"He had to take a call."

"A call? It's Saturday night. We're on vacation."

Solly puts an arm around me and says softly, "Work crisis. Give him a break, okay? It's not like he *wants* to be dealing with this now."

Three years ago, Solly and Peter started a bagel company that aimed to bring New York bagels to Angelenos starved for the real thing. If it doesn't sound like the most original idea, that's because it isn't. But Solly believed that if the bagels were good, and if the marketing was right, and if they could figure out some sort of app for on-demand delivery to supplement the brick-and-mortar spot in Santa Monica for which he'd already signed a two-year lease on a whim, they could make a fortune.

A fortune would be a gross exaggeration, but the business is doing well, and they are making money, though I always suspect Solly is making more of that money than Peter.

Solly brought the business cred to their endeavor; he grew up the scion of a mattress empire and went to Harvard Business School despite having been, according to Peter, who was his college roommate for four straight years, a mediocre student at best. Peter brought the design expertise, having worked at first for magazines, and then for years at a fragrance company, where he developed a staunch aversion to perfume, which is why I no longer wear any.

Peter nailed it with the Boychick Bagels logo—it's simple and retro and you see young people wearing the T-shirts and tank tops and hoodies all over Los Angeles. They went through several ideas for names: Bagel Buds (sounded like they were selling bagels *and* weed), Bagel Bros (douchey), Bagel Boys (only slightly less douchey). Since Peter isn't Jewish, I suggested Bagel Goys, but they decided instead to go full Yiddish, even using a Yiddish-style font for the logo.

At first I wasn't sure about Peter going into business with Solly. He had a solid job with health insurance and a 401(k). We never had to worry about the size of my book advances or my lackluster sales. I worked hard, I contributed to the family, but we didn't have to rely on my income to keep us afloat. Still, Peter wanted to take this leap. He was tired of his job and he wanted a change and of course what I wanted was for Peter to be happy.

Peter never agreed to shoulder the breadwinner burden alone and it's not what I wanted either, for him or for us. We both grew up in households where our parents took on traditional gender roles. Our fathers never changed a diaper and they made the money and all the big decisions. Our mothers didn't work until they both found themselves middle-aged and divorced. Peter and I set a different course for ourselves, and yet when the opportunity to start the business with Solly arose, it forced us to take stock. I realized we'd slipped quietly into something resembling a 1950s marriage—he made the money, I made the house run smoothly.

We agreed this would have to be a family endeavor with both of us firmly on board. *I need you*, Peter said. He pointed out that I managed our finances and paid all our bills and had a far better understanding of what was reasonable and what was fantasy for Team Carlson. So together we did the research. We looked at the numbers. We learned that four out of five businesses fail in their first year and that the ones that survive can take years to turn a profit. We had some savings, sure, but for us, the risk was huge. If Solly's whim didn't pan out it wouldn't make a difference to him—he'd just fall back comfortably onto his piles of mattress money. What would happen to us?

As usual, Solly had answers. He and Peter would be equal partners but he'd put up the seed money. Peter would start drawing a salary right away. We'd keep our health insurance. Our 401(k). The venture wouldn't fail. Overhead would be low and the markup high. By year two, Solly swore, they'd be in the black and they'd be splitting profits down the middle.

The business is now in its fourth year. It is, by start-up standards, a smashing success. And yet, even though I know Solly has his money to recoup, it still doesn't seem like Peter is an equal partner. He's more like Solly's right-hand man. I've stopped mentioning this to Peter; it's a sore spot between us so I leave it alone. All I know is that Peter works tirelessly and puts in longer hours than Solly. I've watched Peter grow from a talented designer into a marketing guru and brilliant entrepreneur. He's my husband, so I'm allowed to brag.

The on-demand option is gearing up to go 24/7 and has been a royal headache. The app falls within Peter's domain, as do so many pieces of the company, but still, I don't see what's so important that he'd have to deal with it now, on a Saturday evening on the first night of our vacation, though I do have an inkling about who is on the other end of that phone call.

"Where did he take the call, Solly?"

Solly shakes his head. "Come on, Jen. We haven't even sat down to eat yet. I know how important it is to you that we all dine as one, and so does Peter, so you can rest assured he'll be back in a minute. Have another margarita."

"I don't want another margarita."

A bell rings. Not the doorbell. It's Roberto, ringing a little brass bell. The dinner bell.

"Ding dong," Ivan shouts.

Solly squeezes my elbow. "Take a seat. I'll go grab him."

I so want this vacation to go perfectly. I want everything in-fused with specialness. This isn't only because we spent more money on this trip than we've spent on any other vacation we've ever taken; there's another calculus at play. Peter is turning fifty. We've been together almost twenty years. In two years our daughter will be out of the house. And six months ago my doctor called after my annual mammogram and asked that I come in for a "sit-down conversation." Peter sat next to me squeezing my hand. She told us we were lucky to have caught it early, as if all three of us had stage-one breast cancer, and that with minimal treatment I should be *shipshape*. I worried about trusting my life to someone who would use the term *shipshape*, but I finished radiation three weeks ago and she was right. Things look good and I'm feeling fine. Anyway, all of these factors add up. These seven days are high-value days. Every minute counts double, triple, even. So I let Solly go collect Peter, and I polish off my hibiscus margarita.

I choose a seat next to Clementine, across the table from In-grid, and I ask Enrique to remove the birds-of-paradise so we can all see one another. On the menu tonight: prickly pear cactus enchiladas and jicama salad, rice and beans for Ivan and maybe Malcolm if he's a picky eater, too, but not for Clem, whose culi-nary adventurousness has always filled me with pride.

The food hasn't even been served yet, and Ingrid is frowning at her plate. She picks it up, looks at the back of it, and puts it down again. Enrique is making the rounds with the large dish of enchiladas, so she beckons Roberto over.

"So sorry . . . Do you know . . . Is this pottery lead-free?"

"Lead-free?"

"Yes. Is it free of lead? Much of the traditional pottery from Mexico is made with a lead-based ceramic glaze. It's very dangerous to eat off of plates that contain lead."

Roberto says something to Enrique in Spanish. Enrique says something back.

"Yes," Roberto nods. "It is lead-free."

Ingrid rubs her hand over the plate and examines her palm, like she's checking for dust. "Would you mind . . . Do you have paper plates in the kitchen? I'm happy to go get them myself." She starts to stand up but Roberto motions for her to stay put. "I will get for you."

"Two, please," she says and she takes Ivan's plate and her own and hands them both to Roberto.

Solly and Peter return, taking the seats at opposite ends of the long table.

"Sorry about that, everyone. Bagel emergency. All peachy now. Wow, does this food look incredible. I don't know what this is, but it looks incredible."

"It's enchiladas," Enrique says, holding the dish for Peter to serve himself. "Please."

Peter is the first person to whom I show my writing, my first editor, in part because he has an excellent vocabulary and always catches me when I repeat words, which I tend to do, so I can't help but notice that he just said *incredible* twice.

"Who was calling you?" I'd decided not to say anything. Hadn't I decided that? Didn't I calculate that when the minutes are high value it's important to try not to ruin a single one of them?

"Just someone from the office. We're dealing with a glitch. Let's not bore everyone."

"Just someone from the office?"

Why am I doing this on my vacation? The very time I set aside to escape anxiety and insecurity, to be less controlling, the time I planned to try to be, as they used to say at Clem's preschool, *my best self.* Everyone stares down at the lead-ridden plates.

Peter takes a bite of his enchilada and then looks up slowly and locks his eyes onto mine. "Jonas. Jonas from tech. Like I said, it's all cleared up now."

"Good," I say and manage a smile. We've moved on from Cesária Évora to something a little too clubby for my taste. I dig deep for some of that *sodade,* but it's gone; slipped away, like the sun.

I CAN TELL by the way Peter brushes his teeth that he's still mad at me for grilling him at the table about the phone call. He takes his frustrations out on his molars, and he's not being kind to his gums. He doesn't want to tell me he's mad, because then I'd proffer my side, and we'd both dig in, and this is the first night of our seven-night dream vacation. We're supposed to be having the kind of sex we never find the time to have at home.

"I didn't know that my life was missing prickly pear cactus. But it was. There's been a prickly-pear-cactus-sized hole in my life all these years."

Peter comes out of the bathroom and cocks his head at me. "A prickly-pear-cactus-sized hole?"

"Yep."

He smiles. We've brokered an unspoken deal. We will leave

the earlier events of the evening alone. It's better this way. It's what we both want.

"Can you believe Malcolm?" I ask.

"Believe *what* about him?"

"Can you believe *him*? How grown-up he is. And how handsome."

"He was always a good-looking kid." Peter climbs into bed next to me. "Clem could hardly take her eyes off of him."

"What? That's ridiculous."

"How is that ridiculous?"

"Because she's madly in love with Sean. She excused herself right after dessert so she could go back to her room and spend the rest of the night FaceTiming him."

Peter laughs.

"What's so funny?"

"I just think it's funny that you, of all people, could believe a sixteen-year-old girl wouldn't go all weak in the knees over an older boy who looks like Malcolm. So what if she has a boyfriend? And I hate to say it, because Sean's a good kid, but there's not much of a contest there."

"There is, because she's *in love* with Sean."

"Ha. She's sixteen. What does she know about love?"

"Sixteen-year-olds know plenty about love. They think about love all the time. Their romantic ideals haven't been derailed by things like adult responsibility or the general mundanities of everyday living."

Peter reaches for a magazine and adjusts his reading light. "Maybe," he says. "I guess you do know more about this than I do."

What he means is that because I write about teenagers, I know more about teenagers. What he doesn't mean is that I know more about this because I habitually read Clem's texts including the ones with Sean. Early on, when Clem first got an iPhone, and I first downloaded the app to my laptop that allows me to see her texts, I told Peter about something I'd read that made me concerned that Clem wasn't treating another girl at school kindly. Peter told me to stop reading her texts. He said it was an invasion of her privacy and creepy to boot. Instead, I just stopped telling him, keeping every insight, every revelation, to myself. The result is that I get a window into the lives of teenagers that's useful when it comes to writing about them, and also that I know far more about our daughter than he does.

Clem and Sean have the kind of relationship it would be difficult to put in a book. It's too sweet, too romantic and way too innocent. They're sixteen-year-olds who profess their love for each other incessantly and still haven't ever had sex. It's a mother's dream and no reader would believe it.

"Here's a shocker," I say.

Peter peers at me from behind his magazine. "Yes?"

"Ingrid tried talking to me about her manuscript again. Not five minutes after getting here. She was boasting about her daily word count, clearly angling for me to ask to see it."

"Solly says it's really good."

"What does Solly know about young adult fiction?"

"He said it's for younger readers. Not little kids, but not teenagers either."

"It's middle grade?" How does Peter not know the terminology? I've been working in this field for more than a decade.

"I guess so."

"So what does Solly know about middle-grade fiction?"

Peter folds the magazine and puts it on his nightstand. He props himself up on his side, facing me. He takes my hand, and rubs his face with it. His stubble won't be soft for another day or two. "Why does this bug you so much?"

I sigh. "It's just that . . . I'm sure Ingrid looks at me, at what I do, and thinks: if *she* can do it, why can't I do it?"

He holds my hand between us and squeezes it. "You do make it look easy. But that's just because you're a pro at what you do."

"Yeah, I'm a pro who can't finish her fourth book."

"Come on. You'll figure it out. You always do."

This is Peter's way of trying to sound encouraging, but he doesn't see that he can often come off as dismissive. On some level I've always suspected that Peter sees me as a housewife who found a hobby that occasionally nets her a modest income. That the challenge of writing a book for young readers isn't a real challenge, because people who write for young readers aren't real writers. When I've tried talking to him about this, how it feels diminishing, he accuses me of projecting my own insecurities onto him.

I'm not going to carry your baggage for you is one of his favorite comebacks.

"What happened to Ingrid's jewelry business?" I ask him. "Why doesn't she just stick with that? She made beautiful jewelry."

That's how Solly and Ingrid met. Solly hired her to design a bracelet for Maureen. It was supposed to be a gift for their tenth wedding anniversary, but by the time the piece was finished, so was the marriage.

"It shouldn't matter to you if Ingrid wants to write a book. Live and let live. And I'm sure you're right about Solly's analysis. What does he know? But really, it has nothing to do with you or what you do and you shouldn't let it threaten you."

"It doesn't *threaten* me."

Peter raises one eyebrow.

"Okay. Yeah. I get it. But I'm not going to send it to Laurel. I know that's what Ingrid is after, but I wouldn't do that to Laurel. It isn't fair. Laurel has to deal with more than her fair share of shitty submissions."

"Fine," he says. "I'm sure you'll figure out a good excuse if it comes to that."

"And it's not like Ingrid needs the money. Not that there's much money in publishing anyway. But what little there may be, she doesn't need any of it."

"I thought we were done."

"We are."

"And I thought you liked Ingrid. I thought you two were friends."

"We are." I do like Ingrid. I really do. Despite the fact that she broke up the marriage of a couple I adored, despite the fact that she thinks writing a book is easy, despite her paranoia about lead in her dinner plates, I really do like her. Most of the time.

Peter slides closer to me so that our bodies are touching, then he puts an arm around me and pulls me closer. He presses his face into my neck and kisses me there. Then he puts his mouth to my ear and he whispers, "I know this is our first night here, and it's not that I don't want to, it's just that I'm really tired. Is that okay?"

"Sure," I say.

He rolls away from me and turns off his reading light. "Consider yourself on notice," he says. "You are not getting off this easy tomorrow night."

I'M NOT A GOOD SLEEPER. This wasn't always so. I started having trouble around the time I turned forty, when my doctor kindly told me to get used to it, that poor sleep goes hand in hand with growing older, like growing older wasn't already a raw deal. At home I partake in the occasional puff of medicinal marijuana, and that does help somewhat, but for obvious reasons, I didn't bring any along with me to Mexico.

Peter is snoring away. He's dodged the middle-aged insomnia like he's dodged many of the other afflictions of aging. He isn't getting soft in the middle. He doesn't need reading glasses. Even with the white hair, he still looks like a boy.

I watch him in the dark. The rise and fall of his chest like a metronome. His breath goes in two beats, out two beats. Steady Peter. Dependable Peter.

Most of the worries that keep me up at night are either irrational or insignificant—they grow in the dark and shrink in the light of morning. *Did I say the wrong thing to that mother of Clem's friend* or *Did the electrician overcharge me* or *Did I remember to roll the windows all the way up in the Prius?* I think of my subconscious as a storage shed for worries—most are useless, throwaways, but hidden in there are some real gems. *What if my cancer comes back? Who was Peter really talking to?*

I check the clock on his bedside table. It feels like it should be later, but it's only 11:47. And back home it's only 9:47. So I guess it's no wonder I'm still awake.

Next to the clock sits Peter's iPhone.

Maybe I'll be able to sleep, I figure, if I can just put to rest my stupid paranoia. If Peter were awake, and he knew I couldn't sleep, he'd probably show me the phone himself to prove to me that, yes, it was Jonas from tech who called in the middle of the cocktails and mini shrimp tostadas on the balcony.

I slide out of bed. The tiled floor is cool on my bare feet. I pick up his phone. It's powered down. I turn it on and wait for it to come to life, making sure it's on vibrate so it doesn't wake Peter with an errant *ding*. His lock screen is a picture of the two of us in sunglasses and baseball hats with toothy smiles. It's from a hike we took up Runyon Canyon on New Year's Day. I push the home button and punch in his four-digit security code—Clem's birth date and month—the same code I use on my own phone.

I touch the green icon. The list of recent calls pops up.

On the top of that list, the most recent call, the one that came in at 7:04 p.m. and lasted for almost eleven minutes, not an inexpensive conversation considering we don't have an international calling plan, did *not* come from Jonas in tech.

It came from Gavriella Abramov, Peter's beautiful twenty-eight-year-old assistant.

SUNDAY

Puerto Vallarta sits in the middle of the Bay of Banderas, surrounded on three sides by mountains, with a prevailing wind pattern from the southwest—all of which makes it a rare target for hurricanes.

The conversation about where to go to celebrate the big birthdays began more than a year ago, when Peter turned forty-nine. After much back and forth, we settled on Puerto Vallarta, taking into consideration the substantial bang for your buck, a glowing endorsement from my friend Sarah, and the minimal time difference (we wouldn't want to mess with Ivan's fragile sleep routine). We did not factor in susceptibility to hurricanes, though if we had, it would have been another check in the box in favor of Puerto Vallarta.

Because I'm a planner, and I consider a six-month lead time nothing short of reckless procrastination, we had the house booked and the deposit paid by August, a full eight months in advance.

Then, in October, shortly after that sit-down conversation with my doctor, the most powerful hurricane on record threatened to hit Puerto Vallarta, with sustained winds clocking in at 200 miles per hour and gusts approaching 250. The distinction between winds and gusts is something I still don't understand, despite developing a hurricane obsession over those few days. I watched its every move from my kitchen in Los Angeles, on a weather-tracking website, while the sun shone outside my window. It was a welcome distraction from WebMD, every dark corner of which I'd already exhausted. Of course I worried about the people who lived in Puerto Vallarta and the fragile infrastructure of a town not accustomed to such violent invasion, but I also felt for the tourists who had maybe spent more money than they ever had before, who had probably been looking forward to the vacation for a solid eight months and who were now being forced to evacuate, rushing off to the airport, where more than five hundred flights had been canceled.

The hurricane ended up making landfall near Cuixmala about 180 kilometers south; Puerto Vallarta was spared the brunt of her wrath. Back home, I looked up from my computer and out my kitchen window at my orange tree heavy with fruit, and my freshly mowed backyard, and I breathed a huge sigh of relief.

Now here I sit, alone at the dining room table at Villa Azul Paraiso, at half past seven in the morning, drinking a cup of excellent coffee, glued to the same weather-tracking website. There's another storm, just upgraded to tropical cyclone, hovering over the eastern Pacific basin. Though she is not predicted to impose any threat to our temporary home on this placid bay beyond the possibility of some unseasonable showers, I am watching her carefully and anxiously, because if back in October the experts were off by 180 kilometers, who's to say their calculations won't be off again?

Roberto arrives with a leather satchel slung over his shoulder and a woman who must be Luisa, though I never did meet her yesterday. I found the kitchen empty this morning, and the coffeemaker fully loaded and ready to go, with a Post-it note attached: *Please push button for coffee* and a smiley face.

"Good morning," he says and then says something to Luisa in Spanish. She hurries off toward the kitchen. "You are up early. We will make for you the huevos. Unless you like something else?"

"I can wait for the others. Really. I don't typically eat breakfast right away. I like to ease into my day."

"More coffee? I get for you."

"No, no. It's okay." I want to tell him to relax, to put his bag down and ease into his day, too, but I worry that will sound condescending, or worse, like an order.

I gesture to my computer. "I'm a little worried about the weather."

He looks out at the cloudless morning sky, the calm waters, the palm trees standing perfectly still. He's puzzled. "It is beautiful, no?"

"Yes, but . . . I'm watching this, here." I point to the screen. He comes closer and leans in. "It isn't predicted to come our way, but it could. Because these so-called *experts* are really just in the guessing business."

"It is only a *tormenta*. No worry."

"A *tormenta*? That sounds bad."

"No. It is okay. A *tormenta*—it is only a storm. Not a hurricane. And it does not come here. You will have sun."

"Actually, they say that even though it probably won't come here, we might see some rain as a result."

"Okay. Maybe some rain. But rain, it does not last long. It is quick and then there is sun."

"I don't care all that much about sun. Too much sun is bad for your skin."

"You do not want sun? This is why you worry?" Now he really looks puzzled.

I shut my laptop. "Maybe more coffee would be nice."

"Okay," he says. "I get for you."

I hear Ingrid's voice coming from upstairs. It starts as a whisper-shout. "Ivan? Ivan?" By the time she's in the dining room, messy haired and wild eyed, she's dropped the whisper. "Ivan? Jenna! Have you seen Ivan?"

"No," I say. "I assumed he was still asleep."

She's wearing a white V-neck T-shirt through which I can see her nipples and boy-short-style underwear. "No, he was in our bed, but I just woke up and he wasn't there and he's not in his room and, oh, God . . ."

"Calm down," I say, even though I know it's the very worst thing you can say to anyone in a panic, especially a mother who can't find her child. "This house has three living rooms. Let's check them all. The one on this floor has the satellite TV, maybe that's where he's gone."

We rush to the living room. It's empty. I send Ingrid down to the ground floor and I run back upstairs to check the main living room and the bedrooms. The master door is open; I can see a Solly-sized lump in the massive bed. Ivan's door is open and his bed is untouched. All the other doors are shut. Everyone is still asleep. He's not on this floor.

I run to the top floor, with the Jacuzzi and the chairs for star-gazing. I haven't been up here yet. It would be a great place to have cocktails, there's a palapa-style bar and some fairy lights, but no Ivan. I hurry back down through the house and into the kitchen, where Roberto sits at a table grating a block of cheese while Luisa stands at the stove.

"Have you seen Ivan?" I ask. I put my palm at about waist height to indicate his short stature. "The little one? We can't find him."

Roberto jumps up and follows me downstairs. The pool, thank God, is clear. Too many stories end this way, and truth be told, I volunteered to go upstairs to search because a part of me feared what I might find at the bottom of the pool. The gate to the beach is open. I can hear Ingrid, screaming now, "IVAN!!! IVAN!!!"

"What's going on?" I look up two floors. Peter and Solly are standing at the balcony off the main living room, the place where just yesterday I stood and watched Clem sunbathe with her back to the Bay of Banderas. How could I have let something so small, so inconsequential, bother me?

"We can't find Ivan," I shout up at them. They both disappear from view.

"IVAN!" I hear Ingrid shout from the beach again, but there's a different tone to his name. It's not panic; it's discovery. It's *eureka!* It's relief, with an undercurrent of fury. She's found him.

I pass Roberto on my way out the gate. He pats me on the shoulder. "It is okay," he says. "He is there on the beach."

Ingrid is on her knees in the sand, clutching Ivan, who is trying to wriggle out of her embrace. Malcolm stands next to them with a bright-red bucket in his hand.

"What were you thinking? What the hell were you thinking?" Ingrid is screaming again. Not at Ivan. She's screaming at Malcolm.

"I . . . I . . . He came into my room and woke me up," Malcolm says. "He wanted me to take him to look for starfish." He holds out the bucket and points up the beach, where the cove ends. "We just went over there. Near the rocks."

I feel an arm around my shoulder. It's Peter. He pulls me close and I let him.

"Are you okay, Ivan?" Ingrid holds Ivan at arm's length and looks him up and down.

"Ding dong."

"Ivan. Answer me. Are you okay?"

"Ding dong."

"Ivan!" She shakes him just a little bit.

Solly runs out onto the beach. "There you are, little guy! You gave us a scare!"

"I was with Malcolm," Ivan says.

"Yes, I figured. I looked in Malcolm's bedroom and he wasn't there so I guessed you two were together."

I should have checked the bedrooms. Then again, Ingrid should have checked the bedrooms. This isn't my fault, but I feel bad because if I'd checked Malcolm's room, he wouldn't be standing there looking so wounded.

"Malcolm took him out to the beach," Ingrid says, not screaming anymore, but not doing much to contain her rage either. "He took him out to the beach without telling me, without telling anyone where he was going."

"It was early," Malcolm says. "Everyone was still asleep."

All eyes are on Solly. What I want Solly to say, what I try to send him a telepathic message to say, is this: *Malcolm is Ivan's brother. You don't need permission to take your little brother out hunting for starfish.*

Instead Solly says, "You probably should have let us know, buddy."

Malcolm looks down at his bare, sandy feet. He walks over to Solly, hands him the red bucket with the starfish in it, and heads back into the house through the gate. This time he doesn't stop to rinse his feet in the faucet.

WE ALL RETREAT to our corners for a while. Clem comes into our room and I catch her up on what happened. She texts Sean while I'm talking, filling him in on the drama of the morning. This is a habit she has that I can't stand, texting while listening, but I forgive her today because she is my only child, and I cannot fathom how I'd ever recover if I lost her.

This has all thrown a bit of a wrench in my plan to talk to Peter. Saying I have a "plan" might be an exaggeration. At some point I just figured I'd find a quiet moment to ask again about the call last night and give him an opportunity to tell me privately what he didn't want to say publicly when it was clear I'd had more to drink than I'm accustomed to. That it was Gavriella on the phone. It was Gavriella on the phone even though I'd *specifically* asked him to tell her not to call while we were in Mexico.

It's well established that I'm uncomfortable with the idea of Gavriella. What wife wouldn't resent her husband's gorgeous, needy young assistant? At first Peter laughed it off and even seemed to find my jealousy cute, but as the months have gone on, he has found it less so. He's stopped reassuring me, stopped laughing at the absurdity of a young woman who looks like that having any interest in a white-haired married father pushing fifty. *I'm not going to carry your baggage for you.* Instead he's taken to minimizing any mention of her and, yes, trying to hide when he's on the phone with her during off-hours.

So when I saw that the most recent call was not from Jonas in tech, I wasn't terribly surprised. It wasn't a gotcha moment. It was more of a disappointment. He said he'd tell her not to call on our vacation. So either he never told her, or he did tell her and she chose to ignore him. But bringing up the phone call now, while recovering from the scare of Ivan having gone missing, seems petty and small.

"Poor Malcolm," Clem says. She's wandering around, sizing up the ways in which our room might be slightly better than hers. "He was just trying to be nice. Why did Ingrid have to go and get all mad at him?"

"It's hard for you to understand, because you don't have a child," Peter tells her. "But the love we parents have for our kids defies all reason. I really don't think Ingrid meant to lash out at Malcolm. She was just having a primal moment."

However true that may be, this strikes me as yet another example of Peter's deference to Solly. It extends to Ingrid, and to making excuses for her inexcusable behavior.

"Well, I think it's because Malcolm is black," Clem says, sitting down at the edge of our bed.

"What? Why would you say something like that?" Peter gets up from the armchair in which he'd been sitting and goes to stand in front of her. It's almost, but not quite, threatening.

"Because it's true," Clem replies.

"There are so many things wrong with what you just said." Peter is pacing now. "I don't even know where to begin."

Clem sighs. "Whatever."

"Don't say something incendiary like that and then follow it up with *whatever*. That's just lazy."

Clem and Peter rarely argue. They have a typically uncomplicated father-daughter relationship. She doesn't get under his skin. He doesn't embarrass her nor does he frustrate her with his hovering. They mostly bond over a shared love of Szechuan food, the spicier the better—digestive consequences be damned—and a shared disdain for the kind of sentimental movies I adore. So when they spar like this, I find it fascinating to watch, and maybe just the tiniest bit gratifying, too.

"Well, Dad, what I mean to say is that Malcolm is black. And because he is black, and because he is Solly's son but not *her* son, Ingrid doesn't trust him."

"First of all, Malcolm isn't black."

"He's not?"

"He has a black mother, yes. But he also has a white father."

"Dad. What planet are you living on?"

"You know, Clem, you're always so quick to remind me all the time about how gender isn't *binary*, and how we should stop thinking of everyone as either male *or* female, so why are you suddenly applying a singular identity to Malcolm? How come when it comes to his race he is one, but not the other?"

I can't quite figure out why Peter is tangling with her this way. Yes, I know that there are times he gets annoyed with the aggressive progressiveness of the private school we scrape together the money to send Clem to, with its gender-neutral bathrooms and the way they use *their* instead of *his* and *hers*. But the thing is, Peter *is* progressive and these *are* his values, even if he's not totally made his peace with the gender-neutral new world order. I guess there are some ideas, some movements, it might take a fifty-year-old man a little bit longer to catch up to. But I know that Peter doesn't really want to fight about whether Malcolm can choose to identify or to be identified as black. This is not the Peter I know. *Why is he so agitated?*

Before Clem has a chance to respond, Peter continues, "And second of all, Malcolm is Ingrid's stepson, and she loves him, and he is a part of her family, and to imply anything else is just way off base."

Peter sits back down. Clem isn't looking at him anymore— she's gone back to her phone. She's given up. Or at least lost steam. "Fine," she says. "Sorry."

I try not to let it bother me that she offers her father an apology when she didn't owe it to him, and she has never offered me an apology on any of the multitude of occasions I've rightfully deserved one.

There's a heavy beat of silence before I break it. "Okay, team. This is our vacation. Let's go get some breakfast, shall we?"

. . .

By late morning, a peace and conviviality has returned to our group. Malcolm, Clem and Ivan are all in the pool, playing some sort of waterproof racquet game they found in a closet full of toys. The men have gone for a walk down the beach because Solly read something about a fishing vessel that pulls up into shallow water where you can wade out and buy fish directly off the boat. He's already cleared his plan with Luisa, who is going to turn their haul into our dinner tonight. I'm sitting with Ingrid, watching the kids and a horizon of nothing but blue skies.

Ingrid is reading the runner-up to this year's Newbery Award winner. Clearly she's reaching for the stars with her middle-grade work in progress.

"How is it?" I nod to her book.

"Oh, you haven't read it? It's fabulous."

"No. I don't read much middle grade. Or even YA for that matter."

"How can you not read YA? Don't you need to know about what else is out there? Research the competition?"

"I guess that's not how I think about writing. I don't think about my books as competing with others. I just think about the stories I want to tell and I do my best to tell them in a way that won't bore readers."

I'm sure Ingrid sees right through my bullshit. Of course I care about the competition. I don't read much YA because it makes me insecure about my own writing and I prefer to evaluate myself as a writer in a carefully constructed and protected vacuum of denial.

"Your books are never boring," she says. "And I read a ton of YA so I can tell you, for what it's worth, that I think your books blow most of the competition away. I don't know why they aren't mega hits."

"That's nice of you to say."

"I mean it." She puts her book down on the table between us. She adjusts her chair so that the umbrella blocks out the little sliver of sun that had been creeping up her arm. "Especially your first book."

What a writer struggling to finish her fourth book does not need to hear is that her first book, the one that came out nine years ago, was her best effort. That it's all been downhill since then. Obviously Ingrid would have no way of knowing this since she's never published a book. Maybe I should say something about how the first necklace she designed was her most lovely piece of jewelry. But that would be spiteful. And it would be a lie. And also, she's not even designing jewelry anymore.

"So how's *your* project coming?" I decide there's no way out of this conversation, and anyway, I figure maybe we can get into a halfway decent back-and-forth about craft and process, that maybe it will help light a spark that sends me back to the blank page.

"Well, like I said, since I've been on this new plan with my nutritionist I've been thinking more clearly and I've got more energy and it's really helped me work through the second act of my book."

"So you have your book organized into acts?"

"Oh, yeah. Sure. Of course. Classic three-act structure."

I have never broken down my books into acts. I've never written an outline. Never made character sketches. I don't storyboard or clip images that inspire me from magazines or websites. I'm not a plotter, I'm a pantser—I write by the seat of my pants, which are currently frayed and torn. Maybe if I bothered with acts and structure, maybe if I started a fucking Pinterest page of inspiration, I wouldn't be so stuck.

"Tell me about your book," I say.

"Come on, you don't really want to hear . . ."

"Yes, I do."

She tells me the plot of her novel. It involves a boy whose father has gone missing. His mother, and everyone around him, believes that he ran off with another woman to start a new life, but the boy believes his dad is on a secret mission for the private space exploration company he worked for, and that he's in grave danger. The boy and the two misfit friends he's recruited try to work the interstellar communication device his father spent years building in their garage, certain that the father is transmitting a call for help. Meanwhile, the boy and his friends try infiltrating the company, run by a Russian billionaire, to get some answers. It is a classic tale of kids who believe in the impossible, kids who ignore the wisdom of the adults around them, kids who ultimately save the day. It's a complicated story, full of plot twists, big action sequences and elements of science fiction. I write contemporary YA, typical coming-of-age angsty tales of love and friendship, so none of what Ingrid is writing is anywhere near my wheelhouse, but I do have to admit . . . it does sound kind of great.

"If you want," I say to Ingrid, "I'd be happy to take a look at it for you. But only if you want. And whenever you feel ready. But seriously, no pressure."

Malcolm is carrying Ivan on his shoulders. They're engaged in a battle against Clem, some sort of gladiator fight where they try to knock each other over in the pool with brightly colored foam noodles. I can tell Clem is letting the boys off easy.

"Would you really?" She sits up straighter in her lounger and turns to face me. "That would be amazing."

"Happy to do it." Why shouldn't I give Ingrid some feedback? It doesn't mean I have to send her manuscript to Laurel; I still draw the line at that. Laurel is my agent, not my friend. She doesn't owe me any favors. But I do know something about writing for young readers, I'm good at it when I'm not failing at it and I'm sure I can be helpful to Ingrid. I didn't have anyone to turn to when I first got started, and it would have been nice if I had.

"You're a great friend, Jenna," she says. "A truly great friend."

I REMEMBER the first double date Peter and I had with Solly and Ingrid. Still full of indignation on behalf of Maureen, I went along reluctantly. I'd somehow convinced myself I might get away with icing out forever the woman whom Solly had already announced he planned to marry.

"We'll have nothing to talk about," I told Peter.

"I'm sure you can find some common ground," he said as he ran his electric razor over his chin. "Who knows—you might even like her."

Peter had already met Ingrid a few times, including an evening of drinks at the Beverly Hills Hotel before Solly had come clean with Maureen—and before Peter had shared Solly's secret with me.

"I doubt it," I said. "She's obviously just after his money. What else would someone her age see in Solly?"

Peter unplugged his razor and tucked it away under the sink. He looked at me in the mirror of our double vanity.

"You don't mean that."

"I don't?"

"You know what women see in Solly."

He was right. I did and I do. But still.

I leaned in to apply my lipstick.

"By the way, you look smoking hot tonight." Peter sidestepped closer to me and put his arms around my waist. "Ingrid has nothing on you."

"You're just trying to make me feel better. And probably trying to make tonight go smoothly."

"I'm saying it because it's true. And because I'd never leave you for someone I hired to design jewelry for you."

"Ha. Easy for you to say as you've never hired anyone to design anything for me."

"You've got a point."

I turned around to face him and he kissed me deeply on my freshly lipsticked mouth.

The evening went better than expected, which tends to happen when you dread something so completely. Just like the way the things you look forward to rarely go as perfectly as you'd imagined.

I remember when we came home that night, full on an overly rich multicourse meal and drunk on expensive wine, Peter made love with an outsize exuberance and energy as if he had something to prove; to me or to himself, I wasn't sure.

. . .

SOLLY AND PETER don't get back until we're finished with lunch, which we had served to us poolside. They're loaded down with plastic grocery bags filled with fish packed in ice.

"We have returned!" Solly holds his bags high in the air. He's dripping water everywhere. "We trust you've spent these hours stitching hides together for our shelter, or weaving baskets to carry our water, or whatever you're supposed to do while we've been out hunting and gathering our motherfucking dinner!"

"Solly!" Ingrid points to Ivan, who isn't listening because he's too busy beating Malcolm at Ping-Pong.

I get up to help them bring their bounty to the kitchen. It smells like fish. They smell like fish. I imagine the label Peter might have designed at his old job for this distinctive men's fragrance.

We put the bags down on the center island where Luisa is already at work, with Enrique's help, hand making tortillas. Roberto is at the table folding the colorful cloth napkins from last night's dinner.

Luisa peeks inside the bags. She reaches around, digging through the ice and manhandling all the fish. She says something to Enrique in Spanish.

"This is it?" he asks us.

"What, that's not enough fish for seven of us?" Solly runs his fishy hand through his hair. "Actually we're only six. Ivan won't eat fish."

Luisa is still speaking to Enrique.

"No. Is enough. I ask—this is the only kind of fish you buy?"

"Yes," Solly says. "That's what they had. They caught it this morning. It's super fresh."

"*Es* bonito," Luisa says. "*Es solo* bonito."

Solly grins and slaps Peter on the back. "It's beautiful. She says our fish are only beautiful. Now let's go get our margarita on. We've earned it."

Roberto stands at the mention of margaritas. "I will make for you. But then, if it is okay, we go to town for one hour. We will leave you. For one hour only. Is this okay?"

I jump in. "Of course it's okay. You can come and go whenever you want." I knew it might be a little uncomfortable navigating a full-time staff, but I didn't imagine I'd have to remind them that they are not actually enslaved to us.

"Yes," Roberto says. "I know. We are here for work all day and for all meals. But it is Semana Santa, and today it is Palm Sunday. It is an important day. It is a day we go to church. We will only be gone one hour."

"Go, go! Of course."

"We come back and make the dinner and the appetizers."

"No hurry," I tell him. "We can eat later. It doesn't have to be as early as last night."

"It is beautiful the Church of Our Lady of Guadalupe. It is special day. It is in town. If you like to go, I show you."

"That sounds cool. I'd like to check it out." I turn around to see Malcolm standing in his bathing suit. I hadn't noticed he'd entered the kitchen.

"Buddy," Solly says. "It's church. You don't go to church. You're Jewish."

It is true that Maureen went ahead with having Malcolm bar

mitzvahed despite not being Jewish herself. When she was still pregnant she promised Solly that they'd raise the child in the Jewish tradition, having no idea of course that she'd end up doing it on her own. I'm not sure I'd have kept that promise to Solly given the ones he broke, but Maureen got into it. She found a synagogue that served a diverse community and ended up joining the board. We all went to New York for the service and the party. It was the only time I've ever seen Maureen and Ingrid in the same room. They were equally adept at faking warmth for each other.

Malcolm gives Solly the kind of look I know well from Clem. It's the *you don't know anything about anything* look. "I'm just interested, Dad. We're here in Mexico. During an important holiday. It sounds like something worth seeing. An opportunity to experience some of the real culture."

Roberto has the uncomfortable look of someone who fears he's said the wrong thing. He puts his stack of napkins away in a drawer and pulls out a map.

"Here," he says to Malcolm. "I will show you where is the church. It is not a long walk from here. You will go if you wish. But it is not necessary."

"Cool," Malcolm says and they hunch over the map together, Roberto drawing the path he should walk with his fingertip.

"Maybe you should see if Clem wants to go," Solly says.

"Ha!" They all look at me. I worry that Roberto and crew think I'm laughing at them, at their invitation to church, when I'm only laughing at the idea of Clem showing the sort of curiosity that would require she put on comfortable walking shoes and hoof it nearly a mile in midday heat. "Good luck with that," I say. "Clem's idea of exercise is rapid scrolling through her iPhone."

"That's rather ungenerous of you," Peter says. Funny coming from him when just this morning he showed no generosity for his daughter's perfectly reasonable position about Ingrid and Malcolm.

"It's not ungenerous, Peter. It's simple truth."

Like she's been summoned, Clem appears in the kitchen. Also in her bathing suit. No pink cover-up from the juniors department for her. Was that bikini that small when we bought it together last week? Did she swap it with a smaller one while I searched through my wallet for my Nordstrom charge card?

"What?" she asks. She must have sensed we'd been talking about her. That, or she's responding to the way I'm looking at her suit.

"I was just telling Malcolm that he should see if you want to go into town with him," Solly says. "To go see the church. It's Palm Sunday."

She shrugs. "Sure. I'll go."

"Really?"

"Yes, Mother. What's the big deal?"

PETER AND I go back to our room for a siesta. At some point today, someone has come in and made our bed, replaced our towels, and put fresh flowers on the table by the window. I'm not sure who's responsible for the cleaning. Luisa has her hands full with all the cooking, and yet, given my personal experience with men, it's hard for me to imagine Roberto or Enrique having made this bed so expertly.

Before I've even kicked off my flip-flops, Peter says, "Jen. I gotta tell you something."

I sit on the bed. I try to exude calm, but nobody, ever, in the history of the world, has enjoyed a conversation that begins with that opener.

"Okay . . ."

"Last night. The phone call. The one I took before dinner. It wasn't from Jonas. It was from Gavi."

Gavi. Gavi? I've never heard him refer to her as *Gavi.*

I don't say anything.

"I know you told me you didn't want her to call on this vacation, and I get that, I do. This is your vacation and I know you want a break. You need a break. From your own stresses and anxieties. About your writer's block. About the cancer scare. I also know that those are the things that are *really* bothering you, not this nonsense with Gavriella." He reaches out and he takes my hand. "But we had a crisis at work. A legitimate crisis. And I simply had to deal with it. I'm sorry."

"It wasn't a cancer *scare.* It was cancer."

Peter sighs. He has no way to come back at that. And I need a minute to regain control.

"You lied, Peter. I asked you who called and you lied."

"I did. But you didn't exactly leave me much choice. It was either lie, or have you throw a fit at dinner in front of everyone."

"You didn't tell me last night. When we came back to the room. When we weren't in front of anyone."

"You're right. I didn't. I think probably because I was still a little angry."

"You were angry? *You* were angry?" I yank my hand out of his.

There goes the calmness I was trying so hard to channel. Everything is going exactly as I'd planned—the only deviation is that I didn't even have to bring up the phone call. Peter did that all on his own. He's telling me precisely what I'd hoped to hear, that he's sorry, that he lied only because he could see I was upset and a little drunk and he didn't want to cause a scene. And yet: I'm still furious.

"Yes, Jenna. I was a little angry because I don't want to have to lie about who I'm on the phone with. I want to be able to talk to my assistant about what is going on at work without being made to feel as though I'm betraying you. You are putting me in an unfair, and frankly, an untenable, position."

I hate the word *frankly*. Just like I hate the expression *to be perfectly honest*. Both imply that everything else you've said is a lie. Peter and I keep lists of words or phrases the other is not allowed to use. The forbidden, inexcusable words. Peter knows *frankly* is on my list, so I can't help but believe that on some level, he's trying to needle me.

"It's only untenable if she continues to ignore boundaries. A good assistant knows when to leave the boss alone."

"Really? And what would you know about that exactly?"

Forget needling, that's a full frontal punch to the face. That's Peter telling me I'm useless. Peter telling me I don't know anything about real work. Peter reminding me that he's the breadwinner and I'm just the stay-at-home mom who can't finish my fourth book for young readers. A book for which I'll be paid barely enough to cover half of a single year of the mortgage on our three-bedroom house. This is a retreat into our old patterns. We aren't our parents. We're a team. We waded into the waters of this business endeavor together, hand in hand. The only reason he can put in the hours at work that he does is because I pick up the slack at home. We've talked about this. Ad nauseam.

"Fuck off, Peter."

This is not at all how I wanted this to go. This was not part of my plan. For how to talk about the phone call, nor for how to spend our siesta. Clem has gone off to town with Malcolm. We have this wing of the house to ourselves. Nobody will come knocking on our door. I was hoping we'd make up for last night's missed opportunity. This is vacation. We have a view of the ocean. These are high-value minutes.

I start to cry.

Peter comes over and he puts his arms around me. He reeks of fish. "Shhhh," he says. I choose to believe he's trying to comfort me with his shushing, not scolding me to keep quiet so the Solomons won't hear us fighting.

"Come on, Jen. Please. This is stupid. Fine. Okay. I'll tell Gavi not to call again. Even if the building is on fire. Even if we poison half of the Westside of Los Angeles with a batch of bad bagels. Even if . . ."

"I get it."

He steps back and takes a look at me. He brushes the hair off my forehead. "We good?"

"Sure." I try for a smile.

"I love you. You know that, right? *You* are my person, Jenna. You're my *wife*. I don't like all this jealousy and suspicion. It's not who you are and it's not who *we* are and I guess it just sets me off that I feel like I'm constantly answering for a sin I haven't committed. So I'm sorry if I haven't been patient with you. I adore you. I don't know what I'd do without you and I'm so grateful for all the work you put into making this trip happen and please . . . let's just try and enjoy it?"

He puts his chin on my shoulder and rests his cheek on mine. In his ear I whisper, "Okay."

He takes a deep breath in through his nose. Then he leans away from me and makes a face. "What stinks?"

I tell him. "It's you."

IT'S NOT LIKE I'VE NEVER held a real job, but it is true that since Clementine was born sixteen years ago, I have not woken up in the morning, showered, put on a pair of panty hose and gone off to work in an office. I didn't do this before Clem was born, nor did I ever aspire to; in fact my aspirations involved *never* having to wear panty hose at all. (*Panty hose,* by the way, is high on Peter's list of forbidden words.)

I spent the first few years after college in a string of jobs at which my newly acquired degree was utterly useless. I worked in a clothing boutique, a fancy stationery store and waited tables at two different restaurants. I spent my off-hours sleeping with the wrong people and writing bad short stories. Eventually it felt like it was time to get a real job, something with some responsibility. Something that mattered and might lead me toward a career. That's when I saw the listing on the bulletin board of the YMCA where I'd occasionally go swimming: a city agency was looking for caseworkers to manage teenagers in the foster care system.

I made less than I did at the combination of my meaning- less jobs, but because the agency was overburdened and underfunded, they didn't require that I have a degree in social work. I had a small budget to provide what they called "enrichment experiences" for the kids in my caseload. I'd take them to museums, or to the movies, and sometimes I'd buy them books, which is how I became familiar with the Young Adult genre. My job also required that I drive from home to home and sit with the kids and their foster parents to try to determine whether anything abjectly horrifying was going on, and if it wasn't, I'd say, *See you next month*. If I worried something abjectly horrifying *was* going on, I'd hand the case over to a caseworker with an actual degree in social work.

I really loved the job and lasted longer than most. I connected with my kids and developed a deeper understanding of, and fascination with, teenagers in general. I even went so far as to start studying for the GREs, thinking maybe I'd go back to school and get that social work degree. But in the end, the path just seemed too long and too difficult and I never even took the test.

Peter and I got together when I was still in that job. When he'd introduce me around he'd often lead with: *Jenna is a social worker.* I liked that I impressed him, even if he had to fudge the details.

All along I kept up with my writing. My short stories got better and I started writing essays, too. Eventually I got some freelance work at various teen magazines and phased into writing full time. I ghostwrote a few books in a mass-market series about the dating shenanigans of teenage zombies and one short nonfiction book in a series about teen entrepreneurs. None of this required I don the dreaded panty hose, or go to an office, or negotiate boundaries with my assistant (because I've never had an assistant, so perhaps Peter does have a point there).

Once Clem was born I took on less freelance work and started spending what few precious hours I could find each week on my own writing. My first novel, my bestseller hands down—and also my best book, according to not only Ingrid but pretty much everybody else—is about a girl in the foster care system who falls in love with her foster brother.

After Peter finishes showering off the smell of fish, I decide I should probably shower off the smell of cheap sunblock. When I come out of the bathroom wearing nothing but a towel, he's already sound asleep, snoring just loudly enough that I know siesta time is a total bust for me, so I decide to go for a walk.

The rest of the house is quiet. I don't know where Ingrid, Solly and Ivan are, but I'm guessing they're napping together in the master bed, Ivan sprawled out between them. Or maybe Solly and Ivan are napping while Ingrid soaks in the volcanic tub, balancing the shit out of her pH levels.

I go out to the beach and walk to the right, away from the rocks where Malcolm and Ivan hunted for starfish, toward the northern bend in the cove. On the other side of this bend are more private villas. After this there will be another villa, and then another villa, and then another, and then, eventually, there will be hotels with beaches packed with tourists, which will then give way to broader beaches fronting ritzy resorts.

Three villas share the first beach I come to, all built tall and shallow like ours, one a little shabbier than the others, one a little tackier, and one is flat-out gorgeous, with an infinity pool on the second level. I pat myself on the back for finding Villa Azul

Paraiso, because even if our pool is shaped like a kidney and isn't infinite, at least we don't share our beach with Villa Shabby and Villa Tacky.

I can see people moving around in each of these villas. They are all living, like we are, out in the open, no walls to hide behind. I wonder about them. Are they also celebrating a big birthday? Did they come for the religious festivities? Did they experience a series of travel mishaps on their way here? Are they with their families? Are they groups of friends who gathered to share the same space? Do they have staff making them hibiscus margaritas? Who claimed the master bedroom?

On the second floor of the gorgeous villa, next to the infinity pool, stands a woman. She is tall with long black hair tied up in a bun, black sunglasses and a black sheer cover-up that most definitely did not come from a juniors department. She is glamorous. She is not fighting with her husband. She is not having trouble finishing her manuscript. Nothing is keeping her up in the middle of the night. She looks content. She looks . . . like she is staring straight at me. It's hard to tell with the dark sunglasses. I look back at her for another beat before I stop and turn, continuing up the beach.

I scramble over a few rocks to reach the next stretch of sand. There is nothing here, no hotel, no villas, just a small patch of undeveloped jungle that has somehow managed to survive despite its prime oceanfront real estate. There's nobody here but a young couple, sitting in the sand at the far end of the beach, under the shade of a palm tree. As I draw nearer, I sneak another look at them.

It's Clem and Malcolm.

"Hey, Mom," Clem calls and waves. She doesn't seem embarrassed. She's not behaving as though she's been caught in the act of doing something she shouldn't. She actually looks happy to see me. I probably imagined it was a young couple in the distance because I saw two species—male and female—side by side, and my brain connected the dots. Jumped to conclusions. They are lying next to each other in the sand, yes, but I can see, now that I've drawn close, that there's a good two feet of separation between them.

"I thought you were going to the church," I say.

"We did." Malcolm reaches over and picks up a palm frond and waves it at me. Clem does the same with hers. "It was really crowded—the whole town must have shown up. There were these people in costumes. It was kind of awesome. We didn't stay for the whole thing, though, because Clem got hot and thirsty."

"I did," she admits.

"We decided to take the beach route home instead of the road," he continues. "And then we found this place."

"It feels like a beach on a deserted island. Like in *Lost*," Clem says.

"That show was sick." Malcolm puts his hand up and Clem claps her palm against his.

"Totally."

"Come on, Jenna," Malcolm says. "Hang with us." They inch a little farther away from each other and I squeeze in between them. Clem is right. From this spot you can't see any signs of civilization.

"I haven't even gone for a swim in the ocean yet," Clementine says, staring out at the calm water. "I've only been swimming in the pool. That's, like, what I do all the time back at home."

"You probably don't remember our house, Malcolm," I say. "But we don't have a pool, so I'm not sure what Clem is talking about."

"Mom. God. I'm talking about L.A. and how, like, *everyone* has a pool."

"Not *everyone*." I'm annoying her, I know. But I can't let her go around saying things like *everyone has a pool*. It's tone-deaf and obnoxious. That school of hers teaches kids not to make assumptions about gender identity, but it doesn't teach them not to walk around saying *everyone has a pool*. Of course, Solly and Ingrid *do* have a pool, so Malcolm probably isn't offended by her crass generalization, but still.

"You know what we should do tonight," Malcolm says to Clem. "We should go for a night swim."

"Isn't it scary swimming at night?"

"No," he says. "It's awesome, trust me."

It's always been this way with the two of them. Even if they don't remember that this is their natural order, I do: Malcolm, older by fifteen months, leading the way. Walking, talking, stuffing Cheerios into his mouth by the fistful. Maureen was my first friend to have a baby and I carefully watched every move Malcolm made like those slow-motion nature videos of a flower blooming or a frog catching a fly on its tongue.

Malcolm leans back and closes his eyes. Clem does the same. It's silent except for the water lapping at the sand. It's almost eerily silent. That's when I realize what's missing. The sound of Clem clicking away on her phone.

"Clementine, where's your phone?" I'm trying to quell my rising panic. If she lost her phone in Mexico, we won't be able to replace it, and she'll have a meltdown, and she'll ruin the rest of our vacation with her sullenness.

"I didn't bring it."

"You didn't?" Her phone is like an appendage. Or an organ. It's as if she left the villa without a lung.

"Nah. Sean is off with Ryan and those guys at some soccer game or something so . . ." She shrugs. "Whatever."

"I bet it's nice," I say. "Being out without a phone. Giving yourself a break from ubiquitous connectivity."

"Let's not push it, Mother."

I open my mouth to say something back but Malcolm speaks first. "You know . . . I *do* remember your house, Jenna. I remember it almost as well as I remember my old house."

"We did spend a lot of time together. Your mom was my only friend with a kid. We were in the trenches together."

"Stop trying to make yourself sound like a war hero," Clem says. "You were a mother. Big deal. And anyway, most of the time you just stuck us on the couch in front of a Disney video."

"I remember that couch," Malcolm says.

Clem turns to look at him. "Me too. I loved that couch. But we got rid of it years ago."

I LET CLEM AND MALCOLM go back ahead of me. I'm not quite ready to see Peter and I want a few more moments to myself. I sit cross-legged in the sand and close my eyes. I breathe in deeply. My go-to stress reliever is picturing myself on an empty beach. Smelling the salt in the air. Feeling the breeze. Since that sit-down conversation with my doctor I have imagined myself in this very spot over and over and over again. And now here I am. No more imagining. So why don't I feel the calm an empty beach promises?

Peter and I went straight home after the appointment. He took the rest of the afternoon off from work. He made me an omelet for lunch and he squeezed me some orange juice straight from our tree and he reminded me again and again that the doctor said I had every reason *not* to worry, that with minimal treatment I'd be *shipshape*. But I worried anyway. I pushed the omelet around on my plate.

"I used three different kinds of cheese," Peter said.

"It looks beautiful."

"Don't make me force-feed you."

I took a bite. And then another.

He grinned. "That's my girl."

"Remember, we have that concert at Largo tonight," Peter said later as he rinsed the dishes. "That'll take your mind off things."

Of course I'd forgotten. Solly had invited us to a benefit concert at Largo. "I don't think I feel up to it."

"Jenna, come on. It'll be fun. It's just what you need. A night out. A distraction."

"That may be what *you* need, Peter. But I don't know if it's what *I* need."

"Solly paid a fortune for these tickets. I think we have to go."

"I imagine Solly would understand. After all, I did just find out I have cancer."

He sat down at the table beside me. He took my hand and he kissed it. "I know this is scary. But there are all kinds of cancer, and sometimes it sounds worse than it really is. The doctor said you'd be fine. You have to believe her. She has no reason to lie to you."

"She can't know for sure."

"Oh, honey." He leaned in close and took me into his arms. With his chin resting on top of my head he said, "I love you and I am going to be right here with you for all of this. It's going to be okay."

We went to the concert that night. We had drinks beforehand with Ingrid and Solly at a bar down the street from the club. Ingrid got tipsy—this was before the nutritionist took her off alcohol. We didn't tell them about my diagnosis. We worried it would ruin the mood. Naturally, Solly's seats were front-row center. He beamed up at the stage with Peter beaming along right beside him.

Afterward, in the car on the way home Peter squeezed my knee and said, "Wasn't that fun? Aren't you glad we went?"

It wasn't and I wasn't, but I didn't see why I should spoil what had been a great night for Peter so I said, "Sure."

I **FINALLY GET UP** from the sand to walk back, but only because I realize that after my shower I didn't reapply any sunblock. I'm a sunblock Nazi with my daughter, but I'm not nearly so rigid with myself, when I need it even more than she does to ward off the wrinkles that multiply while I sleep.

At the next beach I see the woman in the sheer black cover-up and big sunglasses who earlier stood on the balcony of her perfect villa and now stands ankle-deep in the calm ocean water, wineglass in hand, staring at the horizon. I pause and I watch her watch the water because she looks like she's standing in a painting and this painting is having the calming effect that eluded me moments ago.

I want to be someone like that—someone who exudes control, elegance and an aura of *I don't give a shit*. This is what I attempted last night at the dinner table upon Peter's return from the mystery phone call, but instead I came off as jealous and small with an aura of *shrew*.

This woman would never feel threatened by her husband's assistant. She can't be bothered with such clichés. When her husband returns from a phone call taken in another room, on another floor, she does not question his need for privacy. She runs a hand through his thick hair and kisses him. He pulls back and looks at her and says, loud enough for everyone to hear: "How did I get so lucky?"

Why can't I be this woman? Is it too late to be this woman? When did I let my life get overrun by the devil grass of domestic obligation and worry?

The woman turns her back to the horizon and starts up toward her perfect villa. I am standing right in her path.

"Hello," she says to me. "It is beautiful, no?" She has sized me up immediately. Tourist. American. No grasp of basic, conversational Spanish.

"Yes," I say to her. It *is* beautiful: the beach, the sea, this woman and the perfect villa she is renting. "It's lovely."

She lifts her black sunglasses to the top of her head. She has large, dark, bottomless eyes. In her stare I feel tiny. "You've been to the service?"

"I'm sorry?"

She gestures to the palm fronds in my hand. The kids left them behind and I picked them up, because even for items I understand to be compostable, I can't tolerate littering.

"Oh, no. I just—"

"It is okay. I did not go either. But I still pray I may be worthy of His love."

"Me, too," I say because I'm not sure what else one is supposed to say in this situation. It doesn't seem like the right moment to preach my brand of atheism.

"Do you stay here?" She points to the villa next to hers, Villa Tacky.

"No," I respond, trying to hide the sting that she could believe I have such dreadful taste. Maybe it's my pink cover-up. Maybe she can see right through me, clear across the ocean and into the juniors department at Nordstrom. "I'm staying at the villa around the bend. Villa Azul Paraiso?"

"Yes," she says. "I know this villa. It is rumored to have once belonged to Carlos Salinas de Gortari. He was the president, but he was very greedy, and also corrupt. He was . . . a disgrace."

"Richard Nixon stayed there, too. And Martha Stewart. I guess it's like a luxury haven for disgraced people."

"This is funny," she says and she smiles, but she is too in control, too composed, for real laughter. "Now it is owned by an old couple from the United States. They call it Villa Azul Paraiso when it should be called Villa Paraiso Azul. This is the proper Spanish. This couple, they live in Wyoming, so maybe they do not know."

"Wyoming? That's strange."

"Yes. I had never heard of this place. But most of the owners of these villas now, they are from somewhere in the United States. There are restrictions for foreigners buying properties, but investors from the US have learned to work around these restrictions. Fewer and fewer of these homes are owned by the Mexican people."

I worried about the weather, about the exchange rate and time change, I tracked the paths of hurricanes, but I did not think to factor in the socioeconomic implications of renting property from a nonlocal owner. My impulse is to apologize but I had no idea who owned the villa. We went through a rental company, and anyway, if I had known that the owners were two old people from Wyoming it wouldn't have made any difference.

"Who owns the villa where you're staying?" I don't want to admit I saw her standing on the balcony of her enviable rental.

She makes a sweeping gesture toward Villa Perfect. "I do."

"You do?"

"Yes. Do you think the only people who live here cook and clean for rich Americans?"

"Oh, God. No. That is not what I meant at all. I—"

"I am only making a joke with you." She smiles again and this time, she laughs.

"Your house is . . . gorgeous," I tell her. "Truly. It's perfect."

"Thank you. You are very kind." She takes the final sip from her wineglass and then shakes the last drops into the sand. "Now I must go back inside. Please. Enjoy your time here in Puerto Vallarta."

. . .

I HAVEN'T CHECKED CLEM'S TEXTS since we arrived in Mexico. I haven't seen the point. It's not like I have *no* respect for her privacy, but I believe it's my job to keep her safe, to know the dangers she might be exposing herself to and to protect her from, or at least help her navigate her way around those dangers.

So maybe there's no justification for me to open up my laptop now and load the app that lets me see her texts. We're twelve hundred miles from her life back home, and we are under the same roof for the entire week—there are no dangers. But I look anyway, because I'm curious. I'm curious what she's telling Sean about Malcolm. I'm curious what she's telling him about our vacation in general. And curiosity, specifically the kind of curiosity a mother has with regard to her daughter, is a mighty force.

When Clem was in third grade, long before the days of iPhones and texting and Instagram and Snapchat, I found an envelope on her desk. I was straightening up for her; she's never been particularly neat or organized. The envelope was sealed and stuck between two books. On the outside she'd written: *PRI-VATE. DO NOT READ. PERSONAL PROPERTY OF CLEM-ENTINE CARLSON.* Underneath, she'd drawn a skull and crossbones.

I managed to hold out for nearly twenty-four hours before I opened that envelope. First I shook it. I held it up to the window. I placed it flat on her desk and shone a light on it. Nothing gave me the slightest clue about what skull-and-crossbones secret that envelope protected.

That night, when I put her to bed, I asked if there was anything she wanted to talk about. She said no. I asked if anything was bothering her. She said no. I asked if there was something she felt she couldn't say out loud, something it might be easier to write down on a piece of paper and then put away someplace safe. She didn't bite.

In the morning she boarded the school bus. I made myself a second cup of coffee. I poached myself an egg and read the news online. Then I went back up to her room, took out the envelope and tore it open.

Inside I found an itemized list of her Halloween candy.

It was three months past Halloween and all that candy had long since been devoured. I threw the envelope away and Clem never asked about it once.

If that should have taught me a lesson, I'm not sure what that lesson was meant to be, because here I am, sitting in one of the extra living rooms nobody ever uses, scrolling through Clem's texts.

She's mostly been texting Sean. There are a few exchanges with Ariella, who is still peeved about her parents' kilim runner, and with her friend Sadie about some new song that just dropped on iTunes.

I scroll back to yesterday and our arrival at the house.

> **CLEM:** this place is sick. massive.
> even bigger than Jasmine's
> mansion.
>
> **SEAN:** lol

CLEM: we're right on the beach.
ugh. wish you were here.

SEAN: me too

I whip quickly through volumes and volumes and volumes of texts and a full rainbow of heart emojis. I see spots where Sean redirects their conversation away from texting to FaceTime or Snapchat.

SEAN: check ur snap

SEAN: FT?

Those are the places I cannot see. They are the mediums of communication to which I have no access. Texting shows me only part of the picture. It's like standing on the beach and peering into someone's open villa—you may think you can see everything from your spot outside in the sand, but there are corners hidden from view, there are rooms with doors that shut.

I continue scrolling up to this afternoon and a long string of texts from an increasingly agitated Sean.

SEAN: where r u?

SEAN: hello?

SEAN: WTF?

Finally, at 4:30, right around the time Clem and Malcolm returned to the villa, she texted him back.

> **CLEM:** sry! i was w my parents.
> made me go to town to see a
> church and leave my phone—
> so annoying.

WHEN WE SIT DOWN to dinner that night, I notice that Clem chooses a place next to Malcolm. I sit next to her, across from Peter, whose beard is softer now, and with all the color he's getting from the sun, it looks like it's coming in extra white. He's handsome, my husband. I don't say that because I've already had two margaritas (mango-orange); it's just a fact. He's tall with broad shoulders and he has strong cheekbones, kind eyes and a warm smile.

I pretty much won the husband lottery. I know this. I know this because that's what everyone tells me, but also, I can see this for myself even if I sometimes forget to look. I know plenty of wives in addition to Maureen whose husbands left them for younger women. I know wives whose husbands won't come to events at their children's schools or who would never set foot in a grocery store or who can't be bothered to pick their underwear up off the bathroom floor. Husbands who have gotten fat and bald, not that one can be blamed for the latter (or even the former—and shame on me for even mentioning it as I'm the one who has gained fifteen pounds in the twenty years we've been together, not Peter). I know wives whose husbands have taken up expensive, boring hobbies. Husbands who have become drinkers. Or worse: excessive watchers of college sports.

Peter had the perfect model for the husband he wanted to be: his father. Young Pete understood from back when he paid more attention to Dungeons & Dragons than girls that if he wanted to be a good husband he simply had to do the opposite of everything his father did. His father was a temperamental, distant, philandering, boorish bastard. Peter can sometimes be a little smug and dismissive, and he can retreat into his own dark moods, but he's steady and loyal, and that he's as sweet and loving as he is, well—it's nothing short of a genetic miracle.

Instead of questioning his relationship with his young assistant, instead of punishing Peter for the small things he does to annoy me or even to occasionally undercut me, I should drop to my knees and pray like my new friend did today on the beach that I may be worthy of his love.

And did I already mention that he's handsome? Especially tonight with the sun on his cheeks and wearing the blue shirt I bought him for Christmas. The terribly unfair truth is that Peter and I are on opposite trajectories—he gets better-looking with each passing year while my own attractiveness trends downward. I find that this is true of men and women across the board, which only goes to prove that God is cruel. And probably a man.

I catch Peter's eye. He shoots me a grin. I point to him. He points at me. It's something we've been doing across crowded rooms across our many years together, it's our private sign language, our way of saying *we belong to each other*.

I look over at Solly. He isn't classically good-looking like Peter. He's shorter and stockier and, at nearly fifty, he's starting to get some gray in the thick head of black curls he wears long and slicked back. Even though his face is getting heavier and drooping like a basset hound's, he doesn't seem to be losing any of his sex appeal.

I know people who see Solly and Ingrid together wonder about their *Beauty and the Beast* situation, and they probably jump to the same erroneous conclusion I did initially—that it's all about his money. But they'd be wrong. Not about the money, because Solly does have a shit ton of money. But they'd be wrong if they believed that's all that attracts women to Solly. Sexiness can be hard to quantify, but Solly is a bona fide member of the 1 percent. It's a strange alchemy, some powerful brew of his charisma and confidence and intelligence and sense of humor, and the way he flirts. It doesn't matter if you're male or female, young or old, beautiful or hideous, when Solly is talking to you he is flirting with you. Who doesn't enjoy that kind of attention?

Solly looks at the dish Enrique is holding out and makes a face. "What the fuck is this?"

Enrique laughs. He isn't taken aback. Solly can even hurl an insult with a certain degree of charm.

We've all served ourselves the fish already. My piece is dark brown in spots and does not have an appetizing smell despite being smothered in onions and peppers and sprinkled with cilantro.

"It's bonito," says Enrique. "It is not a nice fish."

Solly frowns. "I thought Luisa said it was beautiful."

"No," Enrique says. "It is bonito. It is not good."

"Dad," Malcolm says. "*Bonit-a* means beautiful. Not *bonit-o*."

"Well, shit." Solly throws his head back and cackles.

"Well, shit," Ivan says. "Shitshitshitshitshit."

MONDAY

I ngrid's manuscript is waiting for me in my inbox when I wake
up. The time stamp says 1:21 A.M., so I guess I'm not the only
lousy sleeper in the house, although last night I slept like the
dead. I hate the grimness of that expression, but it's far more apt
than saying I slept like a baby. I've had a baby, so I know firsthand that babies wake many times a night screaming and crying,
having shat their pants, and thus are not the sleepers I aim to
emulate, not that I aim to emulate the dead.

The note she's sent along with the attachment says:

J-

I know when you offered to read this, you weren't necessarily
offering to read this NOW on our vacation, but I also know
that if I don't send it, I might very well lose my nerve. So here
it is. For whenever the mood strikes. Your opinion means the
world to me, but please: be brutally honest. No good will
come from trying to protect my feelings.

xx

I don't open the file, but I move it to my desktop. I can tell by the number of kilobytes that her work in progress already far exceeds the length of anything I've ever written. My manuscripts usually clock in between 45,000 to 55,000 words, or 195 to 225 pages. They're slim volumes, yes, but I don't believe this means they lack depth.

Right now I'm stuck around page 120 on a draft of a novel I've owed my editor for weeks. She's kind enough to give me breathing room, which might have something to do with the fact that I told her the radiation made me tired, when in fact it didn't at all, it just provided an ironclad excuse for my lack of productivity. She'll occasionally send me the cheerful email—with news of a mutual acquaintance, or a video about cats she thinks I'll like because I have a cat and our relationship isn't close enough for her to know that just because I have a cat does not mean I am a *cat person*—but she does not ask about my progress. I keep telling myself that the words will come, that the second half of this story will reveal itself to me. I've done the work of giving a voice to my narrator, developing the secondary characters, setting up the central conflict, the love interest, but I just can't seem to keep the story moving toward any kind of satisfying denouement. I go back and I go back, tweaking sentences, adding details to earlier scenes, but there is no doubt about it: I am lost in the thicket. I do not know how this ends.

Whatever the reason for my lack of progress, the file itself has become like a virus on my desktop. Something I'm afraid to touch. A little white rectangular icon of a reminder that there is something wrong with me, something wrong with everything, and clicking on it will only shine a bright, unforgiving light onto all of my shortcomings and struggles. So instead I avoid it. This is easy to do and even expected when one is on a dream vacation, but I've had no such excuse for the past several months.

The title of Ingrid's completed manuscript: *Lost in Space*. I wonder about this. Does the fifteen-year age gap between us mean she's never heard of the television show? I'm too young to have watched *Lost in Space* in its heyday, and when it came to those unsupervised afternoons we children of the seventies enjoyed, where we'd come home from school, gorge ourselves on junk food and watch reruns of old TV shows, I was more of a *Gilligan's Island* and *I Dream of Jeannie* kind of girl. But even if I've never seen a single episode of *Lost in Space*, I'm certainly aware of its existence, and anyway, I think it's been remade several times in the intervening decades.

I try to imagine what shows were on when Ingrid returned home from a day at school, and I realize that by then I was already an adult with a job, so I have no idea what was going on in the world of afternoon television reruns.

She's up before me. Already at the dining room table with a mug of tea, reading a book to Ivan while he eats a breakfast of sliced mango and tortillas slathered in butter.

"Good morning," I say.

"Shhhhh," Ivan says. "We're reading."

"Oops"—I put my hands up—"Sorry."

"Ivan. That's not polite," Ingrid scolds. "You need to say good morning to Jenna. And then you can say, 'Excuse me, but we're in the middle of reading a book.'"

Ivan looks at me with his little brow furrowed. "Ding dong," he says.

"Ivan." Ingrid closes the book. He reaches over and opens it again.

"Read," he orders.

"First say good morning to Jenna."

At this point, I want a cup of coffee roughly a thousand times more than I want an appropriate greeting from Ivan, but I stand there, waiting. He shoots daggers at me with his eyes. "Good morning," he says in a tone no different than one might say "Fuck off."

"There," Ingrid says, rubbing his back. "Was that so difficult?" She kisses him on the head and picks up where they left off.

This is how Ingrid deals with her challenging son—with a bountiful supply of patience. But I also see how she's constructed an alternate narrative, a version of her family story in which her boy is quirky and maybe a little irascible, but by no means is he on the spectrum. At first I mistook him for spoiled, perhaps ruined, for being his mother's sole focus and raison d'être, but I've seen scores of kids who fit that bill, including my own, who are nowhere near as strange and unappealing as Ivan Solomon. It's pretty clear to me that there's something else going on that his mother fails to see and his father, too, but you can hardly blame Solly for misunderstanding his child when to Solly, his children are an afterthought. When I try talking to Peter about Ivan he shuts me down every time because, of course, by virtue of the fact that he carries Solly's DNA, Ivan is beyond reproach. Sometimes I feel robbed. Deprived of the perverse pleasure that comes from measuring your kid against someone else's lesser one, and Peter calls me on that, too.

Our argument typically goes like this:

"There's something off about Ivan," I tell Peter. "Don't you think?"

"No. I don't think."

"C'mon . . ."

"Are you implying that Ivan has a diagnosable social/emotional disorder for which he needs medical attention? Because if that is what you are implying you seem to be inexplicably gleeful while delivering your wholly uninformed diagnosis."

"No, I'm just saying Ivan is an odd duck and you know it, but instead we all have to pretend that he breathes in rainbows and sneezes out fairy dust."

That's around when Peter will leave the room or turn up the radio or fix me with a look of such withering disdain that I'll drop the subject.

I go into the kitchen where I find Roberto and Luisa sitting together at the table, reading a local newspaper and drinking coffee. They both jump when I enter, scrambling to their feet as if I've caught them in flagrante delicto.

"Sit," I say. "Relax."

"I get for you the coffee." Roberto makes a move toward the counter.

"I'm perfectly capable of pouring a cup for myself. Please, go back to the newspaper."

"No, it is okay. I get for you. You like cream but you do not like sugar, this is correct?"

"Yes, Roberto." I'm touched that he knows how I take my coffee. *"Muchas gracias."*

He fixes my cup and he hands it over. I breathe in the aroma and then take the first exquisite sip.

A few days after telling Clem about my diagnosis she asked me how many cups of coffee I drink a day. I told her around three or four. She said I should drink at least five. I had no idea why she'd taken such an interest in my coffee consumption until she explained that she'd read an article online about how women who drink five cups of coffee a day reduce their risk of getting breast cancer.

I didn't point out that changing my behavior to reduce the risk of getting a disease I already had didn't make much logical sense, I just put my arms around her and held her for a long time. When Peter and I delivered the news we were careful to explain all the reasons she shouldn't worry, and yet she'd gone off and Googled *breast cancer*, probably falling down the same rabbit holes I had. Of course she worried. How could she not? She's my daughter. And by that I mean she's *my* daughter. Despite all our differences and all the ways I believe she is in possession of gifts far greater than mine, we are still very much alike. I held her tighter. She squeezed back. I told her that maybe we didn't need to always show each other our bravest faces. *Okay, Mother*, she said.

"What do you like Luisa to make for you?" Roberto asks. "Huevos rancheros? Chilaquiles? She can make a smoothie with all the fruits?"

"No breakfast for me. Not yet. A little bit later."

They're still standing. Waiting for me to assign them a task. Instead I take a seat at their table. I'd rather be in here with them than out in the dining room with Ingrid and Ivan and that book I remember hating when I used to read it to Clementine. I take a look at their newspaper. It's in Spanish, obviously. Above the fold, there's a picture of a large crowd in the streets. A few people are carrying crosses. Everyone is dressed in bright colors.

"What's this?" I ask, pointing to the headline.

Roberto sits back down at the table and gestures to Luisa, who looks around the kitchen, shrugs and joins us, too.

"It is an article about festivities. In town. For Semana Santa. It is a holy week, but also, it is a week for celebration. People come from everywhere. Not just you from United States, but also the Mexican people. It is a place for everyone. The beaches, they are crowded, and the restaurants and bars in town, and church, too. It is a happy time. Jesus, he is crucified, but then he rises and we celebrate."

"Yes," I say. "We have Easter back at home." I immediately feel like a total ass for having said this, but rather than try to fix it, I turn the paper over to look at the articles below the fold. There is a picture of a man speaking into a microphone at what is probably some sort of a press conference. "What's happening here?" I ask him.

Roberto takes the paper and looks at it more closely. He and Luisa have a back-and-forth in Spanish. Then Roberto says, "He is the governor of Jalisco state. That is the state here, where is Puerto Vallarta. He is speaking to the people to say no worry about violence. We are safe."

"Why would he need to say that?"

"There are gangs, you know, how do you say, *against each other*? The ones who compete to win the same thing?"

"Rivals?"

"Yes, rivals. They fight for control of the drug trade in Jalisco state. One member of one group, he kills a member of other one.

It does not happen here in Puerto Vallarta. It happens farther away. And it is only a problem for criminals who are in cartels. We are safe. This is what the governor says."

"Well . . . that's good, I guess?" Warring drug cartels is another item that did not make it onto the list of considerations when we were choosing our vacation spot. I flip the paper back over. I much prefer to look at the costumed revelers walking in the streets.

There's an awkward silence. Then Luisa says something to Roberto in Spanish. She is pointing at me. He laughs. *Are they making fun of me?*

"Luisa, she wants to make for you the breakfast," Roberto says. "She says you must eat. She says you no wait for your husband. She says women, they spend too much time waiting for husbands."

I smile. "Okay. Tell her to make me whatever she wants."

I HAVE NO IDEA how late Peter will sleep; I have no idea how late it was when he finally came to bed. After dinner Clem and Malcolm went for a night swim. Ingrid went to lie down with Ivan. I tried reading in the living room while Peter and Solly talked, mostly about work, but Solly had put on some jazz that was dissonant and building toward a resolution that never came. It made me anxious and I had trouble following what was happening in my novel, a beach read that hardly requires a great level of concentration, so I retired to our bedroom.

"I'll be in soon," Peter said. "I'll just wait until Malcolm and Clem get back."

An hour or so later I went out to the living room again. I didn't want to fall asleep without Peter and also, I couldn't fall asleep knowing Clem was down on the beach with Malcolm. I didn't love the idea of them swimming in the dark. Aren't there strong tides at night? What about stingrays? Are jellyfish nocturnal? I didn't raise these worries with Peter or Solly because I knew they'd make fun of me—*Jenna and her neuroses*—but I also didn't raise my other nagging concern: Malcolm. I know from Maureen that he'd gotten into some trouble back home, but she'd been vague on the details. All she's shared with me is that he's finishing out his senior year in some alternative school where there are only three kids in a class (*It's fabulous*, she wrote, *a much better fit for him*). Peter claims not to know what happened either. He says it's best not to push and to let Solly and Maureen put whatever sort of spin on it they choose. I don't judge them and I don't judge Malcolm; I know being a teenager is hard and it's probably been harder on him than most. I know good kids do stupid things. But still. That's my one and only kid out there on the beach at night.

When I reappeared, Solly had on some Nina Simone, perfectly acceptable reading music.

"Did Clem and Malcolm make it back?"

"Yes," Peter said. "They weren't gone long. Clem complained that the water was too cold. She's such a wuss."

"Aren't you coming to bed?"

Peter gestured to his glass. "Solly peer-pressured me into having another tequila."

"It's excellent tequila." Solly held up the bottle, but didn't offer to pour me any.

I felt foolish standing there in my nightgown. "Okay. I guess I'll see you soon, then?"

"See you soon, honey."

The next thing I knew, it was morning.

WHEN EVERYONE IS FINALLY UP and fed and gathered in the dining room, Solly announces that he's booked us a snorkeling trip to Los Arcos.

"I found the brochure in that binder with all the house information. Fun fact: did you know that Richard Nixon slept here?"

"Yes, Solly," I say. "It's all over the marketing materials. Which I sent you. Months ago."

"Tricky Dick wandered these hallways. Maybe even in his tighty-whiteys. Let's all take a moment to imagine that, shall we?"

"That's going to be a no for me," Malcolm says.

"Ditto," Clem says. "And ew."

"Anyhoo," Solly says. "Back to snorkeling. We'll be on our own private boat. It comes equipped with all the gear. And that boat will come pick us up at our own private beach. How's that for service?"

"What's snorkeling?" Ivan asks.

"It's when you swim around with a mask and a rubber thing that helps you breathe so you can spy on all the fish."

"Is there wi-fi on the boat?" Clem asks.

"Jesus, Clem." Peter gives her a playful shove. I don't know if she's being serious or if she's just so used to playing the part of technology-obsessed teen that she can't break character.

"What?" she says. "It's a perfectly reasonable question."

"What about Jenna?" Peter asks Solly. I get seasick. Solly knows I get seasick. He knows this because we've been friends for twenty years and these are the sorts of things you know about old friends. At the very least he should remember the time he booked a sunset cruise out of Marina del Rey to celebrate Maureen's birthday. While everyone drank champagne and ate oysters standing on the bow of the boat, I was bent over the back railing, leaving a trail of vomit that zigzagged from Marina del Rey to Manhattan Beach to Redondo Beach and back again.

"I got you covered," Solly says. "I talked to the tour company and they have these foolproof seasickness bracelets. At no extra charge! And on top of it, look"—he gestures to our view of the bay—"it's hardly *A Perfect Storm* situation out there." It's another day of clear skies and calm waters. I checked the weather-tracking site this morning. The storm is farther from us today than it was yesterday.

I sigh.

"Jenna." Solly puts an arm around me. "Los Arcos is the best snorkeling spot in all of Puerto Vallarta. And it isn't a very long trip when you're on a private boat."

Peter gives me a pleading look. Does he want me to go because he wants to be with me, or is it just that he doesn't want me to be a killjoy?

"Okay," I say. "I'll give it a shot."

Solly claps his hands. "Great. All right, folks. We set sail at noon. The company provides all the equipment, towels, lunch, and beer for those who are old enough to consume it." He raises an eyebrow at Malcolm.

"The drinking age here is eighteen, Dad."

"Last time I checked you were seventeen."

"Yeah, but nobody even cares."

"I stand by my statement. Beer for those old enough to consume it."

As everyone disperses, Ingrid lingers. "You know," she says to me in a quiet tone, "you don't have to go just because Solly is pressuring you. He can be sort of overbearing."

"Really? Solly? Overbearing?"

She laughs. "Right. Of course. Sometimes I forget how long you've known him." Ivan tugs at her sleeve but she ignores him. "So listen, I don't know if you checked your email or not today." I give her a totally neutral look. I don't let on that I have, I don't deny that I did. "But I sent you my manuscript. Don't feel pressured to read it. I don't want to be a Solly about it. I sent it to you because I was up late obsessing over it, and worrying about getting it just right, then realizing I probably never would get it just right, and it was better to let it go. So I hit SEND. And now I feel guilty."

I squeeze her arm. "I'm glad you did. And I'll read it soon. I promise. I have a few things to finish first. I'm in the final stretch of my latest book and it's absorbing most of my time and energy, but I swear, I'll read it. Don't feel guilty about sending it. It'll be a treat."

"Thanks, Jenna." She takes Ivan by the hand and they trail off in the direction of their bedrooms to get ready.

I try to picture her up late at night working on her manuscript. Was she typing on her laptop in the master bed while Solly and Ivan slept? Did she leave Solly and Ivan tangled together and sneak out to the living room? Then my curiosity shifts gears: With Ivan glued to her side, with Ivan sharing their bed, how do they find time for intimacy? Do they still have sex? Have they had sex on this vacation?

Not that it's a competition: a race to the sheets. But there's something comforting in imagining that Peter and I are not the only ones who haven't used our high-value minutes; that we aren't getting left in their sexual dust.

"Hey, babe," Peter calls from upstairs. "Have you seen my navy swim trunks?"

I go up to show him where, after drying them out in the sun, I folded them neatly and put them away.

THE BRACELET WORKS. I'm not saying my stomach is 100 percent, but I don't feel like crawling in a hole and dying either, so it's a vast improvement on every other time I've set foot on a boat.

From our vantage point in the water, we watch as everything gets smaller: our villa and the ones nearby; and to the north, the crowded beaches with tightly packed striped umbrellas, big blocky salmon-colored hotels, jet skiers and their circular wakes, and parasailers with their multihued billowing chutes.

Solly was right. The trip to Los Arcos doesn't take very long. Our captain steers us to the far side of the rocks, where fewer boats have dropped their anchors and fewer snorkelers float around on the surface of the water.

There's no shade on the boat to speak of. I pestered Clem to wear the swim shirt I packed for her since she refused to pack it herself.

"Ha," she said. "You're funny, Mother. I am not going to wear that because I am not a nun."

"We're all going to wear swim shirts, because that's how we take care of ourselves."

"Have fun with that," she said and pulled her tank top over her bikini.

As it turns out, Ivan and I are the only ones in swim shirts. Solly and Peter wear regular T-shirts with trunks and Malcolm is shirtless. Ingrid wears a man's-style white linen button-down that could be Solly's except that it fits her flawlessly.

Our captain, "Captain Dan"—so identified by the stitching on his royal blue polo shirt—asks if we want to eat or snorkel first. He's a big, ruddy, white-haired guy with a gap between his two front teeth who came to Puerto Vallarta on vacation from Boston ten years ago and never went back.

There's also a Mexican boy on board who looks like he's younger than Clementine and whose name I don't know because he doesn't have his name stitched onto a blue polo shirt; he wears only a pair of ratty black shorts.

We decide to eat first, so Captain Dan says something to the boy in Spanish, who then opens up a small cooler of sad-looking sandwiches and a much larger cooler filled with beer. He tosses around a few bags of chips.

Solly opens a beer for himself and then he pops another one and hands it to Malcolm.

Malcolm grins. "Thanks, Dad." They clink bottles.

"What about me?" Clem asks. "Don't I get one?"

"Here. You can share mine." Peter hands her his beer and she takes a long, expert pull of it. He avoids making eye contact with me. He knows I won't approve. Even if we're aware that Clem drinks sometimes, we don't condone it, and we certainly don't enable it. But Peter wanted to look like the cool dad in front of Solly. And part of cultivating that coolness means not only giving his sixteen-year-old daughter beer but doing so without asking her mother for permission first.

"I want to spy on the fish," Ivan says.

"Soon," Ingrid tells him. "We're just finishing up our lunch."

"I want to spy on the fish," he says again.

I'm not eating because I can't eat on boats, and I'm certainly not drinking, so I offer to take him.

He eyes me suspiciously.

"Come on," I say, standing up and reaching out my hand. "Maybe we'll find Nemo."

CAPTAIN DAN has the Mexican boy rinse and clean the equipment and then fits Ivan with a mask as big as his face and a snorkel tube he can barely get his mouth around. Ivan keeps his life jacket on and refuses the fins because they make his feet "itchy."

I climb down the ladder off the side of the boat and ease myself into the water. Ivan cannonballs in. I help him adjust his snorkel tube and he immediately takes in a big swallow of ocean water, but it doesn't deter him: He just spits it out and tries again. Clem would have lost her shit at that age if she swallowed ocean water, and probably still would. She didn't even learn to swim until she was two years older than Ivan is now because she didn't like getting her hair wet.

It's lovely in the water. Warm and calm; soon, Ivan and I put a sizable distance between ourselves and the boat. We swim under the arc of Los Arcos—a natural archway in one of the two large rock formations. Solly was right to pressure me into coming on this excursion. The snorkeling is top-notch. There's an astonishing world of sea life. If I knew more about marine biology, perhaps I could name some of what we see, but I don't; all I know is that the fish are colorful and fanciful and they remind me of my childhood dentist's office with its huge aquarium in the waiting room.

Ivan points everything out to me with his chubby little fingers. I respond with an underwater thumbs-up.

When we come around to the other side of the rocks Ivan pops upright, pulls off his mask and spits out the tube. His life vest keeps him afloat; I tread water.

"I think I found him," he says. "I think I found Nemo."

"This is so much fun, isn't it?"

"Yes. But I'm done."

"Okay," I say. "Let's go back to the boat."

"I'm done snorkeling."

"That's fine. We can head back."

"I don't want to snorkel anymore." He hands me his mask and tube.

"That's fine," I repeat. "We don't have to snorkel anymore. We can just swim back to the boat."

"I don't want to swim. I'm done."

I reach over and take him by the hand. "Ivan. We have to get back to the boat one way or another."

He pulls his hand away. "Ding dong."

"Ivan."

"I want the boat to come here and get me."

"Well, it can't. So let's go."

"Ding dong."

"Ivan."

His eyes fill with tears and his bottom lip starts to tremble. "Mommy! *Mommy! Help me! Mommy!*"

"Ivan," I say, more harshly than I intend. "Don't scream like that."

"*MOMMY!*"

Two nearby snorkelers poke their heads up and kick their way closer to us with their fins.

"Everything okay?" says one of the guys in a thick Australian accent. "Are you in distress?"

Yes, I think. I am very much in distress.

"I don't want to snorkel," Ivan wails. "I want my mommy."

The snorkelers look at me, puzzled. "I'm not his mother," I explain. "I'm a friend. His parents are on a boat with my family on the other side of the rocks. We made our way over here while snorkeling and now he doesn't understand that we have to swim back."

"I don't want to snorkel anymore!" Ivan shouts.

"Hey," the Australian says. "Have you ever ridden a whale?"

"No." Ivan has snot running out of his nose.

"See my mate Jeff here?" The Australian gestures to his friend, who waves at Ivan. "He kind of looks like a whale, doesn't he? All blubbery and whatnot?"

"Yeah," Ivan says, letting a little laugh escape.

"So take your pick. You can ride to your boat on the back of a whale, or you can ride to your boat on the back of a sleek dolphin." The Australian points to himself with his thumb.

"The dolphin," Ivan says.

"Good choice." The Australian turns around and Ivan throws his arms around his neck. I lead us all to the boat, somehow managing to swim the distance while dragging Ivan's snorkel gear along with my own.

IVAN WON'T LET INGRID go off and snorkel with the others. He clings to her leg and cries.

"It's okay, sweetie," she says. "I'll stay. I'll stay right here with you." She pulls him onto her lap and he buries his face in her chest.

I turn to Solly. "I guess maybe I took him too far. I knew he was a good swimmer, I just didn't think about stamina. But with the life vest . . ."

"It's okay, Jen," Solly says. "He's just tired."

Tired is the catchall for everything when you're a parent of a small child. When your child throws a tantrum, when your child refuses to kiss his grandmother, when your child doesn't say thank you, when your child does anything remotely shitty, you can always just say: *He's tired* or *She didn't get enough sleep last night* and you're off the hook.

Peter, Solly, Malcolm and Clem sunblock up, put on their snorkel gear and take off. I count the empty beer bottles on the boat: there are only three, and two of them have a third of the beer left in them, so at least I know they're sober enough for snorkeling.

The Mexican boy climbs down the side ladder, and eases himself into the water. He's not utilizing any of the snorkeling equipment; he's just taking slow, lazy laps around the boat. Clearly he'll do anything to avoid being on board and under the command of this fat retiree from Boston, and I have to admit, it's far more comfortable for me not to have him sitting here, absentmindedly playing with the drawstring on his ratty shorts while Captain Dan stuffs his mouth with potato chips.

Ingrid and I sit in silence for a few minutes while I watch the boy swim and she rubs Ivan's back. He sucks his thumb and soon he's breathing deeply. I look at the sleeping Ivan. I point to the padded bench. "Do you want to try to transfer him so you can join the others?"

"No," she says. "I want to sit here on this boat, enjoying the peace and quiet. Just us."

"Don't forget about Captain Dan." I nod in the direction of the front of the boat where Captain Dan sits, headphones on, face buried in a magazine.

"Captain Dan, too," she says. "I want quality time with Captain Dan."

I pick up an uneaten sandwich, think about taking a bite, then think better of it.

"Anyway, it's good for Malcolm to spend time with Solly," she continues. "This hasn't been an easy year for him. He could use the influence of his father. God knows what sort of role modeling he's getting at home."

I guess it's no surprise that Ingrid blames Maureen for whatever trouble Malcolm has gotten into. Even though he's the one who decided to go for a do-over on the family front, Solly has always been stingy in his appraisal of the job his ex-wife is doing as the primary parent. Maureen is *controlling, unbending,* a *funsponge.* She's a *stuffed shirt* just because she works for a New York hedge fund. I'm not sure exactly what Solly expected Maureen to do after he left her for Ingrid, but building a thriving career for herself certainly shouldn't be something he faults her for.

While I was waiting tables postcollege, Maureen was at Oxford on a Rhodes scholarship because in addition to being gorgeous, she is a brilliant and highly capable human being. This trifecta—beauty, brains, competence—is what had Solly so smitten from the minute he met her at a dinner party. Peter and I were also in attendance; we witnessed Solly falling hard firsthand. They married within a year. He was crazy about Maureen, until, of course, he wasn't. Until domesticity ruined them and he fell for the young bohemian jewelry designer. Solly raves about Ingrid's free-spiritedness; how she has an artist's soul. Meanwhile he paints Maureen as uptight and boring and a lousy mother to boot. It's Solly at his least generous and most dishonest.

He says he plans to throw a rager when Maureen remarries to celebrate the end of his alimony payments. He says he'd relish the opportunity to walk her down the aisle himself, but I know, and I'm sure he does, too, that Maureen is far too smart to get married again—ever.

Anyway, I can't defend Maureen to Ingrid if I don't even know what's going on with Malcolm. And I do want to know what's going on, because it is my nature to want to know what's going on. So maybe now, sitting on this boat, with Ivan fast asleep and the others snorkeling out of sight, with Captain Dan buried in his magazine and the poor Mexican boy on his umpteenth lap around the boat, without Peter here to scold me to mind my own business, maybe *now* is the right time to finally find out.

"What's going on with Malcolm anyway?" I ask Ingrid.

"I don't want to say too much. It's not my place. But let's just say he's made some bad choices."

"He's a teenager. Isn't he supposed to make bad choices? Isn't that part of the job description?"

"Yes. I suppose so. Within reason. But look at Clem," she says. "Clem doesn't get herself in trouble. She's a grounded kid. She's a good student. She's got that sweet boyfriend."

"Clem is perfectly capable of doing stupid shit." I'm thinking, of course, of Ariella's parents' rug.

"Well, sure. But not like Malcolm, trust me."

She's being intentionally coy. Wielding the power this sliver of knowledge lends her. I decide to abandon my line of questioning; I don't want to ally myself with her against Malcolm or his mother.

And anyway I'm not sure I trust her assessment of the situation. I'm not saying Clementine is right—that Ingrid is wary of Malcolm because he is black—just like I don't believe her issues with Maureen have anything to do with her being black. I think it's that Ingrid doesn't have a teenager of her own, she's never worked with teenagers and she doesn't write about teenagers, so what does she know?

Ivan lets out a big sigh and flips over, still sound asleep. Ingrid adjusts her towel to shield his face from the sun.

"I had a serious boyfriend when I was sixteen," she says. "We were like Clem and Sean. Always together. And when we weren't together we were on the phone. An hour away from him felt like a year."

I was too loud and opinionated, too stubborn, for boys when I was Clem's age. I wasn't interested in doing what I knew I needed to do to get their attention, starting with caring at all about how I looked or what I wore. I spent most of high school hanging around my male teachers, seeking them out for extra help, writing my papers with the goal of impressing them; any praise they'd bestow on me was a small, delicious pleasure.

"I learned everything from him," she goes on. "And I do mean *everything*."

I laugh, because that feels like the right thing to do.

"So . . ." she says.

"So . . . what?"

"So . . . do you think Clem and Sean are having sex?"

It's funny to me that Ingrid thinks it's not her place to say what's going on with Malcolm, but it is her place to ask if my daughter is sexually active.

"No, they aren't."

"They're not? Really?"

"Nope."

"How can you be so sure?"

"Because we talk. We're close." This is true. I have done everything in my power to present myself to Clementine as someone free of judgment, someone who is not a prude, someone who understands teens and sex. She's told me that they aren't ready yet, that she doesn't see that changing anytime soon; and yes, I'm her mother, so of course that makes my heart sing.

I don't tell Ingrid that I also know they aren't having sex because I've seen their texts, and their texts are full of *luv u* and heart emojis and the quotidian details of their teen lives, and are free of talk of anything having anything at all to do with sex.

"I never told my mother I was having sex," she says. "And we were close."

In the silence that follows I notice a buzzing. At first I think it's a mosquito. I didn't bring any bug spray, only sunblock. Don't mosquito bites cause Zika? Or is it dengue fever? Why do I worry about the sun and not mosquitoes?

The buzzing stops. I lean back and close my eyes. If I pretend I'm asleep I won't have to talk to Ingrid anymore.

The buzzing starts again.

"What's that sound?" Ingrid asks. "Do you hear it?"

I get up, because Ingrid can't. I look around. The sound has stopped. Just as I'm about to sit back down, it starts again. I follow it to the other side of the boat where everyone left their clothes in a pile. It's a phone. It must be Clem's. I pick through her things, but her phone is silent. The buzzing continues.

Peter's T-shirt and hat are covering his wallet and phone. I move his clothes aside. His phone is buzzing with an incoming call from Gavriella Abramov.

I decline the call. The screen shows five missed calls from

Gavriella Abramov all within the last few minutes. I stare at the phone in disbelief. It starts vibrating in my hand with a sixth call.

"Who's calling?" Ingrid asks.

"It's Peter's assistant."

"Gavi?"

"Yes."

"Don't answer it. This is vacation."

"She keeps calling."

"So shut off the phone."

I ignore Ingrid and answer the call. "Hello?"

There's silence on the other end of the line.

"Hello?" I say again. I sound angry, which is okay, because I am angry.

"Oh. Jenna? Hi. It's Gavriella? From work?"

"Yes, I know who it is."

"I'm trying to reach Peter?"

I make a quick calculation. I could tell her that she isn't supposed to be calling, that I asked Peter to tell her not to call on our vacation, not under any circumstances, and certainly not *six times in a row*, but if I do this, it will give Peter leverage in the argument we're inevitably bound to have later on today. He'll say I overstepped, that I shouldn't interfere in his communication with someone who works for him, that I should never have answered his phone in the first place. The other factor is that Ingrid is sitting not five feet from where I stand with the phone to my ear and if I scold Gavriella in front of her it will open a window onto a dynamic in my life and marriage I'd rather keep shut.

"He's snorkeling."

"Oh. Okay. Well. Can you please tell him to call me? It's important."

She sounds upset. I realize I could be imagining this, transferring my own emotional state onto her disembodied voice, but still, I'm a woman, and I tend to know when a woman sounds upset.

I look out over the side of the boat toward the rocks of Los Arcos. There are dozens of snorkelers out in the water. I think I can see Peter and the others in the distance, but there's really no way to tell for sure.

"Okay," I say. "I'll let him know."

She's already hung up. The line goes dead.

BACK ON THE BEACH in front of Villa Azul Paraiso, Peter asks me if I have my wallet. I've already started up toward the house, not waiting for everyone to unload. He has to run to catch me.

"Why?"

"Because we need to pay Captain Dan. We owe him a hundred fifty dollars and I've only got a hundred on me."

"Why do *we* need to pay?"

"Because we hired him to take us snorkeling?" Peter is looking at me like I've lost my mind.

"No. Solly hired him. And he hired him without asking us if we even wanted to go."

"Jen." He lowers his voice. "You're being petty. It's not attractive."

"What about the boy?"

"What boy?"

"The boy on the boat. How much money do you think he's getting?"

"I don't know. But I'll make sure to tip him if you'd just give me some money."

"Why don't you tell Solly to peel off a few bills from that fat, impressive wad he carries everywhere in his pocket?"

"Jesus Christ," he says and storms off back toward the water.

I watched Peter carefully when he returned from snorkeling. He toweled off and gave his gear to the Mexican boy. He picked up one of the bottles with a third of the beer left in it and took a swig. He made a face because that beer was probably close to boiling, then reached into the cooler for a bottle of water. He argued with the others about whether that long striped thing that darted under a rock was an eel. He asked if anyone had some ChapStick. He made his way over to his pile of stuff. He put on his T-shirt and hat. He stuck his wallet in the pocket of his wet swim trunks. He looked at his cell phone.

His handsome, bearded, sun-tanned face showed no reaction at all.

I don't really care about the money for the boat. I suppose that's obvious. Even if it bugs me that Solly would make a uni-lateral decision and then count on us to pay half, I normally wouldn't say anything. I'm used to Solly pretending there's no inequity in our financial statuses and I've made my peace with it. Part of the price of being his friend is accepting that he has more money and more power and that he's generous at times with both—like how he invited Peter, who had no business experi-ence, to be his partner—but also that his generosity has limits, like how Peter doesn't seem to benefit as much from the business's success despite his doing more than half the work. But standing there on the beach in front of the villa, I didn't want to tell Peter why I'm really agitated. I didn't want to say her name out loud. I should have just handed him the money. I have my wallet in my bag.

Maybe I am being paranoid without good reason. Maybe I am misdirecting my anxiety about the book I can't finish and the lingering worry about my health onto what is a perfectly normal employer/employee relationship. Maybe I tend, as Peter claims, to look in the wrong places when I'm in a state about things. But the fact remains that she called six times in a row. That must be one hell of an emergency, and if it was an emergency, why didn't he call her back from the boat?

It's four o'clock in the afternoon. Only a few hours until it's time for predinner cocktails, though I could have one now. I could have several. Nobody would judge. Everyday rules don't apply, time collapses—that's what it means to be on vacation.

Instead I decide I need to clear my head. Get away from everybody.

I go and knock on Clem's door.

"What?"

I don't want to get away from Clem. When she was Ivan's age it's all I wanted, but now I know how soon she'll be the one getting away.

I knock on her door and open it. "Want to go for a walk with me?"

"Ha!"

She's lying on her bed. Still in her swimsuit, on FaceTime with Sean. I want to tell her to cover up, but I don't.

"Hi, Sean," I say.

I hear him say "Hi, Jenna," but Clem doesn't turn the phone around, so I can't see him and what he may or may not be wearing.

"Come on, Clem. Come with me."

"Um, that sounds great, but no."

"I want to spend some time with you."

"We just spent several hours together stuck on a tiny boat."

"Please? I'll take you to town and buy you something. Whatever you want."

"That's cool, Mom. But I don't need a sombrero or a colorful wool blanket. I'm good."

I close her door and make a mental note to chastise her later about the sombrero and blanket comment. I go to the kitchen to talk to Roberto. He's there with Enrique and Luisa, all three engaged in various stages of food preparation.

"The dinner tonight," Roberto says. "Chicken mole. It is much better than bonito, no?"

"Anything will be better than bonito," I say.

Enrique looks up from dicing onions. "Bonito is not a nice fish."

"If I wanted to go to town, to walk around a little bit and check out the shops or some art galleries, can you tell me where I should go?"

The three of them confer in Spanish. Clearly disagreeing, but lightheartedly. Nobody snaps at anybody, I see no signs of simmering resentments, no deep sighs, no whispered rebukes. They come to a consensus. Roberto reaches for the map in the drawer.

"Here," he says, circling a several-block radius with a pencil. "It is good this area. For shopping and also for art."

"And can you show me how to walk there?"

"Do you go alone?"

"Yes," I say, since Clem has made perfectly clear she has no intention of joining me, and since there is nobody else whose company I covet.

"Then you take a taxi," Roberto says. "I call for you."

"I think I'd enjoy the walk."

Again there's a three-way back-and-forth in Spanish. This time Luisa talks over the men. I'm starting to understand that she's the one in charge.

"No," Roberto says. "You take a taxi. For a woman alone it is more better."

"I thought you said it was safe here."

"It is safe, yes. But for a woman it is not good idea to walk alone. In town is fine. But on empty roads, no. Is this not true where you live in the United States?"

I don't feel like thinking about this question. It just agitates me more. "I don't have any pesos," I say.

"Is okay," Roberto tells me. "Everyone here loves dollars."

THE NEIGHBORHOOD the taxi drops me in is charming: tree covered, cobblestoned and full of people. All the bright, electric colors of the fruit stands, tissue paper flags, paintings, pottery, T-shirts and, yes, wool blankets lift my spirits. I know there are women who sing the praises of retail therapy; I have never been one of those women. But I do find that getting out, wandering around, interacting with strangers and generally joining the scrum of humanity has a way of calming me and putting things into perspective. At least for the moment.

I stop at a stand where a young girl is selling bracelets made of string with names woven into them. It's hard to imagine that any locals would buy these bracelets and yet all the names are Spanish: *Antonio, José, Miguel*. And then I see the bright red one with *Pedro* in yellow stitching and I feel a wave of warmth for Peter. He loves me. We have built this imperfect but solid life together.

I reach out and touch the bracelet. The girl quickly unhooks it from her display and presses it into my hand.

"*Cincuenta y siete*," she says.

"I'm sorry. I'm not sure—"

"*Cincuenta y siete*," she says again. She is a beautiful child with huge eyes beneath thick black bangs. One of her front teeth is capped in gold.

I take out my wallet. Peter will wear this bracelet when we are in Mexico to humor me but he'll conveniently lose it as soon as we get back home. That's okay. I don't mind.

"*Cincuenta y siete*," she says a third time, but her voice is raspy and adorable and she is smiling in anticipation of the transaction and it doesn't feel at all like she's giving me the hard sell.

I flip through the bills in my wallet but I don't know how much money to give her.

"Three dollars," I hear a voice say. "But I'm sure she'd happily take two."

I turn to see that the woman who is speaking to me is the

woman from the beach, the woman in black. She has on the same black sunglasses, though now she wears a burnt orange silk sundress and wide-brimmed straw hat.

I reach for three singles and hand them to the girl. She makes a move to tie the bracelet onto my wrist but I say, "No, it's okay. It is for my husband. *Muchas gracias*."

I turn to the woman. "Thank you," I say. "I'm hopeless."

"This is not true."

"My husband," I say. "His name is Peter." I somehow feel obligated to explain why I'd buy something so stupid. "We always buy each other tchotchkes when we're on vacation."

My favorite of these gifts is the bedazzled hot pink model of the Eiffel Tower Peter brought me. I keep it on my dresser.

"Tchotchkes?"

"Frivolous things. The tackier the better."

"I see."

We've started walking away from the girl and her stand, down the cobblestoned street, side by side. I'm not sure where we're going. I was about to head home but I no longer feel in any sort of rush.

"I am Maria Josephina." The way she says her name, with the rolling *r* and the *h* where an American would put a *j*—it's exotic and sexy. I didn't look, but I'm guessing her name was stitched onto one of those string bracelets. After all, around here she's just Mary Jo.

"Jenna," I say.

We don't stop our stroll to shake hands.

"It is nice to see you again, Jenna. I hope that you are enjoying your stay here in Puerto Vallarta?"

"Yes," I say. "Very much. It is beautiful."

"Yes, it is."

"We came for a big celebration. My husband and his best friend: they're both turning fifty."

"So this trip. It is for your husband and his friend?"

"Well, it's for all of us, I suppose. Our daughter is with us, too."

"That is nice."

We stop in front of a flower stand and she grabs two bunches of calla lilies. She hands coins to the man without counting them then hands one of the bunches to me.

"Here. For you. To take back to your villa."

I bring them up to my nose and take a whiff.

"They do not have a scent," she says. "This is why I like them."

"Thank you," I tell her. "You are very kind."

"You can bring them to your husband. Calla lilies die in winter and come back to life in the spring. This is why they are the flowers of Easter. A reminder that in death there is always resurrection."

I have never given Peter flowers, and he has never given me flowers. This isn't because he's a hard-hearted husband, it's because we have always, both of us, eschewed the cliché gifts. We discovered this about each other early on in our relationship. It was yet another sign that we were simpatico.

Instead of a ring, he proposed to me with a new bed. A gorgeous wood-carved queen four-poster from an expensive store on Beverly Boulevard. We'd walk by that bed in the window, draped in a striped Pendleton throw blanket, on the way from our duplex apartment to our favorite coffee shop, and I would stop to admire it every time. Back then, we were still sleeping on a futon.

And then one day I came home from work, a visit with a foster family in Reseda, and the drive back over the hill from the valley had taken me more than two hours in traffic. I was sweaty and hungry and I had to pee and I almost ran out of gas. The family I'd visited was so obviously in it for the measly monthly check and didn't give a shit about the kid they were hosting, but that was hardly grounds for kicking the case to a real social worker, in fact in the foster care world it passed for success.

I let myself into our apartment, ready to tell Peter I wanted to quit my job, when I heard him calling from our bedroom.

In here.

He was lying on top of that four-poster bed. He'd lit candles (he wasn't totally above indulging a cliché) and he had Joni Mitchell's *Blue* on the stereo.

He asked me to marry him. He'd even bought the Pendleton blanket.

I wasn't sure I believed in marriage. My parents and the parents of almost everyone I knew had divorced, leaving the women bitter and rudderless. I might not have been someone with clear life goals, but I knew what I didn't want, and what I didn't want was to become one of those women. And yet knowing how it might all turn out, knowing that domestic devil grass is an insidious foe, Peter made me want to take the chance.

Peter was reliable and steady and patient with a strong moral compass and he made me feel safe and loved. But he also made me feel giddy and sexy. And he made me laugh. And we liked the same things—we had many of the same books and we even had the same print from an exhibit at MoMA—and mostly liked the same people, and from the moment we merged our lives in that duplex, it felt, in the best of ways, like we'd always been together. I had the—*ah, of course, this makes sense*—feeling about Peter. And lest this sound too boring or predictable, it's important to point out that in asking me to marry him Peter was taking a huge risk, engaging in a big romantic gesture, because Peter understood my ambivalence. Peter understood *me*.

It would be months before I quit my job. And three years before that bed would get moved into the guest room of our new house so that we could make room for a king-size mattress big enough for the two of us and our nursing baby.

"Do you have a husband?" I ask my new friend as we walk down the sidewalk holding our matching bunches of calla lilies.

"No."

"Children?"

"Oh, *Dios mío*, no. For me, that is not an option."

As I've gotten older I've come to think of unmarried, childless women with a certain degree of pity, which I try to pretend I am not feeling because I am at heart a feminist who doesn't believe a woman needs a husband or a child to feel happy, accomplished or whole. But with Maria Josephina I do not need to pretend—she doesn't stir up in me the slightest hint of pity, only envy.

"Where do you go now?" she asks me.

I think about this. Now I will go back to Peter. I will remember who he is and who we are to each other. I will bring him flowers for the first time in our twenty years together.

"Must you return to your villa?"

I look at my watch. It's almost time for dinner.

"Yes," I say. "I'm afraid I must."

She walks me to the taxi stand.

I GIVE THE DRIVER a tip that is larger than the fare, as I did for the driver who drove me into town, and I ring the buzzer at the villa's massive front doors. Peter answers. I haven't seen him since our argument on the beach where he called me unattractive.

"Hi," he says. "Did you have fun in town?" His tone is conciliatory and warm. As he steps aside to let me in, I see he's been sitting in the living room with Ingrid and Solly, so I'm not sure if his demeanor is an act put on for the audience witnessing our reunion, or if he's genuinely happy to see me.

I nod.

"Good," he says and kisses my cheek. It's a lingering kiss, soft and sweet. He doesn't want to fight. Of course he doesn't. I turn my face and I meet his lips. When he pulls back, he smiles.

"Those are pretty." He's pointing to the flowers.

I reach into my pocket for the bracelet and I dangle it in front of him. "I bought you something."

He holds out his wrist. "I love it."

I tie it on with a triple knot.

Enrique takes the flowers from me and places a margarita into my hand. It is cold and perfect, as always. It sounds improbable, because clearly he does this day in and day out for whoever is lucky enough to temporarily call Villa Azul Paraiso home, but I think Roberto's margaritas are getting better and better.

"Where's Clem?" I ask Peter.

He has pulled me onto his lap and he holds me tight around my waist. I lean into him. We are building a bridge back to each other made of small gifts and affectionate gestures.

"She went to town with Malcolm. They should be back soon."

"She did? She walked to town?"

"They went to get an ice cream," Solly says. "And when Ivan heard the words 'ice cream' he insisted on going too, but Ingrid wouldn't let him, so he had a tantrum. And now he's in our bedroom playing on the iPad." Solly holds his margarita out until I clink mine against his. "Here's to grown-ups."

I know I shouldn't let it sting that Clem turned down my invitation to walk to town only to agree to do the very same thing with Malcolm. If, as a parent, I internalized each slight or perceived insult, I'd spend my entire life licking my wounds. But still, I'm surprised she went with him given that when I last saw her she looked like she was settling into a long, bikini-clad FaceTime session with Sean.

"Poor Ivan," I say.

Solly waves his hand at me. "Nah. Don't shed a tear for that kid. He's got the world on a string. It's just that his mother here thinks he eats too much sugar. She thinks it makes him hyper. I think being a five-year-old boy makes him hyper."

Ingrid smiles at Solly. He winks at her. I wonder if the reason Ingrid wouldn't let him go along is not because she's worried about sugar but because she's worried about Malcolm: that whatever it is he's done, it's serious enough that Ingrid doesn't trust him to take care of Ivan, which of course makes me worry about whether I should trust him around my daughter.

We have another round of margaritas on the balcony and we watch the sunset, which is just as spectacular as it was the last two nights, and so has lost a little of its luster the way all things do once they become predictable.

Roberto rings the bell for dinner.

Clem and Malcolm still haven't returned.

"I thought they were just getting an ice cream. I thought you said they'd be back soon." I'm trying not to sound hysterical.

"They're kids," Solly says, stepping in to answer for Peter. "They're not great at keeping track of time. Or it's possible they found something more enticing to do than suffering through another meal at home with their boring parents."

"Call her," I say to Peter.

"But we didn't buy the international calling plan."

"So what? So it'll cost five dollars. Or ten. Call her."

He pulls his phone out of his pocket and, seeing it, I start to feel my anger from earlier rushing back. It didn't seem to bother him that we don't have an international calling plan when he fielded six consecutive calls from his assistant. He pushes a button, holds the phone to his ear. He shakes his head. "Straight to voice mail. I'll send her a text."

I turn to Solly. "Can you call Malcolm, please?"

"I could, but the boy has never, not once, picked up his phone when I've called. It doesn't seem to matter that I pay for his plan."

"Can you try?"

"Jen," he says, and he puts his arm around me, pulling me into one of his aggressive embraces. "Why are you getting your panties all in a knot? The kids are fine. They're out having a good time. Let's start dinner without them. We will survive if, just this one night, we don't all sit down together."

I look over to Peter. He shrugs. Back at home, in our normal lives, when we don't have an expansive view of the Bay of Banderas, and Solly isn't standing nearby with a margarita, he worries when Clem can't be reached. But right now, right here, Peter plays it cool. "I'm sure Solly's right. They're probably out having fun. Let's just go eat. They'll be back soon."

"Can I talk to you alone for a minute?"

Let's face it: There is no way to utter that sentence that doesn't make every person within earshot extraordinarily uncomfortable. Solly and Ingrid both make the *uh-oh* face.

"We'll go get Ivan," Ingrid says. "See you guys downstairs."

When they're out of sight, I take Peter by the arm and lead him over to the edge of the balcony so that we stand beneath an open sky that is turning dark and just beginning to show its stars.

"I know what this is about," Peter says. "I know you talked to Gavriella. Let's not do this now, okay? Not here. I'm sorry she called. She's a handful. I'm dealing with it. But please . . ."

"Do you really not know what sort of trouble Malcolm got into back home? Did Solly really never tell you?"

"What? No, he didn't. Why?"

"Because our daughter and Malcolm are out together somewhere and I don't know if I should be worried."

"It's Malcolm," Peter says. "You've known Malcolm since the day he was born."

It is true that we were the first visitors to the maternity ward after Maureen gave birth to him. But it is also true that he's been living on the opposite coast for seven years, during which I have seen him only a few times. Maureen reports that he's just been in a *small spot of trouble* and everything's fine now, but I have only her word to go on, and I'm acutely aware that as parents we shape and polish the narrative when it comes to our children, even if it means doing extensive tweaks and rewrites.

"But I don't know him *now*," I say. "None of us does. Not even Solly. Solly barely ever sees him."

Peter looks wounded, as if I've just called *him* out for being a deadbeat father. "What, exactly, are you worried about?"

"I don't know. I'm just worried. I'm worried about everything."

"Please, honey. Try not to be. This is our vacation. You really need to relax."

Right then, the doorbell rings. Peter smiles with his whole face. All the relief is right there for me to see. He might have been playing it cool in front of Solly, in front of me, but it's clear: he was worried, too.

"Ding dong," Ivan shouts as he runs to open the door. He jumps into Malcolm's arms. Malcolm lifts him up and puts him on his shoulders. Ivan grabs hold of Malcolm's tight curls with his little hands.

"I'm sorry we're late," Malcolm says to Peter and me. "Not sure if you know this about your daughter, but she isn't the speediest person on the planet."

"There was live music in the town square," Clem says. "People were dancing. It was so cool. We sat and listened and watched. And then we realized it was getting late."

She's flushed and excited and talking a mile a minute. "I

wanted to take a cab, but Malcolm insisted we walk. What's for dinner? I'm starving."

SOLLY SUGGESTS a nightcap on the roof.

Ingrid has taken Ivan to bed; this is what she must do each night since the boy cannot fall asleep alone. The teenagers excused themselves at the same time Ingrid did, retreating to their own rooms. Solly makes the suggestion in front of both Peter and me, but we all know the invitation is really just for Peter. I've spent many nights over many years third-wheeling in their friendship, so I can tell when what Solly wants is time alone with Peter.

"I'm in," Peter says. Then he looks at me. "Jen?"

What he's asking is not: *Do you want to join?* He's asking: *Is it okay if I go even though we're scheduled for a big blowout fight about those phone calls?*

"I think I've had enough to drink," I say. So have they, but that's beside the point. "You two go ahead."

"Are you sure?"

"I'm sure."

Peter takes my face in both of his hands and looks me straight in the eyes. "I love you," he says.

"I know."

"But I mean it. I really, really love you."

"He does." Solly stands behind me, squeezing my shoulders. Sensing trouble, he's doing what he can to help smooth things over. "He's a fool for you. Always has been. Because he's a very smart man with exquisite taste."

They take the bottle of tequila with them. I sit alone at the empty table, staring out at the bay. It's so dark I can no longer distinguish the sky from the sea.

Roberto, Enrique and Luisa come into the dining room. They have changed out of their white zippered coats and wear jeans and sweatshirts, bags slung over their shoulders.

"We go home now," Roberto says.

He doesn't phrase it like a question, but still I say, "Of course. Go."

"Do you need anything?"

"No, I'm fine."

"We leave on for you the lights."

"You can shut them off," I say. "I'm heading up to bed now."

"It's okay. We keep them on for you."

"Please turn them off." I stand up. "Good night."

"Good night," Roberto and Enrique say.

"*Buenas noches*," Luisa calls after me.

THERE'S NO GOOD REASON not to use this time to try to work on my book. So what if it's late at night? So what if maybe I've had a little too much to drink? I'm typically a morning writer; I do my best work between the hours of eight and eleven after copious amounts of caffeine. But I'm also typically a writer who is able to finish a book she's started, and finish it on time, so all bets are off.

The file is staring at me. I am afraid to move my cursor near it. Opening the file will only remind me how far away from this story I've strayed. Sometimes I think maybe my problem is that

I've said all I can about teenagers and their troubles. That maybe I'm losing my empathy for those who can still start over. Reinvent themselves. Teenagers have their whole lives and an infinite number of pathways stretching out ahead of them. Unlike middle-aged women, for example.

I imagine Ingrid in her bedroom across the house. A veritable writing machine, getting in her thousand words. Is she lying next to her sleeping child, furiously typing away? Fine-tuning her three-act structure? Honing her story arcs? Sharpening her characters and their dialogue?

I click on Ingrid's manuscript.

Lost in Space.

I don't really intend to read it. Not now. I know I owe her feedback, but I've also made it clear it will take me awhile. So I figure I'll just give it a glance. See if she knows how to write a compelling opening sentence. I'm even curious about what font she chose.

I start to read. I read beyond the first sentence, the first paragraph, the first page, the first chapter. I keep reading and reading and before I know it, it's gotten late and I've made some serious headway.

Peter creaks the door open. I can tell he's disappointed to find the lights still on and me wide awake.

"Hi," he says. I can smell the tequila from across the room.

"Hi."

"Jenna, I'm sorry. I'm dealing with this. I really am. It's a complicated situation. She's a great assistant. And I rely on her. But . . ."

"Peter," I say. "I don't want to talk about this. Not now. Not when you're drunk."

"Really?" He looks like I just told him he won the lottery.

"Really."

"Wait . . . are you saying the opposite of what you really mean . . . and then expecting me to know that you're saying the opposite of what you really mean?"

"No. And I don't admit to ever having done that."

"All righty, then. I'll just go brush my teeth."

Peter finishes up in the bathroom and climbs into bed. He reaches over and gives my knee a squeeze. He falls asleep quickly, snoring at full volume without any windup, and I stay awake reading Ingrid's manuscript until I'm nearly halfway done. I'd keep reading it if I could because I want to know what happens next, but I can no longer manage to keep my eyes open.

TUESDAY

I met Solly before I met Peter, and Solly's never let either of us forget it. He mentioned it in his toast at our wedding, and he'll gleefully take whatever opportunity presents itself to interject the phrase 'as *someone who has known Jenna longer*' into any conversation. I met Solly only a few minutes before I met Peter, but still, to Solly, those minutes are pure gold.

We were in a bar. Despite my appreciation for margaritas and alcoholic drinks in general, I was never someone who spent much time in bars, and certainly never someone who went to bars looking to meet men. It's a cliché, I know, and maybe even a little sexist, but I think women who go to bars to meet men are desperate, and men who go to bars to meet women are gross.

What makes our origin story more interesting than the same old story of two people meeting in a bar, what lends it a wee bit of charm, is the fact that the bar in which we met happens to be the oldest bar in New Orleans. There we were, two Southern Californians, drinking Sazeracs, in town for Jazz Fest, both dragged along by friends who cared much more about jazz than we did, which is to say they *cared* and we did not at all.

I was twenty-seven years old. I'd just broken up with a boy-friend after two years together. Some friends from college had organized a meetup. I hadn't planned on joining, but the boy-friend had just moved out because he'd fallen in love with a co-worker, who was actually his supervisor, and he'd decided to hell with the workplace restrictions and to hell with me. So yes, I was able to sublimate my feelings about jazz and spend money I didn't have to join my friends so that I wouldn't have to sit at home alone with the kitten he'd given me as a birthday gift not six weeks before dropping the bomb about the woman from work. (That kitten is now the ancient cat with bladder control troubles I'm paying a neighbor's kid five bucks a day to feed while we're on vacation.)

Anyway, Solly and I were standing next to each other waiting to get the bartender's attention. He turned to me and said, "I understand why he's ignoring me, but you? That makes no sense at all."

I looked good that night and I knew it with the sort of cer-tainty only available to younger women. I'd shed a few pounds in the breakup. I'd gotten impulse bangs that gave me an air of sophistication. I smiled at him while also sending the clearest message I could that I was not interested in getting chatted up, not interested in men *period*, given that they're all pigs who jump into bed with their supervisors.

Solly didn't get my message; he continued to talk to me. But he wasn't chatting me up. Well, he was chatting me up, but only in the way he chats up everyone. I got my first inkling of this when the bartender finally turned to Solly and Solly spoke to him in the same intimate and conspiratorial tone he'd been using with me.

Solly ordered three Sazeracs and the bartender charged him for only two. He handed one to me.

I took it and I took a longer look at Solly and wondered if maybe I was wrong: about men, about talking to men, about meeting men in bars. He winked at me, an unforgivable sin I quickly absolved him of because he smelled good and he dressed well, not like all the other twentysomethings with their ripped T-shirts and backward baseball caps.

I nodded toward his second Sazerac. "You're not messing around."

"Oh, but I am," he said. "That is why I'm here: to mess around. This drink, however, is for my best friend."

I remember thinking: *What adult still uses the term* best friend? And I also remember thinking: *He may not be my type, but I could totally go to bed with this guy.*

"We're turning thirty," he continued. "And we're celebrating by drinking Sazeracs and listening to great music. You?"

I lifted my cocktail. "I'm celebrating the breakup of a relationship." I knew this was flirty. To announce that you are unattached within minutes of meeting a man sends a very strong signal. Like a neon sign around your neck: OPEN FOR BUSINESS.

He looked me up and down. "He broke up with you."

My cheeks burned red. "No. That's not true."

He shrugged. I could tell he didn't believe me. "Either way, it's the best thing that could have happened. You made him feel small, inferior, not because of anything you did, but because he *was* small and inferior. You need to find someone worthy of your strength, and he needs to find someone he can dominate. Someone with whom he can be the boss."

"Actually"—I took a long sip of my Sazerac—"he was fucking his supervisor at work."

Solly threw his head back and laughed. And then I laughed, too. We both laughed and laughed and leaned into each other like two people who've been sharing laughs for years.

"What's so funny?"

I turned to look at the person who was interrupting one of the first moments of genuine fun I'd had since getting dumped. He was good-looking, better-looking than the man I was laughing alongside, but even with his white hair he looked to me like the other boys in the bar.

Solly handed him a Sazerac and nodded in my direction. "She's what's so funny."

"And you are . . . ?"

I stuck out my hand. "I'm Jenna."

He took it. "Peter."

Peter uses this fact, that he introduced himself first, that Solly hadn't even bothered to learn my name, as an argument that actually, he met me before Solly did.

Right then Solly spied a woman across the room—long blond hair, bright red lipstick, probably not old enough to be in a bar— and excused himself.

Peter gestured to Solly's empty seat. "May I?"

It's raining.

The storm, the *tormenta*, which took a turn away from us, turned back again because *tormentas* will do what *tormentas* will do without taking into consideration the wishes of any particular vacationer. It looks as though it will stay offshore, churning up the seas, wreaking havoc on the lives of those colorful fish who today probably wish they lived in the aquarium at my childhood dentist's office rather than in the Bay of Banderas.

I get up and close the wooden shutters to stop the water from getting in and then I climb right back into bed again. I open up my laptop and I read Ingrid's book until I finish it. By the end, I'm tearing through it—it's suspenseful and exciting. It's sad and also hopeful. I mostly forget that I'm reading something written by Ingrid Solomon because it's so improbable that Ingrid Solomon, former jewelry designer and second wife to Solly, could have written this book. I'm not saying it isn't derivative, because of course it is—what book isn't? But it's good. It's *really* good. And I can't even criticize the ending for being too tidy. Yes, the boy and his group of friends rescue his father, take down the evil corporation and save the day, but the boy has to grapple with the truth that his parents' marriage is over, that the cracks were there already—how else to explain the mother's willingness to so quickly and completely accept that her husband ran off with another woman?

When I'm done, I stare at the last page for a very long time.

"Is that Ingrid's book?"

I hadn't noticed Peter had woken up. I snap my laptop shut like he's caught me watching porn.

"Yep."

"How is it?"

"I haven't really read it, I was only skimming it. Just getting a sense of what she's been up to."

"And?"

I put the laptop on the side table and get out of bed. "I don't know yet."

Peter looks at the closed shutters. "Is it raining?"

"Yes."

"Cozy."

"Cozy? This is a beach vacation. We don't want rain on a beach vacation."

"I love rain."

"I know you love rain, Peter. But can you really say you love rain *now*? Here? Today?"

"I love rain any day," he says and he pats the empty spot next to him in the bed.

I climb back in and lie down and he spoons me, resting his soft bearded cheek on top of mine. I play with the string of his *Pedro* bracelet.

"I'm really sorry about yesterday," he says. "I talked to her. I told her she can't call me again. I don't think she will. Things are complicated at work. And they are complicated with Gavriella. I know you'd be happy if I'd just get rid of her, but I can't. Not without creating a serious crisis."

I don't say anything. He breathes into my ear.

"I need you to trust me," he continues. He pulls me tighter against him. "Trust that I'm trying my best. To handle a situation that is exceedingly thorny."

I pull away and roll over onto my back. I stare at the ceiling fan as it slowly moves the chilly air around the room. The rain is falling harder now and I can hear the palm trees blowing in the wind.

"Are you sleeping with her?"

"That's ridiculous."

"No, it isn't. You aren't leaving me much of a choice but to ask you flat out. You're hinting at something without saying it. So—are you?"

"No. I am not sleeping with her."

I turn to look at him. We stare at each other silently for several rotations of the ceiling fan. I can tell he's telling the truth.

"So what's going on?"

"Jen, I just told you. I can't really talk about it. It wouldn't be appropriate. Or fair to the people involved."

"Wait . . . is this about *Solly?*" The words come out before I've thought it through. It's as if I put the puzzle together before looking at the picture on the box. But as soon as I say it, I know I'm right. This *is* about Solly. This is about Peter cleaning up Solly's mess. This is about Solly abusing his friendship with Peter.

"Jenna."

"Is Solly sleeping with her?"

There is a long beat of silence. Peter doesn't nod. He doesn't even meet my gaze. He stares up at the ceiling fan.

"Fucking Solly," I hiss.

"I really, really don't want to talk about this. I've told you. I'm trying to handle things and I don't think she will call again while we're on vacation. There are legitimate problems happening at work but I've told her to take them to Kim. Kim can handle everything while we're away. Please. Can't we just parking lot this?"

"I can't believe you just said that."

"Said what?"

"I can't believe you just used *parking lot* as a verb."

He laughs a little. "You never told me it's on your list."

"You should *know* it's on my list. It's the new version of *let's put a pin in it.* Just another one of those idiotic things they say at Clem's school."

"Well, they say it at start-ups, too. I'm sorry. But you owe me one. You described the way Roberto set the table as *festive.*" He grabs me again and pulls me back into spooning position. He buries his face in my hair. He kisses my neck and my shoulder. He lifts up my T-shirt and he kisses the small of my back. He flips me around and then he kisses my stomach. He removes my shirt and then his own. He slips off my pajama bottoms and my underwear. He wriggles out of his boxers. He climbs on top of me and pulls the covers up to our chins.

There's a clap of thunder.

"God, I love the rain," he whispers.

ROBERTO AND ENRIQUE have lined the edges of the open living spaces with towels to soak up the water. I guess this is what they meant when they said the house was built for comfort as well as luxury. *We may not have doors or walls to protect you from the elements, but we will have our staff line the floors with threadbare towels so you don't slip and break your necks.*

Everyone else is already at breakfast. Clem has wrapped herself in the blanket from her bed.

"I am sorry," Roberto tells me as he hands me my coffee. "I know you worry about weather. I know you do not like the rain.

But it will not last longer than one day. That is what it says in the newspaper. Tomorrow there will be sun."

"It's okay," I say.

As Roberto retreats to the kitchen Solly leans in close. "I can't believe he let it rain on our vacation. It's so hard to find good help these days."

"Shut up, Solly." I'm not in the mood for Solly's humor. I don't even want to look at him right now.

"You shouldn't say *shut up*." Ivan is sitting at the table building something with his LEGOs.

"I was joking," I say to Ivan. He doesn't bother to look at me. "But you're right. Saying *shut up* is not okay."

I wait for one of his parents to step in and explain that after twenty years of friendship, and when you are an adult, you can tell each other to shut up and nobody takes offense.

"You two slept in," Ingrid says. "That must have been nice. This one"—she pats Ivan on the head—"up since six a.m."

"I want to go snorkeling," Ivan says.

"Ivan, you hated snorkeling," I tell him.

"I did not!"

I know better than to get into an argument with a five-year-old. I know that facts and evidence don't matter. I know that he probably doesn't even remember his epic freak-out in the water yesterday. And besides, the way he carries on refusing to look up from his LEGO set makes for excellent psychological warfare.

"Well, sweetie," Ingrid says to him. "It's raining today and—"

"Ding dong."

"And we need to find things to do indoors."

"But I want to snorkel," he whines.

"Look—" Ingrid points out to the bay, but he still won't take his eyes off his LEGOs.

It is gray and choppy and white-capped. "You don't want to go out in that."

"So, Peter," Solly says. "On your last day in your forties, the last day of your first half century of life, rather than bathe you in sunbeams, God has decided to piss rain upon you. What did you do to get on his bad side?"

"I don't know," Peter says with a huge smile. "But isn't it perfect?"

"Pish." Solly waves him off. "While you and your bride slept the morning away, the rest of us debated what we should do. We have two votes for a movie marathon scrapped together from Villa Azul Paraiso's random collection of VHS tapes." Clem and Malcolm raise their hands. "One vote for a LEGO build-off." Ingrid takes Ivan's arm and raises it for him. He quickly yanks it away. "And the final two votes go for long, uninterrupted nap time." Solly and Ingrid high-five each other.

I know everyone is looking to me. I am the default planner. The one who books vacations eight months in advance. The one who recognizes that the minutes are high value and cannot be wasted sitting inside complaining about the weather. Surely I have some idea of what we should do?

I take a final bite of my breakfast and bring my coffee cup into the kitchen.

Luisa is cleaning the stove. Roberto stands up from the table. He refills my cup and shows me the paper. Up in the corner is a little graphic. There is a sun and then a cloud with rain and then another sun.

"See? Yesterday there is sun. Today there is rain. Tomorrow there is sun."

I nod. "Okay."

"I am sorry."

"Please don't apologize about the weather."

"Yes," he says. "I will not."

"I'm wondering if you have any ideas of what we should do today. What do people do in Puerto Vallarta on rainy days?"

He and Luisa exchange a few words in Spanish. She doesn't appear to be particularly sympathetic to my situation.

"The guests here, they like to enjoy the house. Stay inside. Read books. Be together. We have games. Some miss pieces, but some have them all. Or, you go to town. We give you umbrellas. You visit the church or the galleries. There is a movie theater. It is near to where Mr. Solly makes the reservation for your dinner. They sometimes show movies in English."

"A reservation for dinner?"

"Yes. He says that tomorrow it is the birthday for your husband. He wants to do something special. We tell him about the restaurant in town that is the best. He asks us to make a reservation. It is confirmed. So we do not cook the dinner for you tomorrow."

"Okay." I suppose this is something I should have thought of: a night out. It's the right way to celebrate, even if we've paid for all of our meals already. I feel foolish. For not having thought of making a plan for my own husband's birthday, and for standing in the kitchen asking the staff for advice about how to enjoy a rainy day in a luxury villa.

I pick up Roberto's paper and look at the little icons again.

I flip the paper over. There is the face of the man I saw yesterday. The governor. This time he is sitting in a red velvet chair next to another man, with flags in the background. They both wear blue ties.

"What's happening here?"

Roberto takes the paper. Luisa comes and looks over his shoulder. They discuss the article. Luisa jabs at the paper with her finger a few times.

"The governor. He meets with the interior minister for Mexico. They speak more about the drug cartels and the violence."

I take a closer look. The interior minister looks Asian.

"He is Mexican. He is Miguel Chong. His mother is from Chinese descent, but he is from Hidalgo state." Roberto says.

I don't bother trying to defend myself or deny that this is exactly what I was wondering. Roberto knows I expect all Mexicans to look the same, as if mine were the only multicultural country. And here I've been scolding Clem about her insular worldview.

"What are they saying about the drug cartels?"

"They speak of increasing police presence in Jalisco state. Because of violence between gangs. They do not like the recent activities of these two cartels. They do not want Puerto Vallarta to become like Acapulco. But here it is still safe. Mr. Chong, he wants to control production of flowers from where they make the heroin. The poppies? So if the government controls the flowers, and makes drugs for medicines, it stops trafficking and weakens the gangs. But it is still far away and maybe happens never. For now, they bring in more police to stop the drug trade."

"Do you worry about all this?" I ask him. If I opened my local paper every day to this sort of local news I might never leave the house.

"Like I say, it is safe here. And the violence, it is between gang members only. So no. I do not worry. And you do not worry."

"So you feel like it's a safe place to live? With a family?"

Luisa says something to Roberto. He replies with a long string of words—I can't even tell when one sentence ends and another begins. As I have many times in my life, I feel embarrassed for having elected to take French instead of Spanish in high school— an indefensible choice for a Southern Californian.

"Yes. We live here always. Our son, he is now in Mexico City. He is student there."

"Your son?"

"Yes."

"You mean, you have a son . . . with Luisa?"

They share another quick exchange and a laugh.

"Yes. She is my wife."

"I didn't know that."

"And Enrique," he says. "He is my brother."

I didn't know that either. I'm not sure why this surprises me. It's not like I spend my time in the kitchen asking them about their lives, I'm far too concerned with where to go shopping and what to do when it rains. I haven't spent a single minute imagining who they are outside of this house. I caught a glimpse last night when they passed through the dining room in jeans and sweatshirts, but I didn't let my imagination follow them beyond the large wooden front doors.

"Is Enrique married, too?"

"Yes, but his wife takes his children to the United States. He does not see them, but he will soon we hope. Enrique helps to take care of our parents here."

I wonder if Enrique's absence from the kitchen means that right now he's off making all our beds, putting fresh flowers on our tables; if maybe I was wrong about the woman's touch.

I feel like I should say something more, but I'm not sure what, so I take my empty coffee cup to the sink and I wash it and place it on the counter.

"*Gracias para los* breakfast, Luisa," I say.

She smiles at me. "*De nada.*"

I FIND INGRID ALONE, reading in the main floor living room. She's on to another children's book. Another Newbery runner-up. Another book I haven't read.

I ask her about it.

"I love it," she says. "I'm not sure what the committee was thinking this year. All of the silver medals are far better than the book they actually gave the award to."

"I guess consensus is difficult. Maybe it was a compromise?"

She shrugs, pulls the throw blanket up to her chest and puts the book down on the table. She's settling in for a nice long chat. I hesitate to sit down with her. I'm still rattled by what Peter told me about Solly and Gavriella. The weight of that knowledge is a boulder in my stomach.

When Solly started his affair with Ingrid, Peter didn't tell me. He kept Solly's secret. He didn't want to put me in an awkward position with Maureen, who, unlike Ingrid, was a true, close friend. Peter told me later that he pushed Solly to come clean, that it would have gone on much longer had he not spent many nights over many drinks with Solly playing out the different scenarios and convincing him he needed to make a choice. I always wondered if Peter tried talking Solly into choosing Maureen, into staying married to his wife, to the woman he once loved so fiercely that he sobbed through his own wedding vows.

It didn't matter that I didn't know about the affair; on some level I know Maureen still holds it against me. Our four lives were interwoven in such a way that our relationship couldn't avoid some collateral damage from such an ugly implosion. And by virtue of the fact that I am married to Peter, I am forever a part of the universe of Solly from which she needed escape. But once she resettled in New York and things starting turning out as well as they did for her—new job, new friends, new gorgeous apartment, new string of boyfriends ending in one serious, unreasonably handsome one—we started to rebuild what we'd lost, text by text, email by email, and brief visit by brief visit. But of course, things were never quite the same between us.

I sit down in the chair across from Ingrid and I push what I know out of my head. What do I know anyway? Peter didn't really tell me anything. I chose to take Peter's silence in response to my question about Solly as a *yes*, because in all our years together we've developed a shorthand. But I don't know for certain, do I? And if I don't know something for certain, how can I tell her about what I don't know?

"The Printz winner, though," Ingrid says. "Now, that's a book that deserved the gold."

I haven't read this either so I just nod in agreement. There's really no excuse for a writer of YA fiction not reading the book that's been crowned best book of the year written for young adults. Before I wrote my first book, I'd never even heard of the Printz Award. It's better that way. Who needs to know about the awards you'll never get? But clearly, Ingrid is doing her homework. She's devouring the prizewinners. And who knows? Her book could very well wind up with a sticker on it one day, too.

I look at Ingrid stretched out on the sofa. She's just a bit too long for it so she bends her knees and props her feet up on the armrest. She's wearing gray sweatpants and a blue long-sleeved T-shirt, not a hint of makeup. Her hair is wild. With all those proteins and the limited complex carbohydrates, with the absence of all that sugar and alcohol, her skin glows even more than usual. She's written a book I stayed up late reading and woke up early to finish. And yet, when I look at her, what I feel is pity. She's thrown her lot in with a man who will never give her the whole of his attention and affection, a man whose appetite is too large, a man for whom there is never quite enough of anything.

"I started your book last night," I say.

She sits up quickly and the throw blanket falls to the floor.

"Oh. Wow. I'm . . . nervous."

"Don't be. It's really good so far. I really enjoyed what I've read."

"For real?"

"Yes, for real."

"Because, like I said in my email, I don't want you to protect my feelings."

"Don't worry," I say. "I'll be honest."

"Brutally honest."

"I'm against brutality."

She laughs. "Solly is the only one who's read it and he says he loves it, but you know Solly. He's such a softy. He loves everything I do."

Oh, Ingrid. Poor Ingrid. Beautiful, naïve, talented Ingrid. I decide to dole out a little bit more.

"Well, from what I've read so far, I think you may be onto something pretty special."

She brings her hands up to her face to cover her huge smile, like Clementine and her friends used to do in middle school, like smiling is shameful, something to hide.

I debate saying more. Admitting I've finished it. Admitting I admire and envy her talent. Admitting I haven't stopped thinking about her book except for when I've been thinking about the fact that her husband may be cheating on her. But I don't. For whatever reason, I'm not ready yet. I need to look at it again. Make sure I'm not so disenchanted with my own unfinished book that any completed manuscript shines like a polished diamond.

"Jenna, I don't even know what to say. This means . . . everything."

"Of course," I say, and I wonder if maybe Solly sobbed through his wedding vows because promising fidelity to one person for the rest of his life was too unbearably sad.

· · ·

I FIGURE THIS HOUSE has to have a Scrabble set somewhere so I go down to search the TV room and find Malcolm looking through a shelf of old tapes.

"I'm trying to curate the perfect double feature," he says. He holds *A Nightmare on Elm Street* in one hand and *Meet Me in St. Louis* in the other. "What do you think?"

"I think that never, in the history of humankind, has there been a viewing of those two movies back-to-back."

"They also have a copy of *Grease,* but it's in Spanish and it's called, no joke: *Vaselina.*"

"Now, *that* I would like to watch."

"Wanna join? Clem is on her way."

I think for a second about taking him up on his offer, but this was their plan for the rainy day, not mine. I don't want to intrude. I shouldn't intrude. "No, thanks. I have a date to kick my husband's ass in Scrabble."

He sits down on the arm of the sofa. "Well, I wouldn't want to get in the way of a good ass kicking." His smile is wide. The kid drew a full house: he's got his father's magnetism and his mother's looks.

"You know, Malcolm, it's really nice to spend some time with you. I'm sorry I don't get to New York to see your mom as often as I'd like."

"Well, it's not as if she comes out to L.A. to see you, so you probably shouldn't beat yourself up."

This is true. As far as I know, Maureen hasn't returned to Los

Angeles since she filled a New York–bound extralong moving truck with half of their marital property.

"So how do you get on with Bruno?"

Malcolm shrugs. "He's chill. And his place is sick. Or I guess it's our place now. It's, like, a block from the High Line. So that's cool."

"Sounds like you got pretty lucky with the stepparents."

"Bruno isn't my stepdad. He's just my mom's boyfriend. But, yeah. I guess so."

Is that hesitation I hear in his voice? And is that hesitation I hear about Bruno or is it about Ingrid?

"It can't be easy for you," I say. "Living so far away from your father. And your little brother. I'm sorry you've had to go through that." I'm drawing on my days working with foster kids. All those hours spent in temporary living rooms practicing the listening and reflection skills I learned in the mandatory two-day training I attended before getting handed a full social worker's caseload. *I hear how this is hard for you. I hear that you are unhappy. I hear that you wish your life was different.*

"You don't need to feel sorry for me, Jenna."

"That's not—"

"I mean . . . I consider myself to be pretty lucky."

"I was just saying that I hear you. I hear that it hasn't been easy."

"You heard that? Because I don't think I said that."

Clearly, I'm out of listening and reflecting shape, my training in dire need of a booster class.

I wander over to the shelf of tapes. I notice that they've gone full hog on their collection of Nixon films: *All the President's Men*, Oliver Stone's *Nixon*, *Frost/Nixon*, *The Assassination of Richard Nixon* and even a movie called, simply, *Dick*. Underneath the tapes is a cabinet with board games. Scrabble is at the top of the pile. I stick it under my arm and start to move toward the door, but then I turn back around and sit on the side of the sofa opposite the one he's perched on. "So you're good? Life is good?"

He shrugs. "Sure."

"And your mom? I haven't talked to her in a while."

"She's great." There's that smile again. "And you?" He pauses. "I mean . . . are you feeling better? I heard about your diagnosis. My mom said it was the kind of cancer that, like, isn't all that serious."

"Yes, I'm feeling fine." I don't tell him that it felt serious *to me* and that I don't understand everyone's impulse to diminish my experience. But I get it. Cancer is scary, and we want to protect our children from scary things, so I can see why she'd present it this way to her son.

Maureen called me every week for the first two months to check on me. And she sent a beautiful basket of treats from Zabar's. We still have a loaf of uneaten rye in the freezer. I told Peter we should save it to eat with the lox we'll get sent when my cancer comes back. He told me he didn't think that was funny.

"Which movie are you going to start with?" I ask.

"I'm not sure. I'll have to consult Clem."

"Maybe I'll stay and watch with you for a bit."

"Seriously?" Clem has appeared in the doorway. "I thought

you were going to, like, play games or whatever with Dad. You
don't want to watch stupid movies with us, Mother. Trust me."

"You're right." She is right. I know an exit line when I hear
one. "I'd better go see what your father is up to."

THE RAIN LETS UP in the late afternoon. It's still cloudy with
only a smattering of blue. The bay continues to churn up the
dregs of its bottom, but the chill is gone and the air is thick and
muggy. I've spent the day eating too many tortilla chips and finally diving back into my unfinished manuscript, rereading the
pages I have, each sentence a reminder of the sharpness of Ingrid's book.

Everybody stuck to his or her original plan. Malcolm and
Clem settled into their movie marathon. Ingrid and Solly disap-
peared for a long nap, leaving Ivan to build his LEGOs on the
floor of the living room. He let me work on a fortress with him,
undoing my contributions only a few times, and nodding his approval of a few others. I think plying him with chips all day has
thawed the ice between us.

At one point I went downstairs to see if Malcolm and Clem
wanted me to bring them something to eat and found them
sharing the same blanket and corner of the long sofa. They didn't
jump away from each other when I entered, so I don't think
anything untoward was going on, but I did stare at Clem a beat
too long while Judy Garland was crooning "The Boy Next Door."
Clem returned my stare with a *what's your problem* look.

"We do not need a snack, Mother," she informed me. "Because
we are not five years old."

Back upstairs as Peter was annihilating me in a game of Scrabble, Ingrid appeared in tiny spandex shorts and a cropped tank top.

"Solly is still napping. I'm going to go do some yoga," she said. "Wanna join me?"

"I hate yoga," Ivan said without looking up from his LEGOs.

"I was asking Jenna, sweetie."

"Jenna is a pro," Peter said. "Good luck keeping up with her."

Peter bought me a twelve-session package of yoga classes at a fancy studio in Santa Monica shortly after my diagnosis. It was something the doctor had mentioned might help with stress and anxiety. With Clem's guidance he'd even picked out some yoga clothing along with a mat and bag. I was really touched by the gesture and I knew he wanted me to love it, but I didn't. I haven't had the heart to tell him I still have nine classes left.

"Thanks," I said, "but I think I'll try and do a little more work."

"Are you sure?"

I looked at Ingrid in her getup. I imagined how I would look next to her in downward facing dog.

"Yes, I'm sure."

After finishing the bloodbath of a Scrabble game with Peter I went back to my book, not adding anything new, just scrolling through what I already had, second-guessing every choice I'd made and beating myself up for each clumsy turn of phrase. I tried convincing myself the path out of this thicket existed somewhere, somehow; I just had to find it. I closed the manuscript. *This is my vacation.* I shouldn't have to worry about the thicket on vacation.

Finally, even though I had no reasonable excuse to do so, I

logged on to check Clem's texts. She sent a message to Sean around noon telling him that we were going on a family outing and that she wouldn't be able to text again until dinnertime. He responded with a crying face and a heart with an arrow through it.

I know that kids throw around the word *love* (or *luv*) willy-nilly. Clem and her girlfriends are always saying they love/luv each other. Clem and her eighth grade boyfriend Brett told each other they loved/luved each other about twenty times a day. But I believe that Clem does genuinely love/luv Sean and that he genuinely loves/luvs her. Their relationship, what I've seen of it, is real. It is true. And I adore Sean, not only because he hasn't pressured my daughter into having sex but also because he is attentive and sweet and he treats her with respect. Her feelings for him should be stronger than the pull of an older, handsome boy who was once like a brother and is now a stranger. Clem isn't thinking. She's developing some kind of Stockholm syndrome born from captivity in this luxury vacation rental where everyday rules don't apply and time collapses.

I try talking to Peter about what I saw when we take margaritas to the hot tub on the roof. We've sent Ivan back to his parents. Solly is finally up from his nap and Ingrid is slick with yoga sweat and they're prepping a bath for mother and son in the volcanic tub.

"This is what I'm talking about," Peter says. "This right here." He holds up his margarita. He raises his voice to be heard over the sound of the hot tub jets. "This is vacation."

"Clem and Malcolm were sharing a blanket," I say. "And they were snuggled up together on the couch."

"What? They were snuggling? Get my shotgun!"

"Peter, come on. Be serious."

"About what?"

"Clem has a boyfriend. She has Sean. Sweet Sean. And she's been lying to him."

"Lying to him? How?"

"Well, for starters, she tells him she's unavailable to talk when she is available. She tells him that she's spending time with us when she's really with Malcolm."

Peter puts his head under water, remerges and shakes it out. "Do I want to know how it is that you know this?"

"It doesn't matter. What matters is why. Why is she doing that?"

"Seriously, Jen. You need to mind your own business."

"She *is* my business."

"Well, she's also sixteen. And you can't control her whims. Following your whims is the very best part of being sixteen, maybe the only decent part. So leave it alone."

I take a sip of my margarita. I lean back against the side of the hot tub and look up at the patchy sky. The bubbles are too loud. I reach over to the dial and switch it to OFF.

Peter pouts.

"Sorry," I say. "Did you want them on?"

"It's okay."

We sit in silence for a few minutes.

"Do you really not know about Malcolm?" I ask him.

"What do you mean?"

"I mean about what kind of trouble he's in. I know you've told me you don't, but I can't help wondering if this is one of those times where Solly confides in you and you don't confide in me."

"Jenna."

"What? I know he's your friend and I know you keep his secrets. That's fine, generally. But now our daughter is involved. And I want to know what's going on."

"How is our daughter involved?"

"*Because*, Peter. She's snuggling up to Malcolm on the couch."

"Again with the dreaded snuggling."

"You aren't answering my question." I fix him with a look. "Do you know or not? And please. Don't lie to me."

He takes in a big breath and blows it out into the water, creating bubbles of his own.

"Yes," he says. "I know."

"So? Tell me."

"I don't want you to freak out."

"Peter. If you don't want me to freak out, don't tell me not to freak out."

"He got busted for drugs."

I'd already run through a few scenarios in my head. This was one of them. I figured it must have something to do with drugs or alcohol or cheating at school or maybe getting a girl pregnant. On the scale of bad to horrible, this falls someplace in the middle.

"For . . . *dealing* drugs," Peter says.

Okay, so maybe this moves the needle in the direction of horrible.

"Was it weed?" I know from Peter that Solly used to be the

weed guy in college. He didn't sell it, because he didn't need the money, but he always had tons of it and he was the go-to if you wanted to get high. Maybe Malcolm is just following in his father's footsteps.

"No. Not weed. He was selling pills. Opioids."

And a brick drops on the scale.

"Jesus."

"He never took the drugs. He's an athlete. He's super serious about his martial arts. But somehow he got his hands on some pills and he saw an opportunity with all his rich classmates and he took it. Solly says half the kids in his prep school take drugs and Malcolm is far from the only one who was selling, but he's the only one who got caught and expelled and Solly thinks it might have something to do with the way Malcolm looks. He wanted to sue, but Maureen talked him out of it. And now he's in that alternative school and everything is fine."

"Why didn't you tell me?"

"Solly didn't want anyone to know."

I wouldn't want anyone to know either.

"Malcolm is a good kid. Please resist the urge to judge," Peter says. "And most important, don't say a word. To anyone. Not Solly. Not Clem. Promise?"

"Promise," I say.

"More margarita?" Roberto has appeared on the roof with a pitcher in his hand, just as my glass goes empty.

I'M DRUNK AT DINNER. A lunch of tortilla chips followed by several margaritas consumed in a one-hundred-degree hot tub will do that to you. The food looks delicious but I can't taste it. My face is warm and flushed. I wonder if anyone notices. What I need is water. I reach for the glass and take big gulps and it runs down my chin as I drink. I wipe the water away. I wonder if anyone notices. Solly is holding court. He's saying something about a playlist. A death playlist. He's talking about what songs he wants to listen to on his deathbed. I think that this day can't come soon enough. I love Solly. I hate Solly. I think I'm glaring at him. I wonder if anyone notices. Enrique is standing next to me. He is offering me more food. He is offering to take my plate away. I do not know what he is offering. I do not know what to say to him so I say thank you. Thank you, Enrique. *Muchas gracias.* Enrique is Roberto's brother. He is younger I think. At least he looks younger. But that could be because he is rounder and rounder people don't show their age the way that thinner people do because rounder faces don't show wrinkles. I want to touch Enrique's face but I know I shouldn't. Ingrid isn't round *and* she doesn't have wrinkles. That is because Ingrid is young. Ingrid is beautiful. Ingrid is talented. Poor Ingrid. I am staring at her now. Solly is still talking. I could suggest some songs for his playlist. There are lots of great songs about people who cheat but I can't think of any. The only song that comes to mind is Stevie Wonder's "Part Time Lover" and that's a terrible song. I love Stevie Wonder. Why did he write such terrible songs? "I Just Called to Say I Love You" is another terrible song. Solly said something to make Malcolm laugh. Malcolm loves his father. You can tell by the way he is looking at him as he laughs. He loves his father even though his father sees him only twice a year. Would Clem love me if I saw her only twice a year? Why do I have to work so hard for her love when Solly does jackshit for Malcolm and gets his love anyway? Why do you do jackshit for your son, Solly? I don't ask this out loud. If I did, everyone would be looking at me and they aren't. Nobody notices. I know why Clem wants to be near Malcolm. She probably senses that he's a little dangerous. Danger is sexy. I should stop staring at Malcolm. I turn and look at Peter. My husband. He isn't dangerous. He is reliable. He is dependable. He has white hair but he looks younger than fifty. I look older than Peter even though he is three years older than me. Peter is looking at Solly. He is looking at Solly the way Malcolm is looking at Solly. He loves Solly. Everyone loves Solly. Why does everyone love Solly? I hear a sound. It is a screechy unpleasant sound. Now everyone is looking at me. Everyone notices. The sound is my chair on the hard marble floor. I am pushing it back and I am standing up and I am saying something out loud.

"I'm going to go lie down." This is what I say. "I'm not feeling well at all."

I WAKE UP AT 10:34. At first I think it's morning, but then I see that it's dark out. My mouth is dry and tacky and I go into the bathroom and put my head in the sink and take a long greedy drink right from the faucet. I straighten up and look at myself in the mirror and remember that I am in Mexico and that I shouldn't drink from the faucet and I try to spit out the water, but it's too late.

I've probably made myself sick, I think. And then I think: *If I get*

sick from the water I could blame that sickness for my strange be-
havior at the dinner table.

Peter hasn't come to bed yet. Why should he? It's only 10:34.
He's on vacation. These are the last few hours of the first fifty
years of his life.

I turn the faucet back on and take handfuls of cold water and
splash it on my face, careful not to get any of it into my mouth.
I look at myself in the mirror again. There are dark purple semi-
circles under my eyes, but that's nothing new. I check my roots
and think I should use that brown touch-up I brought but I can't
be bothered with that right now. I'm presentable enough, I decide, to venture out and see what everyone else is up to.

Ingrid and Ivan have gone to bed, of course. Solly and Peter sit
in the living room, close but not snuggling. Steely Dan is on the
playlist, which probably means Solly wants something from Peter, or maybe he's just indulging Peter on the eve of his birthday,
because I happen to know that though Peter is a huge fan, Solly
hates Steely Dan. They stop talking when I enter the room.

"Hey, party girl," Solly says. "Up from your power nap?"

I stretch. "Yeah, I was feeling . . ."

"I believe the word you're searching for is *wasted*."

I debate arguing this point, defending myself, but there's
really no use.

Peter pats the spot on the couch next to him. "Come sit."

I do. He puts an arm around me. It's a little awkward, the
three of us sitting so close.

Solly holds out his glass of tequila. "Little hair of the dog?"

I shake my head. "Where are the kids?"

"Ivan is sleeping with his mother," Solly says. "Sadly, he gets to do much more of that these days than I."

"I meant Clem and Malcolm."

"Night swim," Peter says.

We sit through half a song without saying anything. They obviously don't want to go back to their prior conversation. I get up from the couch.

"Heading back to bed?" Peter asks.

"No, I think I'll go down to the beach. Check on the kids."

Peter fixes me with a look I ignore by avoiding eye contact.

"I'm sure they're fine," Solly says. "They don't need to be checked on."

"I can check on my kid if I want to check on my kid," I say and I think, *Maybe if you did more checking on your kid he wouldn't be a drug dealer who has to finish up his senior year in an alternative school.*

He puts his hands up. "Well, then by all means, check away."

I walk downstairs, through the darkened dining room and past the darkened kitchen where Roberto and his family have left everything neat and tidy and ready for tomorrow, and down one more flight to the ground level. The pool lights are on and the kidney glows a not particularly inviting blue-green.

I unlatch the gate to the beach and step into the sand wet from a day of rain. It is completely silent. The bay has returned to stillness. The sky displays a blanket of stars the likes of which you'd never see even on the clearest, quietest night in Los Angeles.

I walk into the water until it reaches my ankles and I scan the flat, dark horizon for Clem and Malcolm. All I see is the reflec-

tion of the moon. I turn back and look at the villa. It appears
even taller, wider, grander, at night. The lights shine from the
main floor living room where Solly and Peter will have returned
to their conversation, speaking freely now that I am gone.

Where are Clem and Malcolm?

I walk down to the end of the beach where the starfish live
in the rocks. I am trying to do several things at once. I am searching for my daughter. I am fighting off panic that I don't see my
daughter anywhere. I am trying to appreciate the exquisite beauty
of this beach at night. I am battling nausea from the earlier margarita fest.

When I reach the rocks I turn around and head north toward
the other end of the beach, where if I continued through the
dark I'd pass Villa Perfect, the home of my new friend Maria
Josephina, and eventually reach the town and the hotel beaches,
which are probably full of revelers, even this late at night. The
water slips up under the soles of my feet, erasing any trace of my
footprints.

I see no sign of my daughter. The most likely explanation for
this, I decide, is that Solly and Peter were so deep into their conversation and that bottle of tequila that they didn't notice the
kids return from the beach. Their swim would have been brief.
As Peter has pointed out, Clem is a wimp about the cold.

As I turn to head back to the villa I see two figures coming up
the beach toward me from the direction of the starfish rocks. In
the dark they do not look like Clem and Malcolm. The height is
right, but the figures are both too thick, too broad. They don't
look lithe and graceful like our daughter and Solly's son.

I'm frightened, but this lasts only a second, because as they draw closer I can see that in fact they are our kids, and that they don't look like themselves in the dark because they're each wrapped in a large blanket.

"Hey, Mom," Clem says. "What are you doing out here?"

"I was just getting some fresh air."

"Really? There's lots of fresh air in the house because, like, there aren't any walls."

"Well, I wanted to be outside and then when I came out here and I didn't see you I got a little worried."

"Why?"

"Because it's late at night."

"It's not that late, Mother."

"Why are you carrying blankets?"

"Because," Clem says, "last time we swam at night I was really cold when we got out of the water."

"Did you go swimming?"

Clem and Malcolm exchange a look. I can't tell what kind of look because it's too dark out to read faces.

"No," Malcolm says. "Clem thought the water wasn't warm enough so we went for a walk instead."

"With blankets?"

"Yes. We had them with us, so."

"So . . . what? Finish your sentence."

"So we brought them along. Jeez," Clem says. "Are you still drunk?"

"I wasn't drunk."

She scoffs. "Whatever."

We stand there, the three of us, while I decide what to say next. Whether to continue with my interrogation. I want to know

where they walked to—I went to that end of the beach and I
didn't see them. Did they scramble to the other side of the
rocks? What's on the other side of the rocks? Did they turn in-
land? Make their way through the jungle patch? Don't they
know that it's dangerous to be out at night? What's with the
blankets?

Am I still drunk?

"I think I'll head inside," Malcolm says.

"See you in there," Clem tells him.

He turns and heads up to the house. Clem and I stand silently,
facing each other. I want to wrap myself inside the blanket with
her, to feel that sort of closeness, but she wants the opposite of
that.

"What's your problem?" she asks. "Why are you out here?"

"What's going on with you and Malcolm?"

"What? Why are you asking me that? God, Mom. You are so
annoying."

"Clem," I say. "What about Sean? He's a nice boy. You have
such a nice relationship with him."

"You know what your problem is, Mother?"

I shouldn't let her talk to me like that. I should scold her. Take
away her phone. Do something. Instead I just say, "No. What's
my problem?"

"You have absolutely no idea what you're talking about. You
think you know everything. You think you have it all figured out.
But you're wrong." She turns her back on me and starts up
toward the villa. Over her shoulder she calls, "The problem with
you, Mother, is that you don't know anything about anything."

WEDNESDAY

You would think that after nearly twenty years together, it would be easy to find the perfect gift for your husband on his birthday.

Peter insists that this trip is enough. That we've spent so much money we should cut back where we can, but more than that, he claims there's nothing in the world that could top a week on a luxury vacation with the people he loves most.

"Things are just things," he told me. "I never liked things that much in the first place, and as I get older, I like things even less."

This, of course, is not entirely true. There are things Peter likes. He likes good bourbon. He likes a good pair of socks. He likes fancy chocolate, the darker the better. He likes big door-stopper books about military history. He enjoys a cigar every now and then. None of these things fits the occasion. Peter is turning fifty. These things are just things. And anyway, with the exception of the socks and maybe the chocolate, these things proved problematic to pack along on an international trip.

So the short of it is, I have nothing. Nothing to give my husband on his fiftieth birthday.

The best birthday gift I ever gave Peter was when he turned thirty-one, the first of his birthdays we spent together. We were already living in a Spanish-style duplex in West Hollywood planning a wedding nobody knew about yet.

We spent nearly every minute together in the days that followed that night at the bar in New Orleans. Everything about Peter Carlson took me by surprise. I hadn't come to New Orleans to hole up in a hotel room with a man I'd just met, but he had a beautiful smile and he barely took his eyes or his hands off me and I'd never before been the focus of such intense, intoxicating attention. I loved the way he smelled and his sunburned arms and I loved his white hair and the thin trail of darker hair below his belly button. I liked how he worked as a designer for a magazine—it seemed edgy and sophisticated and very adult. Despite all of this I told him I was just getting out of a relationship and that whatever was happening between us wouldn't go anywhere. This wasn't a ploy to make myself more desirable, and yet there was no denying Peter's desire.

We skipped the music. We never went to another bar. We ate from stands where you ordered food on the street so you could continue on with the revelry, which for us meant having sex, nonstop sex, and talking. We told each other everything. The entire story of the years that led up to the night we met.

We bonded over being the children of divorce, and discussed how my experience made me unsure if I ever wanted to get married while his made him want to have the kind of marriage that eluded his parents. He held my new bangs off my forehead and put them back again so he could weigh in on which look was better. (The bangs.) He loved my raspy voice and made me read aloud from the Bible he took from the hotel nightstand. My job with teens in foster care impressed him, and hearing myself describe it to him, I felt real pride in the work I was doing. I told him I wanted to write, and he asked me why I didn't, and I said I didn't know how to be a writer, and he shrugged and said I guess you just have to sit down and do it. This is still the best piece of advice about writing that I've ever been given.

The friends I'd come to New Orleans with were having their own wild adventures, and Solly didn't mind Peter abandoning him because Solly meets people everywhere he goes, and there was no shortage of young, beautiful, unattached women in town for Jazz Fest.

As we lay naked on one of the nights or mornings or afternoons, Peter told me about the View-Master he'd lost when he was nine. I'd had one, too, as a child, the red plastic toy into which you'd slip a white cardboard disk of tiny photographs to click through. I had some assortment of cartoon character disks, Mickey Mouse or maybe Snow White, I couldn't remember. But Peter remembered his very well. He had a collection of travel disks, from Saudi Arabia, Kenya, Antarctica and less exotic locales like Washington, D.C., and Yosemite. He used to lie in bed and look at these places and fantasize about visiting them with his sister, who didn't give him the time of day, and his parents, who were in the midst of a spectacularly bitter divorce. Somehow, in the back-and-forth between his boyhood home and his father's new apartment, Peter lost his View-Master. Each parent blamed the other parent for misplacing it. Neither parent offered to buy him a new one.

So for his thirty-first birthday I tracked down a vintage seventies View-Master. This was just around the time eBay was getting started, but I didn't yet know about eBay, and so I spent months searching antique shops before I finally struck gold at a tiny place in the Valley. Then I found a film developer who took a series of photographs I had of Peter and me from our first year together and converted them onto a white cardboard disk that fit into the View-Master. He charged me four times what the vintage toy cost, but it was worth every penny. Peter cried when I gave it to him. It was the first time I'd ever seen him cry.

I knew I'd never top that gift, and that seemed just as it should be: You put your best foot forward, give the greatest gifts at the beginning of your love story, so that you have something to look back on and say, "Remember that time . . ." But now, twenty years later, I wonder if I had it wrong. If maybe we should save our best gifts for the middle, for the times when you both need reminding that you are special to each other.

When Solly arrives at the breakfast table with a gift-wrapped box for Peter, I'm livid. This isn't fair, I know. Peter didn't tell Solly not to buy him anything. He didn't tell Solly that this trip was enough. How could Solly know that to Peter *things are only things*? That as he nears fifty he cares less for things? Only a wife would know that.

And what did Solly get him anyway? Not bourbon. Not cigars. I can tell by the shape of the box that it isn't a book.

Solly puts the present down at the empty place where Peter will sit when he's done with his morning bathroom routine, a routine that has gotten longer and louder over the course of our stay in Mexico; also something only a wife would know.

"How nice," I say. "What's in the box, Solly?"

"You'll see." He smiles at Ingrid. She knows, too. I'm the only adult in the room who doesn't.

"What did *you* get him, Mother?" Clem asks. I know that Clem knows that I didn't get him anything. She was there for the conversations about how this trip was to be his big fiftieth birthday present from all of us.

"This trip is his gift," I tell her. "You know that."

"You didn't get him anything? Nothing to open on his birthday?"

"Did you?" I ask her.

"No. But I'm not, like, married to him."

"So? You're his daughter. You could use the occasion to give something back, considering how much he's given you every single day of your extraordinarily charmed life."

I know that the last thing Peter wants for his birthday is to show up to breakfast to find his wife and daughter bickering, but sometimes Clementine can be so selfish.

Clem leans closer to Malcolm and says something to him under her breath to which he shows no reaction at all. He smiles at me weakly.

Peter enters the dining room and everyone applauds. He takes a theatrical bow. He looks happy. Content. Wanting for nothing.

He slides into the seat in front of the wrapped box. "I thought we said no gifts."

"Nobody said anything to me about no gifts," Solly says. "And for the record, I would like gifts on my fiftieth birthday. Many gifts. No expense should be spared. And no joke gifts, please."

"Duly noted," Peter says.

Enrique comes to pour Peter some coffee. *"Feliz cumpleaños,"* he says.

"Thank you, Enrique."

"Here in Mexico we have the tradition of *la mordida*. Where you go to eat the cake with your hands behind your back like this"—Enrique mimes eating without hands—"and then your family, they shove you into the cake so that you get it all over your face and in your hair."

"As inviting as that sounds," Peter says, "I think I'd like to start with some eggs over easy."

Enrique takes the empty plate from his place and heads toward the kitchen. "As you wish," he says.

Peter studies the box. He picks it up and gives it a little shake.

"Careful," Solly tells him.

"So it isn't a snow globe?"

"Right. Nor is it a pair of maracas."

"What could it be?" Peter says as he tears into the paper, revealing a black box, which he opens on its hinges. The inside of the box faces him, so the rest of us can't see its contents. "No. Way," Peter says. "No way!" He turns the box around. It's a watch.

Peter has never worn a watch for as long as I have known him.

"This is amazing, Sol. Really." He takes the watch out of the box and straps it onto his wrist, the one on which he isn't wearing the string bracelet I gave him, and he stares at it. I think, though I find it hard to believe, that I see tears in Peter's eyes.

"So when we were in college," Solly starts, "I used to wear this watch. It was from my father's business. It said Solomon Mattress Company on the face. I still can't figure out why he had them made. They weren't for sale. And what employee would want one? I guess he made them for family, a reminder of the ship our good fortune sailed in on. Anyway, Peter used to make fun of me for wearing it. He thought it was terribly bourgeois, though he never used that word, because as you can probably discern, *bourgeois* is a word beyond the limits of Peter's simple vocabulary."

Peter lets loose a sharp, staccato laugh.

"Someday, I told him, maybe you'll be lucky enough to own a business worthy of a watch face." Solly reaches over and takes Peter's wrist and turns it so we can take a closer look at the watch. On its face: the logo of Boychick Bagels.

"This is . . ." Peter takes his wrist back and stares at the watch again. "Amazing."

"But wait," Solly says. "There's more."

Of course there is. With Solly there is always more. With Solly enough is never enough. He reaches into his pocket and he retrieves three more watches. He straps one to his wrist, hands one to Malcolm and one to Clementine.

"It seems only fitting that our progeny should wear them, too. Like I wore the watch from my father's mattress company. And if anyone tells either of you that you are bourgeois for wearing it?" He wags his finger at the teenagers. "You be sure to tell that person to go fuck himself."

"Ding dong," Ivan says. *"Go fuck himself."*

"You tell 'em, Ivan." Solly pulls Ivan onto his lap; he quickly wriggles out and retreats to his mother, who is doing little to hide her disapproval.

"Thanks, Solly," Clem says, fiddling with the band. "I love it."

Clem is particular about everything she wears, careful to never make a fashion statement someone else didn't make first. I don't know if watches are *in* among Clem's peers, but I doubt it given that they're never more than arm's reach from their phones.

"Don't worry, baby," Ingrid coos at Ivan. "Daddy had one made for you, too."

Ivan shrugs. "I don't care."

"We're just saving it to give it to you later, when you're a little bigger." She strokes his hair. "Because you're his progeny, too."

I SPEND SOME TIME on the website for the restaurant Solly booked us for Peter's birthday dinner.

It's the opposite of what I pictured. Not to sound like Clem with my gross generalizations, but I imagined a palapa roof, colorful tablecloths, massive margarita glasses, maybe a wandering mariachi band.

Instead the restaurant is modern and rustic. Sleek and simple. It looks like one of the many hipster places that have popped up over the last few years in downtown L.A. where Peter and I always talk about going, but then we consider traffic on the 10, and the lines to get in, and we just go to the same Italian restaurant in Westwood we've been eating at for years.

I imagine Solly would have selected this restaurant for its name alone, even if it hadn't come so highly recommended by Roberto, and even if it didn't have reviews in *Bon Appétit, Sunset* magazine and a mention in the *New York Times*.

It's called El Cabron Suertudo: The Lucky Bastard.

All of the text on the website is in Spanish; they promise *una experiencia gastronómica.* There are a few photographs of the food—definitely Instagram worthy. It's the kind of restaurant my father would call "schmancy."

I close my laptop and head downstairs to join everyone else at the pool. It has returned to postcard-perfect vacation weather.

There are six loungers and every one of them is occupied. I expect Ingrid to tell Ivan to move to make room for me, but she doesn't. She is reading a book to him as he lies in the lounger next to hers. Malcolm and Clem have pulled their chairs close to each other and Peter and Solly have done the same. They are all lost in their own conversations. Their own little universes of two. I sit at the shallow end of the kidney and dangle my feet in the water.

I stand up and say, "Well, I guess I'll go for a walk on the beach."

Peter is the only one who responds, which he does without looking my way. "Okay, honey. Have fun."

I WALK NORTH, toward town, though I have no intention of going that far. I don't have my wallet. I don't even have on any shoes. Just my bathing suit and the gauzy pink cover-up I thought was cute when I first bought it but now plan on leaving behind.

I round the bend to the three villas. Nobody is on the beach. Nobody swims in the glassy water out front. Nobody stands on the balconies. Is it siesta time?

In front of Villa Perfect a hammock hangs between two trees, completely still, with no wind to move it. I don't remember seeing this hammock. Its U shape is a smile, beckoning me.

Come, it says. *Lie here in the shade of these trees. Rock back and forth like a baby in my cradle.*

I oblige its call and climb in. I'm weightless like in the ocean. It's heavenly.

I close my eyes. Maybe a siesta will finally rid me of this nagging, lingering hangover. It's Peter's birthday. I will need to toast him tonight. I will want to toast him tonight. He is fifty. We have spent two fifths of his life together.

I reach my toes into the sand and kick the ground so my hammock swings side to side, side to side, rocking me back and forth, back and forth.

I think about how when Clementine was a baby, she loved Johnny Cash. His was the one voice we could count on to soothe her. His version of "You Are My Sunshine" was nearly foolproof, even in the midst of a catastrophic meltdown. I never understood why such a gloomy song became a favorite lullaby, not only of my daughter's but of generations of children.

In my state of almost sleep I see Solly's face. He opens his mouth and out comes Johnny Cash's voice. He sings the forgotten verses in which it becomes clear that this child's lullaby is about infidelity. It's about the narrator's pain and desperate loneliness in learning that Sunshine has been cheating. He or she—it never is clear—is willing to forgive and forget if Sunshine will just leave the new, undoubtedly younger and more attractive love object and come back home again. No questions asked. The song ends before we know what happens, but, let's face it, the melancholy melody gives us a big fat clue about what Sunshine decides to do.

Fucking Sunshine. What an asshole.

"Jenna?"

It's Maria Josephina.

I open my eyes and try sitting up, but that's no easy feat in a hammock. I pull my pink cover-up down over my exposed thighs.

Was I singing along with the Solly / Johnny Cash mash-up?

God, I hope I wasn't singing out loud.

"Oh, hello!" I climb out of the hammock with less grace than I'd like. "I'm sorry. I just saw this hammock here and there was no chair left by our pool and I guess I was more tired than I realized and—"

"You are welcome to it. The hammock is here on the beach and the beaches belong to everyone."

"Thank you."

"Tell me," she says. "Did your husband like the bracelet?"

"Sure. But it was just a little gesture."

"A tchotchke."

"Ha. Right!"

She sits down, with her legs crossed, and rests her back against the trunk of the palm tree that holds up one end of the hammock. She is wearing a beige linen skirt and white T-shirt straight out of a Clorox ad. I sit near her in the sand. I can feel it sticking to my bare legs. We both face the ocean.

"Today is his actual birthday," I say. "Peter, I mean."

"Your husband."

"Yes. I didn't buy him a gift."

"Other than the bracelet."

"I just . . . I guess I thought this trip would be enough."

"And it isn't?"

"It should be, shouldn't it? But I don't know. He turned fifty. And I'll be fifty soon. In three years." I have no idea how old Maria Josephina is. She could be thirty. She could be sixty. It's nearly impossible to tell. I've barely seen her without her huge black sunglasses.

"Fifty is not the end of living."

"No. I don't suppose it is."

We watch a flock of birds land at the water's edge and then quickly take óff again just as a small wave threatens to lap at their feet.

"Have you been to the Malecon?" she asks.

"I don't think so. What is it?"

"It is our boardwalk. By the sea. With many not very nice shops. But still it is lovely. There is a sculpture, there are several, but my favorite is one by Sergio Bustamante. It is called *En Busca de la Razón.* Searching for Reason. You should go and see this sculpture."

"Maybe I will."

"It is of a ladder. And on this ladder two figures climb, and one stands on the ground, arms open. Maybe to catch the climbers if they fall. Maybe to say, *Come back, it is safer here on the ground in the life we already know.* When I see this statue I think that I would like to be one of the climbers. Even if I do not know where this ladder goes. I always want to keep climbing. To keep moving toward whatever is next."

"It sounds beautiful."

"It is."

I'm not sure who I am in this sculpture. I think neither the one on the ground with open arms nor the one climbing into the unknown. I'd probably be the one checking each rung of the ladder to make sure it isn't about to break.

Maria Josephina sighs. She looks up at her perfect villa. "And now, I think it is time for a glass of wine. Would you like to join me?"

I would. I would very much like to join her for a glass of wine. "I can't," I say. "I should go back to the others. Back to Peter."

"I understand. Perhaps there will now be a chair available by the pool."

Perhaps. But I suspect they're still ensconced in their universes of two. I suspect that they will hardly notice I've been gone.

WE EAT A LATE LUNCH because our dinner reservation isn't until nine o'clock.

Ingrid is far from thrilled with this plan.

"That's when Ivan goes to bed," she says. "I don't understand how you couldn't have taken that into consideration."

"Because, my darling," Solly tells her, "it was either nine o'clock or five o'clock, and though Peter is fifty and I will be soon, we are not quite ready to feast on the early bird special with the rest of the blue-hairs."

"So what are we supposed to do about Ivan?"

Solly shrugs. "Make him take a nap."

"Ding dong," Ivan chirps. "No nap."

Ingrid gives Solly a *told you so* look.

"So, he'll stay up later than usual. This is a special occasion. We're on vacation. We're celebrating. This is a party. You like parties," he says to Ivan. "Right, champ?"

"I like parties," Ivan says.

"That's the spirit."

Ingrid shifts in her seat so that her back is to Solly. "We'll just have to see how it goes."

Ingrid and Solly rarely quarrel. Not publicly at least. I always attribute this to the newness of them, though at seven years into their relationship, they can be considered new only from the vantage point of someone who has been with her husband for twenty years. It makes me like Ingrid a little bit more when I catch a glimpse, however fleeting, of her losing patience with Solly.

Roberto, who has been making the rounds with seconds of avocados stuffed with chicken, bravely wades into the controversy. "In Puerto Vallarta it is more better going to dinner late. It is when the town is busy. The streets, they fill with people. And the restaurants, too. People will be going to the clubs for dancing. And during Semana Santa it will be even more like celebration."

Ingrid manages a smile at him.

"At five o'clock"—his voice is apologetic—"it is not good. At nine o'clock it is much better."

Solly slaps his back a little too hard; Roberto almost loses his grip on the tray of avocados. "Thanks for backing me up, amigo."

"Dancing could be fun," Clementine says. "At one of the nightclubs?"

She is looking at Malcolm. The invitation is for nobody else but him.

He nods his head. "Totally."

"I will tell you where is the best one," Roberto says. "It is not far from the restaurant where you go to eat."

Clem looks at me pleadingly. *Don't say no. Don't kill the fun. Don't wield your parental power arbitrarily like you do.*

I decide to try out Ingrid's line. "We'll just have to see how it goes," I tell her.

INGRID ASKS ME if I'd like to go to town with her early to look around a bit before meeting the others at the restaurant.

"I'll let Solly be the one to wrestle Ivan into his nice shirt," she says. "I love him, but I haven't had a minute away from him since we got here and I think I could really use the space."

Is she talking about Ivan? Or is she talking about Solly?

Roberto calls us a taxi. We are two people: by his earlier calculus it should be safe for us to walk, but when you factor in that we are two women, and that it is getting dark out, and that Ingrid is wearing heels even though she's already annoyingly tall, a taxi makes sense.

We get dropped at the main square. It's lit up with colored spotlights and a nine-piece band plays salsa or samba or some kind of music in the gazebo. Couples dance. Men get their shoes shined. Old women feed pigeons. Children chase each other in zigzags.

"Isn't this fabulous?" Ingrid puts her arms out and spins around. "It's so nice to be out and unencumbered."

We wander around the periphery of the square and then onto the smaller streets, where the shops are still open and vendors sell food, sweets, toys and souvenirs from carts. Ingrid links her arm through mine. It's a friendly gesture and practical, too—cobblestones aren't easy to navigate in heels.

We stop so she can buy a bottle of water. Back on the sidewalk she opens it, takes a long drink like she's just run a marathon and then fixes me with a look.

"So how *are* you, Jenna?"

I try to figure out what she's trying to ask. I've been with her around the clock since Saturday, so this isn't just your default conversation opener. Is she wondering how I'm recovering from drinking too much last night? Is this about my writer's block? My breast cancer? My shame over not buying my husband a birthday gift? My unease with Clem's sudden and increasingly obvious infatuation with Malcolm?

"I'm good," I say with a little too much pep. "I'm great."

"Good," she says. "That's . . . good."

"Why do you ask?" To this she just shrugs her shoulders. "I mean," I try again, "why do you ask *like that*? Like things maybe shouldn't be good?"

"Oh, no. No. I don't think that. I'm just . . ." She takes my arm again and we continue our slow stroll. "I guess, I'm just, I'm not very good at this, am I? At this friendship thing? I've always been a little intimidated by you. Or maybe in awe of you. And I used to think you hated me, because, you know, of how Solly and I got our start and Maureen and everything. But now, I feel like we're friends. We *are* friends, right?"

"Of course we're friends," I say.

"Good. That's how I feel, too. So I guess I was just trying to be a good friend. I was checking in with you. I'm afraid I've done all the talking on this trip about my manuscript, and the stuff about Malcolm, and dealing with Ivan, and I just wanted to make sure that I took the time to see if there's anything *you* wanted to talk about. You haven't said much about yourself or how things are going for you."

This would be a whole lot easier if Ingrid would just have a drink. Then we could go to a bar rather than wandering through the streets with her arm in mine like I'm her doddering old grandmother. We could pull up some stools and settle in for a real conversation. It's been ages since I've done anything like that. Life is so busy. There's hardly time anymore for friendship. And maybe Ingrid could be a real friend. Maybe I could finally forgive her for banishing Maureen to the opposite coast. Maybe I could finally see her for who she is: a mother like me, a wife like me, a writer like me, a woman trying to make sense of it all like me.

But if Ingrid is a real friend, then what to do with what I know about Solly?

"And you're feeling well? After all the . . . you know."

"Treatment? Radiation? *Cancer?*"

"Yes. That. You're back to your old self?"

"Pretty much."

"That must have been so hard. Even though your prognosis is good, it doesn't make it any less scary, does it?"

"No. It really doesn't. Thank you, Ingrid, for recognizing that."

"I just . . ."—she shakes her head—"think you're amazing."

"Well, that's very nice of you to say." It is nice. Ingrid is nice. She's so, so nice.

"You're such a great mother. And of course you're such a great writer, too. How you've managed to raise a child and write four books—"

"Three," I correct her. "I'm still working on the fourth."

"Fine. How you've managed to raise a child and write *three* books is beyond me."

"Wait a minute," I say. "You're raising a child and you've written a book. Sounds like you're on the same track."

"Yes, but I'm just messing around. It's a hobby. I'm not an author, like you. I have no idea what I'm doing." I don't think Ingrid is fishing. Her undervalued opinion of her own work strikes me as genuine. As does everything else about Ingrid. "Ivan, yes," she continues. "I'll take credit for him. He's a good boy. I'm managing to do that part well."

I stop. I take her arm out of mine and I turn her to face me. "Ingrid," I say. "Your book is great. You are going to find an agent and then you are going to find a publisher and that publisher is going to have to win your book in a bidding war because everybody is going to want it."

She looks confused. "What?"

Given what she is going to have to face in her own marriage, it can't hurt to give her a little sliver of hope about her future as a writer. "I finished it. I love it. It's so, so good."

She puts her hands up to her face. "No."

I nod. "Yes."

She reaches over and she puts her arms around me. It's a big, strong, Solly-style hug. "You aren't just saying that? Remember, I told you no good will come from protecting my feelings."

"I am not protecting anything. What I'm doing is telling you I think your book is really good."

She squeals. "I can't believe it. I just can't believe it."

We start strolling again. This time when she links her arm through mine she pulls me closer, like we're lovers. "This has been such a great trip, Jenna. I know how hard you worked finding the house and setting everything up and I just want to say thank you. Thank you from all of us. You're our captain, and I fear you don't get enough credit."

"I don't need credit," I say.

"Oooh, look!" She pulls me toward a brightly lit jewelry shop. "Let's do a little browsing, shall we?"

We go inside. The woman who owns the place is a painter as well as a jewelry maker and the walls are lined with her paintings of dogs and chickens and children. They're bright and fanciful and not at all cheesy, though they so easily could have gone in that direction. Ingrid heads straight for a case of necklaces.

"*Por favor?*" Ingrid says. "Can I see this one?" She points to a big chunky necklace of silver and some sort of red stone, not clear like a gem, but solid like a rock.

"Of course," the woman says in perfect, unaccented English. "This is one of my favorite pieces. You have a good eye."

"Do you make these yourself?" Ingrid asks.

"Yes," the woman answers. "Most of what I sell here I make. I have a workshop in my home. Some of the pieces, not this one, but some of the others I buy from *artesanos*, local artists. For those I only keep five percent of the sale price."

"Oh, good." Ingrid says. "I don't mean to be nosy, but it matters to me where and how things are made."

"I completely understand," says the woman. "It matters to me, too."

Ingrid holds the necklace up to me. "With this outfit?" she says. "It is perfect on you."

I take a quick look at the price tag. "I don't think so," I say. I'd spend that kind of money on the painting of the chicken that everyone in the family could enjoy before I'd spend it on a piece of jewelry for myself.

"I'm getting it for you," Ingrid says. "And I'm getting something for me, too. I'm not going to argue with you about it. Everyone else got a watch today and what did we get?"

She points to another necklace in the case, a similar one but with green stones cut into round rather than square shapes. The woman hands it to her and she fastens it around her neck. It looks like she's been wearing it forever.

She pulls out her credit card and hands it to the woman.

"Ingrid. Wait."

"Nope," she says. "No arguments."

I catch a glimpse of myself in the mirror. The necklace isn't something I ever would have picked out, but I have to admit, I love how I look in it.

"Thank you, Ingrid," I say. "You're too nice."

SOLLY NEVER DID MANAGE to get Ivan into his good shirt. Nor into a pair of pants. Ivan arrives at the restaurant in pajamas with cowboys and cacti on them.

"This is what the boy wanted to wear." Solly looks at him proudly. "And when I say wanted, I mean insisted."

"But I packed that shirt special for tonight," Ingrid says. "When is he going to wear it?"

"I'm going to go out on a limb and say . . . *never*."

"Dammit, Solly. I asked you to do one thing."

We're still waiting to be shown to our table. The area by the hostess stand is small and cramped and I'm quite literally in the middle of Solly and Ingrid's argument. Clem has already acquired the wi-fi password and she hunches together with Malcolm looking at something on her phone. Peter catches my eye and rolls his, just a little. Not enough for anyone but me to know what he's trying to say: *Look at Solly and Ingrid bickering over a shirt. Remember when we used to do stupid shit like that? Now we're better. We fight only about things that matter. And right now we aren't fighting about anything at all. Yay us!*

He reaches over and pulls me into him.

"You look beautiful," he whispers into my ear.

"Thank you," I whisper back. It's probably the necklace. "I hope you're having a great birthday."

"It's the best. It couldn't be any more perfect."

We follow the hostess into the large, loud, crowded dining room. The ceiling is tall, the floor is concrete and the walls are white and covered with bottles of wine on old wooden shelves. The Californian in me can't help but look at this decor and imagine the nightmare earthquake scenario.

We're shown to a round table. I sit in between Clem and Peter.

"So, Mom." She throws an arm around me. "The club Roberto

told us about looks really cool. Check it out." She hands me her phone. She's pulled up the Yelp page. The club gets four-and-a-half stars. I had no idea you could Yelp a Mexican nightclub.

I hand her phone back to her.

"Well?" she asks. "What do you think?"

"About?"

"About me and Malcolm going there after dinner. It's only three blocks away. It looks super fun. Please, Mommy?"

"Don't 'Mommy' me, Clementine."

She does a pouty face. "It's just that it really looks fun. And I really want to go. And this vacation has been great, don't get me wrong, but we haven't done anything for, like, people our age."

"How old do you have to be to go to this club?"

Clem and Malcolm exchange a look. "Well," she says. "Technically you're supposed to be eighteen, but online and in the reviews and stuff they say that nobody in Puerto Vallarta checks ID. They don't care."

"They may not care, but I do."

"Why? What do you think is going to happen? I just want to go hear music and dance and stuff. I swear we aren't going to drink or anything like that. I promise you. Right, Malcolm?"

"Totally," he says. "We won't drink. You have my word."

"Or anything else?"

Malcolm puzzles over this, eyeing me, like *I'm* the one who's been caught selling drugs. "Or anything else," he says.

Now that the three of us are in conversation we've attracted attention from the others at the table.

"Dad says it's fine with him if it's okay with you," Clem says. "Right, Dad?"

I glare at Peter. He gives me an apologetic shrug. He's set me up.

"Aw, come on, Jen," Solly chimes in. "Let the kids go have a little fun. I'd offer to chaperone, but I'm afraid I'd slip a disk, or tear a rotator cuff, and anyway, let's face it, the music is going to suck."

Now it's a full-on ambush. I'm not left with much of a choice.

"Fine," I say. "But this doesn't mean you should rush through your father's birthday dinner."

Clem leans over and kisses me on the cheek. "We won't. I swear. Thanks, Mom."

Malcolm and Clem grin at each other. They look like they're in a toothpaste commercial.

"What are we eating tonight?" Solly asks, opening his menu.

"What are we drinking?" I reply, gesturing for the waitress.

AT 11:15 IT'S JUST Solly, Peter and me left at our table. Clem and Malcolm have headed off to the nightclub against my better judgment and Ingrid took Ivan home before dessert, which did not make him happy.

We've stayed to drink a final toast to Peter.

I watched Solly walk Ingrid out to the street and help her into her cab. I watched him hold her hand and stroke her hair. I watched him act contrite about the shirt fiasco, ever the doting husband.

I never had to watch Solly put on a fake show for Maureen while he cheated with Ingrid because I found out about the affair after Maureen did. Now I see why Peter kept that secret from me and tried keeping this one: it is excruciating to watch a woman whose husband is cheating when you know it and she does not.

Why does Solly always covet the new, shiny object? Why is he never happy with what he has? Maybe I should feel sorry for Solly: who wants to live in a state of perpetual dissatisfaction?

I watch as he puts his hand on the waitress's forearm while he orders our round of tequila. *Get your hand off her, Solly,* I want to say to him. *Not everything is yours for the grabbing.*

When the tequila comes, Solly holds up his glass.

"Peter," he begins. "You have been my best friend for thirty-two years. I cannot fathom why the powers that be in freshman housing conspired to pair us together, unless it's that they'd watched too many episodes of *The Odd Couple.*"

Solly turns to me and adds, as an aside: "In case it isn't clear, I'm the Oscar in that scenario."

I don't say anything. He waits. I manage a fake smile.

He continues, "You have made my life richer in every way. And let's be honest: I was plenty rich to begin with."

Big belly laugh here.

God, I hate Solly.

"So I make this toast to you," he says. "My best friend, my brother. You make turning fifty seem like a walk in the park. And I look forward to following you, as following you is something I have always done, in one way or another, since the day we first met. *L'chaim.*"

Solly throws back his shot of tequila. Then Peter does the same. They both stare at me, waiting. I glare at Solly. There is fire in my cheeks. I know this probably isn't the right moment, but when is it ever the right moment to call someone out for being a fucking pig?

I take my shot of tequila. It burns going down, an exquisite, delicious sort of burn.

"Solly."

He looks at me inquisitively. Peter is looking at me, too, with no admonition, no pleading—he has no idea that I'm about to confront Solly. This will infuriate Peter, whose first allegiance is not to me but to his best friend. He will see this as a betrayal of my trust, a trust that's shaky to begin with. If Peter really trusted me I wouldn't have had to squeeze the information about the affair out of him, or the truth about Malcolm's troubles. Peter might say this is none of my concern, but he'd be wrong. This affair isn't only about Solly and Ingrid, it's also about the business. *Our* business. Solly is jeopardizing all of our futures.

"Solly," I repeat. "I—"

Solly isn't listening to me. He's no longer paying attention. He's looking out the window to the street. He's like a kid with ADHD.

"What's going on?" he asks, but he isn't asking me. This isn't about what I've been building up the courage to say. This is about what's happening outside the restaurant.

The sidewalk is full of people, as it has been all night, but now the people are running. The people are shouting. You could easily mistake this sort of action and energy for revelry, for a celebration in the streets, but if you look more closely you see that there's no order, no sense. It's chaotic. Pure panic.

The noisy restaurant gets suddenly, eerily quiet. Sirens wail in the distance. Competing from all directions.

The check is on the table. Solly picks it up, looks at it, reaches into his pocket, pulls out four hundred-dollar bills and throws them down.

"Let's get out of here."

We follow him outside, leaving the quiet for the chaos. There are others like us, standing on the street, dumbfounded, trying to make sense of what is happening. And there are those who run. They are running in both directions. I can't tell who's running away from the danger and who's running toward it.

We try shouting at strangers. *"What's happening? Why is everyone running? Please? Someone? Anyone? Tell us what's going on?"*

The sirens are drawing nearer to us and nearer to one another. They no longer sound like they're coming from all directions, they sound like they're gathering to our right, to the east, at least I think it's the east, as it's the opposite direction from the bay.

"The nightclub," I say. "Which way is the nightclub?" *How did I not get the address of the nightclub from Clementine?*

"I don't know," Peter says.

"It's that way—" Solly points in the direction of the sirens. He grabs a man who is moving quickly past where we stand in front of the restaurant.

"What's happening?" he screams at the man.

The man looks more frightened than annoyed that a stranger would put his hands on him like that.

"Un secuestro! Ha habido un secuestro!"

"What?" Solly shouts. "I don't understand you."

The man wrenches his arm free and runs away, and we start

running in the opposite direction, toward the club, toward the screeching sirens.

We make it two blocks before we have to slow because the crowd is getting thicker. I take Peter's hand and he takes Solly's and the three of us worm our way through the sea of people, nearer to the flashing lights of the police cars.

I pull out my phone with my free hand and call Clem. Straight to voice mail. I text her with my shaking thumb: where r u call me now

We've made it as far as we're able. Police are blockading the street and there's already crime-scene tape going up around the perimeter of a big white building with tall windows. People are filing out of the open doors, slowly and calmly, but they are holding on to one another, and some of the women are crying. The people are young and attractive and dressed to reveal as much skin as possible.

"Is that it?" I scream. "Is that the nightclub?"

Solly and Peter have their heads close together. They are speaking so I can't hear them.

Peter lets go of Solly and puts both of his hands on my shoulders. "Yes," he says quietly. "But don't panic. Look. Look at me." I focus my eyes on his. "The police are here. All those people are coming out of the club and they're fine. We will find them."

We push farther through the crowd until we reach a line of police officers in helmets holding machine guns.

I try asking them, shouting at them—what is happening and I need to find my daughter—but they stand still, shoulder to shoulder, and stare straight ahead, as if I don't exist. They part to let people through who are coming from the club, but the flow goes in one direction only.

We cannot get any closer. I scan the dozens of faces moving toward us for my pale daughter and Solly's dark-skinned son. My eyes are darting everywhere, trying to see everything at once, desperate to put things into order, to make some sense of what is happening.

Time is both racing forward and moving in slow motion.

Time is collapsing.

Peter has stopped a young man who has made his way out of the club and he's trying to ask him what's happening, but Peter is shouting, and he sounds angry and threatening, and the man just wants to get away, to keep moving. The man says the same words: *un secuestro.*

If my hands weren't shaking and my heart wasn't racing and if there was wi-fi in the middle of the street or if I'd paid for a fucking data plan I could look up *un secuestro* on my phone, but none of these things is true, and so I shout to nobody, I scream into the electric night air: "WHAT IS *UN SECUESTRO?*"

"A kidnapping."

I turn. There is a young woman standing next to me. She is tiny and looks no older than Clementine. She is holding on to the arm of a young man who appears far more upset; she is calm and she speaks clearly.

"There has been a kidnapping. Inside the nightclub. It happened very fast. Inside it was very frightening. There were gunshots fired. Into the air. I do not think anyone was shot. The police arrived after it was over. After they got away."

"A kidnapping?" I say, only inches from her face. "Who did they kidnap?"

"I don't know," she says and she holds on to my arm. Her touch is gentle. She's barely more than a child and yet she's trying to comfort me. "There was a large group of men. All dressed in black. With masks on their faces. They took many people. It all happened very quickly."

"My daughter," I scream. "My daughter was in there."

"I do not think they took your daughter," the woman says. "They seemed to know who they wanted. They took people from the VIP section of the club. People who were together. It did not seem random. And I think they took only men, but I can't be sure."

"My son," Solly says. I didn't know that he'd been listening to us. "My son was in there, too."

"I'm sorry," she says. "I have to go now. My family will be worried. You will find your son and your daughter."

She turns and, with the young man on her arm, disappears into the crowd. I wish I'd hugged her, if only so that I could be sure that she'd been real. Without her in front of me I can't be sure of anything.

The flow of people from the nightclub has stopped. Now it's only the police swarming the building and the sidewalk out front.

I move along down the barricade and Peter and Solly follow. I try again with a different officer.

"Please," I say. "I am trying to find my daughter."

Nothing.

I try another officer. And then another. I know I am screaming. I am not being polite. I am not behaving with respect. I am
not showing deference to their roles, nor to their culture, nor to
their language.

"PLEASE," I shout.

Nobody will help me. I turn around to scream at Peter and
Solly because I need to scream at somebody, but the bodies next
to me that I thought belonged to Peter and Solly belong to
strangers. They look nothing like Peter and Solly.

Where are Peter and Solly?

The crowd isn't thinning, if anything it is growing, it is swell-
ing, and now I can't find my husband. I don't see Solly. I am totally and completely lost.

I pull out my phone and call Clem again. Voice mail. I call her
again. Voice mail. She must have turned her phone off, or put it
on airplane mode, or maybe she's been separated from it, from
this essential piece of her.

I am separated from her, this essential piece of me.

I move back through the crowd to where I can be certain I
last stood next to Peter and Solly. Can I be certain? When was
this? Minutes ago? Hours? I remember there was a woman. She
was young and beautiful and she told me that everything was
going to be okay. She told me the kidnappers did not take my
daughter. Where did she go? I would like to find this woman
again.

"CLEMENTINE," I shout. "PETER."

The crowd is closing in on me.

I used to claim I had claustrophobia because I don't like elevators packed with people. Who likes elevators packed with

people? I was only being dramatic. Assigning a diagnosable con-
dition to a mild dislike. Now I close my eyes. Everything swirls
around me. A tornado made of noise. Light. Heat. Breath. Fear.

This is claustrophobia. I have to lie down. I am going to lie
down. I cannot hold my body up any longer. I am falling down.
The pavement will cool my skin. I need to feel the ground.

But no. Instead of falling, I am lifted up.

I feel arms around me. In this cluster of people, there are
helping hands. Strangers' hands. They are holding me. They are
guiding me through the tornado.

In my ear: "It's okay. The kids are okay. We found somebody
who knows. This way."

I know this voice. It is Solly. My old friend Solly.

And there is Peter. He is standing with an officer who holds
his helmet under his arm and has slung his machine gun onto his
back. His posture is peace. Succor.

"There you are," Peter calls out to me. Solly delivers me to
Peter's embrace. "This is Officer Delgado. Officer Delgado, this
is my wife, Jenna."

He nods at me. Peter is squeezing me so tight now I'm having
trouble breathing. In his effort to comfort me I can feel his fear.

"Officer Delgado says the kidnappers are from a drug cartel
and the men they abducted are from a rival one. They entered
quickly, fired some shots, grabbed the men, loaded them into
waiting SUVs and were gone before the police arrived. Nobody
in the club was hurt. And everyone who was taken was a member of the rival cartel."

"Yes," the officer says. "This is true. There are no injuries.
There are no innocent victims. These men who were kidnapped,

they were here for celebration, for Semana Santa, but they are not innocent."

"So where's Clem?"

"We still don't know. But Officer Delgado assures us that everyone made it out safely. Nobody was hurt. The club is empty now. Maybe we just missed them in the crowd. They probably headed home."

"You should go back home now," the officer says. "And you should stay there. We are still looking for the men who did this, and we ask that, for now, everyone stay inside."

"How do we get home?" I ask. Nothing seems possible.

"We ask that everyone stay inside and that is for taxi drivers, too. Can you walk?" Officer Delgado asks. "Is it very far?"

"No," Peter says. "It's not far. We can make it. Thank you for your help."

They shake hands. Officer Delgado extends his hand to me and I hold it in both of mine and I tell him the words of Spanish I know. *"Muchas gracias."*

"Let's go," Solly says, putting one arm around Peter and one around me. "My kingdom for an Uber."

We start off on the long dirt road to Villa Azul Paraiso.

No place ever has seemed so far away.

THURSDAY

Peter fumbles with the key in the lock of the big front doors and we burst into a darkened, quiet house. Without saying a word, Peter and I run to the right, toward our wing, while Solly runs to the left toward his.

We throw open Clem's door and there she stands, half naked.

"Jesus," she screams. "Don't you knock?"

I throw my arms around her. She has no shirt on, just a bra, and a tiny pair of cotton shorts that stand in for pajamas. Peter is holding her, too. She squirms her way out of our embrace and grabs a T-shirt off the bed, holding it up to her chest.

"You're okay," I say. "You're okay."

"Of course I'm okay. God."

"We tried calling. I texted you."

Clem gestures to her phone next to her bed. "I ran out of power."

Peter takes one more look at her and then races off, presumably to check on Malcolm. Clem slips on her shirt.

"You told us our curfew was one o'clock." She looks at her

new watch. "It's twelve-twenty. We got home early. What's your problem?"

"The club . . ." I start, but the relief is so overwhelming, it's like I'm under water. I can't fill my lungs. I sit down on the edge of her bed.

"Yeah, the club was lit. It was super fun. Thanks for letting us go. But I got tired. So we grabbed a cab. We just got home, like, five minutes ago."

"Wait. I don't understand."

"What don't you understand, Mother? We went to the club. We danced a bunch. We didn't have anything to drink or take any drugs just like we promised and then we left and we came home. Early, I might add."

"You just left the club?"

"Yeah. Like twenty minutes ago."

"You took a cab?"

"Yeah."

Peter and Solly appear in the doorway.

"Thank God," Solly says. "What a night."

"Sounds like you just missed it," Peter says.

"Missed what?" Clementine asks. "What is everyone talking about?"

"Well, sweetie," Peter says. "If Malcolm hadn't gotten sick and you hadn't left the club after only half an hour and come straight home you would have been there for a really terrible scene. You were so lucky. We're all so lucky."

"Except for Malcolm," Solly adds. "Just goes to show you there's no correlation between a meal's cost and its cleanliness. Poor kid. It must have been the ceviche."

I'm still under water. Still struggling to fill my lungs. To find the surface.

"What happened?" Clementine asks.

"There was a kidnapping. At the club. The whole downtown is chaos. There aren't any cabs. We had to walk home. It was torture," Peter says. "That was the longest walk of my life."

"Didn't you hear the sirens?" Solly asks. "Maybe not. Ingrid and Ivan are sound asleep, so I guess you didn't hear them here."

"No," Clem says. "I guess we didn't."

She won't look at me.

Solly lets out a huge sigh and stretches his arms above his head. "Well, I'm going to bed. I'm wrecked. What a fucking night. I love you all. Even you, Clementine. We don't tell each other enough so I'm saying it loud and clear. I love every single one of you three idiots. And you know what else I love? Food poisoning. I have never loved food poisoning until tonight. All hail food poisoning. I love you, bad ceviche."

Solly steps across the threshold of Clem's room and he kisses her cheek, then he bends down to where I sit silently on her bed and he kisses mine. He goes and he hugs Peter and they hold on to each other for a long time before pulling back and kissing each other's cheeks.

"Good night, Carlsons," he says and heads off toward the master bedroom.

"Come on." Peter reaches a hand out to help me up from Clem's bed. "Let's go. I feel like I could sleep for days."

I keep my hands folded in my lap. "In a minute," I say.

He smiles at me. *I understand*, he is telling me. *You just want to sit awhile with our beautiful, perfectly fine daughter.*

"Good night, Clementine."

She allows him to embrace her now that she's clothed. "Good night, Daddy."

Peter closes the door and I continue to sit. I continue to wait for her to look at me. I continue to feel both the heavy weight of relief and the complete and utter confusion that arrived alongside the first scream of that first siren.

Clem goes over to the dressing table in her room. She opens a drawer, takes out a package of disposable makeup wipes, sits down on the stool and starts removing her mascara and eyeliner. She has her back to me, but we can see each other in the magnifying mirror.

She finally meets my gaze. "We did just get home about five minutes before you. I wasn't lying about that."

I don't say anything.

"Malcolm doesn't have food poisoning."

I still don't say anything.

"And we did go to the club. But only for a little bit like Malcolm said."

I wonder if she's trying to say as many true things as she can that aren't incendiary, that don't have consequences. She's listing a string of facts as a way to protect herself, building a fortress of truth into which she can retreat from whatever attack I have planned.

But I do not have a plan of attack. I have no idea what's happening. I'm confounded. I am lost like when I was in that crowd, but I am not afraid because my daughter is sitting in front of me, within arm's reach, and now that her makeup is off, she is brushing her beautiful hair. Maybe I'm supposed to be summoning up some anger, but anger feels very far away. It lies on the pitch-black bottom of the ocean and I'm just coming up to the surface, just reaching the light.

"Tell me," I say. "Tell me what happened tonight."

She shifts her gaze so that she is looking hard at herself in the mirror. She frowns. "I don't want to."

"You'll forgive me for saying that I don't really give a shit if you want to or not." The calm in my voice surprises me. And I think it unnerves her. She can fight with me when her first line of defense is that I'm crazy or I'm irrational. But that line isn't available to her as I sit here exuding reason and patience. It is the wee hours of the morning, and I have nothing but time.

"Well, okay. But don't freak out."

"Why does everyone keep telling me not to freak out?"

"Because, Mom. You tend to freak out."

"Okay," I say. "I won't. I promise."

She turns around on her stool so that the magnifying mirror is no longer doing the work for us. We look directly at each other.

"We went to the club. That part is true. And it was really fun. That part is also true. We danced. True. And we did not drink or take any drugs. All true."

I sit and wait. I am patience.

"And then we left," she says. "We left because we wanted to go somewhere and . . . be alone."

Calm. Project calm.

"We figured you'd probably be home and even if you hadn't gotten home yet, Ingrid and Ivan would be here, so we had to find someplace else, you know?"

"Someplace else to . . . *be alone.*"

"Yes. So we went to that beach. The one where you found us on the first day. The one that's totally private. The one that looks like it's in *Lost*. And that's where we were. We were there up until about five minutes before you came back. I was wondering why you guys were out so late, but then I just figured: whatever. You were probably out drinking."

She is safe. She wasn't at the nightclub. This is all that matters. This is all I should care about. I should stand up and give her a hug and tell her I'm relieved that nothing bad happened to her and I should tell her to go to bed and get a good night's sleep.

"Why did you and Malcolm need to *be alone?*"

She stares at me. I watch as the signs of repentance start to vanish and her edges return. "Do you really need me to spell this out for you?"

"I guess I do."

"Malcolm and I wanted to be alone, Mother, because Malcolm and I wanted to have sex." Now her bottom lip starts to tremble a little. She's trying so hard for defiance, but she doesn't have it in her.

Something is wrong.

A single tear works its way down her cheek. I fight the urge to reach out and wipe it away with my fingertip. I am afraid to do or say anything. Afraid to scare her off. I wait for her to say more, but she doesn't.

"Are you okay?" I ask.

"Yes."

"Do you want to come sit next to me?" I pat a spot on the bed.

"No."

"Do you want to tell me what happened at the beach?"

She swallows. She looks down at her hands. She still doesn't say anything. I can't help myself: I search her. I search every inch of her. She is sitting before me in a tiny T-shirt and even tinier shorts. Even after days of sun, her skin is so pale, so delicate. I am looking for a sign that she's been hurt. I look for scratches. Bruising. Deep purple or maybe beige since the bruise would be so recent. There is nothing. She is flawless. She is perfect.

"It didn't really go how I'd imagined it would," she says finally.

Another tear. She turns back around to face the mirror, grabs the balled-up makeup wipe and rubs her eyes with it. She leans in close and inspects herself, looking for traces of eyeliner or mascara, but there's nothing left.

"What happened, Clementine?"

Now she starts to cry in earnest. She keeps her back to me and she shields her face from the mirror but her shoulders are shaking. She looks so small and vulnerable. I let her cry for a little.

"What did he do to you?" I ask finally. My voice is barely more than a whisper.

She straightens up. She turns around. Her face is a red, blotchy mess.

"What?"

"Did he hurt you?"

"No. Mom. God."

"Did he force you to do something you didn't want to?"

"Mom. We didn't have sex."

Relief floods me. I exhale and collapse a little. I'd been sitting up straight. Rigid. I didn't realize how tautly I'd been holding every muscle in my body.

"Why are you smiling?" Clem asks.

Was I smiling?

"I guess I'm just relieved." I lean forward and I reach for her hand, but she pulls hers back.

"Mother. We didn't have sex because he didn't want to. He rejected me."

"No, that can't be right."

"God. Why are you so clueless? Of course it's right. I wanted to have sex and he didn't. That's rejection. He rejected me. He rejected me because I'm not good enough for him."

The calm and quiet is leaving the room. The reason, the understanding, the connection we'd forged, is packing its bags. I am no longer patience.

"Clementine. Why would you want to have sex with Malcolm? Why would you want your first time to be with him? With someone you don't really know all that well? Why wouldn't you want your first time to be with somebody like Sean?"

"Lol," she says, though she is not laughing out loud. She is not amused in the slightest. She is saying *lol* but she means the opposite of *lol*.

"What's that supposed to mean?"

"I mean it's funny that you think that this would have been my first time."

"I don't understand. . . . I thought you and Sean weren't having sex."

"And why did you think that?"

"Because you said you'd tell me if you were. You promised you'd come to me before you made that decision."

"And you really thought I'd tell my mommy before I had sex with my boyfriend? Do people even do that?"

"Yes, Clementine. They do."

"Ha. I don't think so, Mother."

We sit silently, wrapped in our own grievances. I reach for the calm, the patience. When I speak again I bring the volume down several notches. Back to where we began.

"I thought you and Sean weren't ready. I thought you were just enjoying the love part of your relationship without the sex."

"I think you thought that because you read my texts." Now I'm the one avoiding her stare. "And since we both know you read my texts we're careful about what we say to each other."

I sigh. "Oh, Clem."

She sniffles and clears her throat. She is done crying. She is pulling herself together. "I thought Malcolm was into me. He sure seemed like he was. But then when it came down to it, to you know, *doing it*, he stopped. He said he didn't think it was a good idea. He said I have a boyfriend, and that his life is complicated, and that we probably won't see each other again for another four years, and . . . I'm just really embarrassed."

"Oh, Clem," I say again. "It sounds like he was being thoughtful. And kind. And mature about it."

"No, Mother. He was rejecting me. Obviously I'm not attractive enough or whatever. I'm gross. If I was hot enough, he wouldn't have been able to stop himself."

I pat the spot on the bed next to me. "Please?"

She rolls her eyes, but then she lifts herself off the stool and she collapses into me. Her head is on my shoulder. I put my arm around her and I kiss her beautiful hair.

"Honey," I say. "You shouldn't be embarrassed. Malcolm was just trying to do the right thing. He's a good kid. I'm sure he wanted to. I see the way he is with you, the way he looks at you. But sometimes the right thing to do is to hold back, to stop ourselves from doing what we want, from acting on every impulse we have. Sometimes we have to look ahead. To try and predict the ways in which our choices may affect us later."

I want to add that Malcolm certainly did not learn this from watching his father, but of course I don't.

Clem's breathing is slow and steady. She is seconds from sleep. Like Ivan when his thumb is in his mouth.

"I'm so tired," she says.

She scrambles away from me, up and underneath the covers of her bed. I rise and walk over to her and pull the blanket to her chin. I stroke the hair off her face. I reach to turn off the light, but before I do, I look at her closed eyelids.

I take a moment to see what my daughter looks like sleeping.

I WAKE UP AT NOON. This has never happened. Not even in college when everyone slept half the day away. Peter is still snoring next to me. Sleeping late has never been a problem for him.

I go downstairs. I've missed breakfast. I wonder if they're already preparing lunch. If it's too late to ask for a poached egg.

There's nobody in the dining room so I head for the kitchen. There's nobody in the kitchen either. The coffeepot is half full. Someone has pushed the button and brewed the pot Roberto prepares before he leaves for the night. And someone has left dishes on the counter. A half-eaten bowl of cereal. Two plates with crusts of bread and the rough husk of a pineapple wedge.

There are never dirty dishes on the counter. Luisa won't stand for it.

I go back to the dining room and walk out to the edge of the balcony. I look down one level to the pool. Ivan lies on an alligator raft, surrounded by a rainbow of foam noodles. Solly and Ingrid sit side by side in loungers, holding hands.

"Morning," I call down.

"Is it?" Solly calls back. He looks up at the sun. "Because it feels like afternoon to me."

"Where is everybody?"

"Malcolm is sleeping off his food poisoning," Solly says. "And I assume your people are still upstairs filling their eyes with golden slumbers."

"What about Roberto, Enrique and Luisa?"

"They didn't show this morning," Ingrid calls. "So I made us some breakfast. There's plenty of stuff in the fridge. Solly filled me in on what happened last night. Oh, my goodness. So scary."

"Do you think the roads are closed?" Solly asks. "That maybe that's why they aren't here?"

"I don't know," I say. "I'll go see what I can find out online."

"Don't bother," he says. "The wi-fi is down. Better just grab yourself a cup of coffee and something to eat and join us by the pool. Out here"—he holds his arms out wide—"it's still paradise."

I do as I'm told. I pour some coffee. I make some toast. I cut up what's left of the pineapple. It has been five days since I have

prepared anything for myself or anyone else and it feels labori-
ous. I marvel at how quickly one can adjust to doing nothing.

I join the Solomons poolside. They seem calm and relaxed.
Blissed out. They continue to hold hands.

"Look at me," Ivan shouts. "Mommy, Mommy, look at me!"

"That's amazing, baby." She pulls her hand out of Solly's so
she can clap at Ivan's unimpressive underwater trick. "*You* are
amazing." She slips her hand back into Solly's.

I stare at Solly's hands. I think of how last night they lifted me
up, pulled me from the crowd. How they guided me toward
Peter and the kind officer. I think of Solly's steady voice in my
ear. *It's okay. The kids are okay. We found somebody who knows.
This way.*

I loved Solly last night. I do love Solly. But I hate him, too.
And I hate to see how he holds Ingrid's hand as if to say *I am
yours. We belong to each other.*

I lie back and I close my eyes to the sun. Ivan splashes in the
pool. Solly hasn't put on any music in deference to the sleepers.
The air is still, but not silent. I hear sirens. At least I think I do.
They are in the distance, so far away that they could be the sirens
from last night. My brain could still be processing the noises and
reverberations, the chaos.

"Do you hear that?" I ask.

Solly and Ingrid both sit up straighter. Ingrid cocks her head.
"I think so," she says. "Are those sirens?"

"Sounds like it." Solly lies back down and sighs. "You know
what I could use right now? I could use a cold drink."

"I'll get one for you." Ingrid stands up and wraps a towel

around her bikini. She wags a finger at him. "But I'm warning you it will be light on the sugar and free of alcohol."

"Fine, Nurse Ratched. Be that way."

"Ivan," she calls. "Do you need anything from the kitchen?"

"Don't leave," he says.

"Don't worry, love. I'll be right back."

Solly and I are alone. Ivan is still in the pool with his array of rainbow-colored noodles, absorbed in his underwater world. I try to remember how I gathered the confidence and the courage to confront Solly last night. I was ready to unleash on him. It was only a matter of seconds. It was all right there, an itch on my tongue.

Solly, I had said.

And then: sirens.

I know where at least some of last night's confidence and courage came from; it came from the tequila. From that final drink in honor of Peter's first fifty years. I have none of that tequila left in me. I've even slept my way through the hangover.

"Solly," I try again.

"Yeah," he says. He's not paying attention to me; he's watching Ivan. In Ingrid's absence, he's on high alert.

I don't follow up, and Solly seems to forget I've said his name.

"Look at him." He points at Ivan. "He's part amphibian. I could swear he's got gills."

The faint sirens still hover in the place between present and memory.

"Are you worried?" I ask.

"About Ivan? No. Not really. He's got his quirks, sure. But who among us doesn't? He's a solid kid. A little sensitive. Maybe he'll be an artist or a poet."

"That's not what I meant," I say, though I'm surprised to hear Solly acknowledge that his son is anything but perfect. "I mean about whatever is happening out there. Whatever it is that's keeping the staff away. Do you think we're safe? Do you think we should consider leaving early?"

He lowers his sunglasses and takes a long look at me. "Are you serious?"

"I'm just wondering."

"Jenna. We're on the vacation of a lifetime. We've got everything we need right here. Sand, sun, surf. We've even got a volcanic tub! So maybe things are a little sketchy in town. We don't have to go into town again. We can stay right here. And if it comes down to it, I'll make the margaritas."

"Solly, Officer Delgado told us to stay here, to stay away from town, so that's hardly a choice we're making for ourselves. We're following an order. From the fucking police."

"So?"

I'm getting angry at Solly all over again. At the way he compartmentalizes everything. He's doing to our situation what he does in his personal life. He's refusing to connect what's happening outside with what happens inside, because the act of connecting these two worlds—of recognizing how one informs the other—creates an inconvenience for him.

"And anyway," he says. "We go home the day after tomorrow. I don't see how we could get out of here any quicker than that. Did you see all the luggage we brought?"

"Yoo-hoo," Ingrid calls from the balcony. "Look who I found!"

She stands flanked by Roberto and Luisa.

Roberto waves at us. *"Buenas tardes.* We are sorry we do not come this morning to make for you the breakfast."

"It's fine," I call. I feel a rush of relief. Like the grown-ups just arrived to fix everything and make it right again. To set us back on our axis. "We all slept late anyway."

"Speak for yourself," Solly grumbles.

"We go now and we make the lunch," he says.

"Is everything okay?" I ask. "In the town? Outside? Are the police still searching for the men who did the kidnapping?"

"We go now," Roberto says. "And we make the lunch."

He and Luisa disappear from view.

I CHECK ON CLEM. I check on Peter. They're both still sleeping. They're both so beautiful. Almost unbearably so. I want to stroke their faces. Kiss their cheeks. But I don't want to disturb them.

I go to the kitchen, where Roberto and Luisa have emptied the entire refrigerator and Roberto is making a list of its contents. There's a pot of soup warming on the stove.

"What's going on?" I ask.

"We check on the food we have for next two days. The stores, they are all closed. But it is okay. We have food. We do most of the shopping already. We cannot get the steak to make the carne asada for dinner, but we have chicken from the freezer. We can also make many things with beans."

Luisa says something to Roberto and his response sounds snappy. She turns her back on him and begins reloading the refrigerator.

"Where's Enrique?" I ask.

"He goes to be with our parents. He brings for them the food. He will stay there. He does not come here to work but it is okay because Luisa and I, we can do everything ourselves."

"What's happening, Roberto? Did the police find the kidnappers? The victims? Why are the stores closed? Did you bring a copy of the newspaper?"

Roberto talks to Luisa. His tone has softened. She stops, with the doors to the refrigerator open, letting the cool spill out into the kitchen. Her voice rises at the end of each sentence as if she were asking him a long string of questions.

He sighs. I know he'd rather that I leave them alone to do their work. To the cooking and the table setting, the cleaning and the drink making. He'd rather not be charged with bringing in the news from the outside world.

"The cartel, they cause more troubles. They light gas stations on fire. They throw a bomb into the banks. They block roads and highways with burning cars. The police, they now have to put out fires and empty the buildings and it is difficult to go after the cartel. This is just what the cartel wants."

"If the roads are blocked, how did you get here?"

He looks at Luisa before answering. "We walk."

"How far away do you live?"

"It is not too far. It is maybe seven miles."

I sit down at the table in the kitchen. "Oh, God, Roberto."

"It is okay," he says. "It will be safe to go outside soon. But first, the police, they must get control."

"Why did you come here?" I ask him.

Again, he and Luisa speak to each other in Spanish. Then she makes a move to leave the kitchen.

"It is okay," Roberto asks, "for Luisa to go make the beds now?"

"No," I say. It comes out more harshly than I intend. She stops and looks at me. "Please. No. The others are still sleeping. And anyway, we will make our own beds today. You don't need to do that. We're perfectly capable of doing it for ourselves."

He translates this to Luisa who doesn't put up too much of a fight. She goes back to stirring the pot on the stove.

Roberto pulls up a chair and sits down at the table with me.

"I am sorry," he says.

"Why are you apologizing?"

"I tell your daughter and Mr. Solly's son about the club. I did not know. There has never been trouble before. The club, it is one of the nicest in Puerto Vallarta. I am very, very sorry."

I reach my hand out and place it on top of Roberto's. He doesn't pull his away, but I immediately feel uncomfortable for having touched him this way. I leave it there for a beat and then I take it back.

"It's not your fault," I say. "And the children are fine. They're safe. They weren't even there when it happened."

"No?" Relief floods his face. "Mr. Solly's wife, she tells me they are fine, but she does not tell me they were not there." He relays all the information to Luisa. She draws her hands to her chest.

"*Gracias a Dios,*" she says.

"So please," I say. "Don't feel badly. You couldn't have known."

He nods.

"So why *did* you come in today?" I ask again. "With all that's going on, with the roads closed, with the directive to stay indoors, why did you walk all the way here?"

He looks puzzled. "It is our job," he says.

"Yes, but . . . sometimes things happen."

"We must come to work. We must take care of the villa and its guests. It is very important for us to be here."

"But what about later? How will you get home tonight? You aren't going to walk another seven miles, are you?"

"No," he says. "If it is okay, we stay here."

"Of course," I say. "You know Ivan doesn't use his room at all. He sleeps with his parents. You can have Ivan's room."

"No," Roberto says. "We do not stay there."

"Well, then you can stay in one of the living rooms. I haven't looked to see if any of the couches fold into beds." I jump up, like it's my own house I need to make up for unexpected guests.

"No," he says again. "It is okay. We stay in the room downstairs. The room by the pool."

There is no room by the pool. The only space downstairs is an outdoor living room. The one with the Ping-Pong tables. Even in a house designed for openness and exposure, that space is not habitable. Not for sleeping overnight.

"Outside?" I ask him.

"There is another room," he continues. "Come, I show you."

I follow Roberto down to the pool level. Ivan has roped his parents into a Marco Polo–like game in which he makes up the rules as they go along.

"Here," Roberto says. He leads me to a door I hadn't noticed. He reaches into his pocket and pulls out a cluster of keys and he opens the lock. He flips on a light. Inside there's a bed and a tiny bathroom with a toilet and shower. There are no windows. It's basically a glorified storage closet. "This is the room for us when we need it. And we stay here tonight. We will not be in your way."

There's a recurring dream I've had since I was little in which I discover a door in my house I didn't know existed that leads to a room I'd forgotten or never even knew about. I used to have this dream about my childhood home, and inside I'd discover toys, books, an oversize dollhouse. I have this dream about the house I live in now, and when I discover this room I think: *This would make the perfect office*. Why haven't we ever done anything with this room? Why do we let it sit here untouched?

In my dreams this forgotten room is always lovely, always expansive. It is an astonishing surprise.

This extra bedroom is not that room.

"Wouldn't you be more comfortable upstairs?"

"No," Roberto says. "We stay here."

PETER WANTS TO GO for a swim in the ocean. He argues that we won't be in direct violation of Officer Delgado's orders, that our little patch of beach is probably not a hot spot for the fledgling drug cartel.

Clem hasn't emerged from her room. I keep peeking in on her and suspect that when she hears the doorknob she feigns sleep, though with the wi-fi still down, I'm not sure what she's doing in there. Malcolm came downstairs shortly after Peter. I watched Solly fuss over him, rubbing his back: father of the year.

How's your stomach? Can I get you anything? Would you like some white rice? My poor, sick boy. Then Malcolm excused himself to the kitchen, where I'm certain he ate a hearty meal.

Out in the water, Peter and I float side by side on our backs, weightless. The temperature is perfect. The sun is warm, but not hot. There's no wind. With my ears submerged I hear nothing, only a deep echoing silence. In the absence of all external stimuli I can finally feel myself relax.

Peter is right. We are safe here.

We stay like that, floating side by side, for what feels like forever before Peter reaches out and takes me by the hand, breaking my trance. I switch from floating to treading water and look back at the villa. We are much farther away than we were when we started floating.

"It's nice out here," Peter says. "I needed this. That was quite a night."

"It sure was."

"Everything okay with Clem? She seemed rattled. But I guess maybe she was just mirroring our hysteria."

Though Clem didn't say so specifically, I understood that our conversation last night was to remain between us. She confided in me, and even if that confidence was forced by my having caught her in a lie, it doesn't mean I should betray her by repeating what she told me to her father. She loves Peter, sometimes I suspect she loves him more, and it is both in spite of and because of this that I cannot tell him what she told me.

"She's okay. I think it all just sounded scary to her. We shouldn't have let her go to that nightclub in the first place."

"You're probably right."

"So *now* you admit it?"

"What does that mean?"

"It means that you allowed yourself to be bullied by Solly. I know you, Peter. I know that if it wasn't for Solly pressuring you, if it wasn't for his whole *aw shucks let the kids have some fun* routine, you wouldn't have told her it was okay with you for her to go to a nightclub in a foreign country with a boy who's a drug dealer."

I don't know why I threw in that line about Malcolm. I don't blame Malcolm for his troubles. I feel for Malcolm. I understand him. And Malcolm turned out to be the hero of the night, not the villain. But I just wanted to put a fine point on Peter's recklessness with his own daughter.

"That's not fair. You told her it was okay to go. Why are you blaming me?"

"Because you put me in a situation where I couldn't say no without being the bitchy uptight mother."

"Is anything ever your fault, too? Do you ever take any responsibility or share any blame for anything?"

We bob in the water side by side without looking at each other. The silence is no longer calming. The temperature suddenly too hot. My bathing suit, my skin, everything, feels tight.

He lets out an exasperated sigh. "Why are we even fighting? Nothing happened to her. It all turned out fine. Can't we just be grateful for that?"

"Yes," I say. "We can. You're right. This is a stupid fight." I open my mouth to say I'm sorry, but then I decide that I'm not really sorry, because everything I just said to Peter is true.

"Solly told me that you suggested we pack up and go home

early," he says. "Is it really about the violence? Or is it just that you're sick of everyone?"

"I'm not sick of everyone."

"You're sick of Solly."

"Is it that obvious?"

"You're hardly the queen of subtlety, Jenna."

I dunk my head under the water. When I come back up I feel calmer. Cooler.

"I guess I'm just having a hard time playing along with the charade of Solly as the perfect husband—not to mention father. I already felt sorry for Malcolm, and now I can't help but feel sorry for Ingrid. It's hard to watch her be the cuckquean."

"The what?"

"It's the opposite of a cuckold. It's when a woman has an adulterous husband."

"Oh, for fuck's sake."

"What?"

"I never told you Solly was cheating on Ingrid. You're jumping to conclusions. As usual." His voice is loud enough now that if we weren't floating out in the ocean it would draw the attention of people in other rooms. "Really," he continues. "Stop it. For once can't you just mind your own goddamn business?"

I try channeling Maria Josephina in her perfect black cover-up and glasses. I can even see her villa from our spot out in the water. How would she handle this? How would she keep her calm? What sharp comeback would she employ?

"Peter," I say. "This is how you explained Gavi calling you. Disrupting our vacation. Six times while we were on the boat. You said you were dealing with a situation. You basically admitted it was Solly. That you were cleaning up his mess as you tend to do. Look, Peter. I know you pride yourself on your gift for keeping Solly's secrets. But you let this one slip."

"What I told you is that we had a legitimate crisis at work."

"So, then, what was the crisis? Come on, Peter. It's not like I don't know anything about how the business works. And I also know, like you said, that Kim can handle anything. So I know this wasn't about bagels and it wasn't about the app."

"Fine. It's Solly, okay? But please, stop thinking you know *everything*. He's not cuckqueaning his wife or whatever your fancy, all-too-clever word is."

"So he just slept with her? It was just sex? It isn't a full-blown affair?"

"Jenna. I'd rather not—"

"And if it isn't an affair and it isn't just sex, what is left? What is it?"

Peter has never been a door slammer, but this might be the moment in an argument where Peter would get up and leave the room. I can tell he's had it with me, and yet I won't retreat. This is our family venture. We've staked our future on Boychick Bagels. If Solly is jeopardizing the health of the business by engaging in a sexual relationship with a subordinate, I have a right to know.

"It's complicated," he says. "Gavi, she can be a little . . ."

"Needy."

"I guess you could say that."

I already told him she was needy. And he told me I didn't know what I was talking about.

"This could ruin everything, Peter. Gavriella could sue Solly and she could sue you, too."

"Jen. Honey." His voice is softer now. "The situation is under control. Can't you please just stop your constant worrying? Can you stop seeing the worst-case scenario in every place you look? Can't you just try and enjoy what's left of our vacation?"

I don't respond. My silence is my answer. I can do none of the things he's asking me to do.

"You worked so hard to put this together. You deserve this trip after everything you've been through. . . . Why can't you just relax and be happy?"

I think about the figures in the sculpture Maria Josephina told me about. The ones climbing up the ladder to the unknown. Why is Peter asking me why I'm not happy, what I need, as if I were alone in the pursuit? As if I were the only one on that ladder?

"Why are you angry?" I ask.

"I'm not angry."

"You seem angry. You seem angry that I dare to point out that your friend Solly isn't the shiny idol at whose feet you worship. He's risking everything for a stupid affair and on top of it all he works you to the bone, treating you like an employee when you're supposed to be a partner. He uses you, Peter."

"You have no idea what you're talking about."

"That's what you always say."

Peter glares at me. "Let's go back."

"Peter."

"I'm done," he says. "I'm going back."

He begins the long swim toward the shore.

I stay where I am treading water. I think about how different things might be if Peter hadn't quit his job at the perfume company. If we hadn't decided, together, to take the risk of starting the business with Solly, Peter wouldn't have needed an assistant. And he wouldn't have hired Gavriella Abramov. And Solly would never have met her, and never given into whims, like a teenager. Never fed his hunger, his impulse to *take, take, take*. I wouldn't be out here treading water worried about our financial future and I would be back to envying Ingrid rather than feeling sorry for her.

Every choice we make has far-reaching, entirely unknowable consequences.

How many chances do we get in our lives to start over? To do something entirely new? Peter is fifty. Boychick Bagels is very likely his last chance to start fresh. To begin again.

I worry he squandered that chance and I wonder how our lives would look different if he had held on and waited for something better, something to come along he didn't have to share with Solly, because sharing with Solly always means taking the smaller half, even if you have to pretend, like with a slice of cake divided for competing children, that both halves look the same.

"I CAN'T STAY HERE ANYMORE if there's no network and no wi-fi," Clem is telling Peter.

"Really. So where are you planning on staying instead?" he asks.

"I just can't, Dad. Okay? There's no way. This isn't working for me." She's crimson. Breathing heavily. Teetering on the verge of a full-blown temper tantrum.

When Clementine was a baby, her skin was so pale, so transparent, that at the first whimper, the first sign of discomfort, her entire body, from her little toes to the top of her crusty blond scalp, would turn scarlet in seconds. This earned her the nickname "Big Red." Though we no longer see it happen to the whole of her, her face gives her away. She is morphing into Big Red before our eyes.

Peter is having none of it. "I'm sorry that this expensive international beachfront vacation *isn't working for you*, Clementine. That's really a shame."

"Dad. God. You don't understand. I can't be without wi-fi."

"You're right. I don't understand. I don't understand how I could have raised such an entitled child."

I have walked into this battle, merely a spectator. They are standing in the hallway between our two rooms. Clem is still in the T-shirt and tiny shorts from the wee hours of this morning. She hasn't brushed her hair and I'm pretty sure she hasn't brushed her teeth either.

"Mom. Help me. You get it. You understand how important this is. I know you do."

They both turn to me, eyes filled with rage. I'm still wrapped in my towel. My feet are wet from rinsing off the sand. I swam slowly back to the beach trying to listen for sirens in the distance but hearing nothing.

I'd like to hold on to this moment for a little longer. To live in this space where Peter is angry at his daughter rather than at me. Where my daughter thinks I understand her, that I understand teenagers, that her father is the clueless one. It's an upside-down world.

"If you need to make a phone call—" I start.

"No," Peter interrupts. "The network is down, too. I'm not get-ting any service either. This is contributing to our daughter's crisis."

I turn to Clem. "Let me talk to Roberto. See if we can find out what's happening with the wi-fi. If he can do something to get it fixed."

"Thanks, Mommy." She gives me a squeeze and retreats into her room.

Peter stares at me. "That's how we handle this? By trying to meet her unreasonable demands?"

"She's sixteen. Cutting off all connection is like cutting off her oxygen. I'm not saying I approve, I'm just saying it's the real-ity of being sixteen."

"I guess you'd know since you're the expert. But I'll remind you there's a fucking breakdown of civilization happening out-side. Not sure the breakdown of network connectivity in our villa ranks high on Roberto's to-do list, but go ahead and see if he can help."

Peter turns and goes into our bedroom, closing the door be-hind him. I'm left standing alone in the hallway, in nothing but a towel and a wet bathing suit.

I stare at the two closed doors, debating for a minute behind which one I'm more likely to find refuge. I choose door num-ber two.

I knock and then let myself into Clem's room.

"Can I borrow your bathrobe?"

She's lying on her bed with a tear-streaked face. More soft pink than Big Red.

I don't wait for her response. I take her robe off the back of her chair and put it on. Then I attempt the Houdini-like feat of getting myself out of my wet tankini without exposing myself to my daughter. I may not be an expert on teenagers, but one thing I know for sure is that they have no interest in seeing their parents naked.

"Are you okay, honey?"

"Yes," she sniffles.

"Why don't you get dressed? Or maybe go for a swim. The water is lovely."

"No, Mother. I don't want to swim. I don't care if the water is *lovely*. I just need to get on wi-fi. I need to text Sean. He's gonna be worried. You said you'd fix it."

"That's not what I said. What I said is that I'd go talk to Roberto."

"Well?"

"Well . . . I will. But I also think you should get up. It's after five. You can't stay in your room all day and all night."

"Watch me."

"Clem. Come on. What's going on?"

"Nothing is *going on*, Mother. I just don't feel like being social, okay? I don't want to sit down to another long, boring meal and play nice with your friends."

"This is about Malcolm, isn't it? I told you that you shouldn't feel embarrassed."

"God." She flips over and buries her face in her pillow. "Please just leave me alone."

"Honey—"

"Please. Just go. Stop trying to force some kind of meaningful talk with me. Just go fix the wi-fi."

Back out in the hallway I reach for door number one. I made

the wrong choice. Why did I think I'd find solace with Clementine? My daughter who burns hot and then runs cold without warning? Who creaks her door open only to slam it shut again? Someone who, like Peter said, can't control her whims?

I knock. I wait for him to invite me inside.

He's in the bathroom, checking his face in the mirror, razor in one hand, shaving cream in the other.

"No," I say. "Don't. That's your vacation beard. You can't shave it yet. We're still on vacation."

"I don't know. . . . I think it makes me look old."

"I think it makes you look handsome," I say.

He turns around and cocks his head at me. "Really? You think I'm handsome?"

"Of course I do."

"Sometimes I'm not so sure."

"Peter." I reach for his cheek. "Of course I think you're handsome. I adore you."

"It's nice to hear that every once in a while."

"Do I not tell you that I love you enough? Or fawn over your obvious good looks? Is that why you're sulking?"

"I'm not sulking. You don't need to belittle me."

"I'm not belittling you. I'm just trying to figure out what I've done wrong."

He sighs. He puts his razor and the shaving cream down on the counter. "You can never just say you're sorry."

"Your bracelet," I say to him. "You're not wearing it."

He looks at his naked wrist, the one without the watch. "I guess I lost it in the ocean. Please don't try and read something into it."

"Okay. I won't. *I'm sorry*. See? I can say it. I'm sorry." I fold my arms across my chest, but inside I don't feel defiant. I feel genuine remorse. I feel like I'm failing everywhere. As a writer, as a mother, as a wife, as a planner and executor of the perfect vacation.

"I'm sorry if I'm punishing you for Solly's actions, okay? And I'm sorry if sometimes I'm too stressed out or bogged down in my own shit or whatever it is to give you the right kind of attention . . . or to just let go and—"

While I've been speaking, in his own Houdini-like feat he's been untying the knot in my bathrobe with one hand. With the other he pushes the robe off my shoulders. It falls to the floor. I am totally naked. He looks me up and down. I stand feeling both heat and ice from his gaze. Then he pushes me.

I take a step backward.

He pushes me again.

I take another step.

He gives me another push until I step into the bedroom, where I fall back onto the bed, Peter landing heavily on top of me.

I open my mouth to say something, but he covers it with his hand. We don't speak, not even a whisper.

My hair, too short for a ponytail, can still be grabbed by the fistful.

His beard, though soft now, can still burn.

He isn't gentle with me. I'm not careful with him.

We are still on vacation.

This is what you are supposed to do on vacation.

· · ·

IN THE KITCHEN, Roberto and Luisa listen to the radio. Someone with a deep, authoritative voice is interviewing two people, one man, one woman—both slightly hysterical, breathless and, by the sound of it, not in agreement.

Roberto reaches to shut it off, but I gesture for him to leave it on.

I stand at the counter and listen. Luisa is shaking her head. She speaks to Roberto over the reporter. He shushes her. She slams down the knife with which she'd been chopping garlic on the counter. She doesn't appreciate being shushed.

The story breaks for a commercial and Roberto turns down the dial. He knows I've got questions, so he avoids eye contact with me. This is fine because I'm certain that anybody looking at me right now can tell what I've been doing behind door number one for the last half hour. I smooth down my hair. I rub my cheek where it's red.

"The wi-fi isn't working. We can't get online," I say to Roberto. "Is there any way to fix this?"

"No," he says. "I am sorry."

"No?"

With his look I know Peter is right. This is not high on Roberto's list of priorities in light of what the people were just shouting about on the radio.

"It is a problem everywhere. Not just here. It is Telmex."

"Oh," I say. "I see."

"But we still make for you the dinner."

This feels like a non sequitur until I realize it's his way of asking me to leave them alone in the kitchen. Or maybe it's his way of saying *Shut the fuck up and be grateful that we're still going to feed you.*

I start for the door but then I stop and pivot to face him again. "Is there anything we should be doing?"

"I do not understand."

"I mean, you know, about what's going on. Are there steps we should be taking for our safety? Should we be thinking about trying to get out tomorrow?"

He and Luisa exchange a few words back and forth. I think it's about the food and not my question because she's holding an unidentifiable squashlike vegetable in her hand and she's pointing to it.

"You just enjoy vacation. It is like rainy day. You spend time indoors. There are games. And books. And it is okay to go by the pool and beach in front is okay, too. But do not go anywhere else. We will cook for you the food. You will leave Saturday. That is the schedule. By then the airport will be open."

"The airport is closed?"

He sighs. He says something to Luisa, and this time I know it isn't about the mystery vegetable. She shakes her head and shrugs.

"Yes. It is closed now. But it will open soon. Police will get control. They are bringing more officers. Everything will be okay. You go now. Soon I bring margaritas."

As I turn again to leave, admittedly a little stung by Roberto's dismissal, I hear a sound I haven't heard all week. It's the sound of a telephone ringing. It's been longer than a week since I've heard this particular sound; it's been years. Maybe even a decade. It's an old-fashioned phone with an old-fashioned ring, not a cell, not a cordless, but a rotary telephone, the kind you never see anymore. I hadn't noticed it attached to the kitchen wall.

Roberto picks it up. *"Hola."* It's mustard yellow. Richard Nixon probably used this phone.

I stand and watch him. So does Luisa.

"Yes," he says. "Yes, is okay. Yes. Is fine. Yes, we are here."

He sees me staring at him and he puts his hand over the bottom half of the receiver.

"It is owners," he whispers. "You go now. I bring you margarita soon."

I **HEAD DOWNSTAIRS** to collect the sandals I left next to the faucet when I returned from my swim with Peter. I find Malcolm, alone, hitting a Ping-Pong ball against the wall.

"Are you feeling better?" I ask him.

He catches the ball in his hand and turns to face me. "Yeah. I guess I just needed some rest."

I've never been able to raise one eyebrow, despite a fair amount of practicing in a mirror when I was a child, so instead I shoot him my best skeptical look, eyebrows stitched together, mouth tight, pulled to one side.

"What?" he asks.

"You weren't sick, Malcolm."

He turns back to the wall and starts hitting the ball again. I watch him. He's shirtless. His back is smooth and hairless, unlike his father's. As he moves between *forehand, backhand, forehand,* his skin ripples over the young, expert machinery of his muscu-lature. I go over to the other side of the table and pick up a racket. He assumes the position across from me.

He sends a ball over to my side of the net. I lob it back. We continue like this, gently, silently, except for the sound of the hollow *thwack* of the ball.

"I know what happened," I say. "Clementine told me."

He still doesn't speak. *Thwack . . . Thwack . . . Thwack . . .* He's probably trying to figure out if I'm calling his bluff. Setting a trap. If I've arrived at this Ping-Pong table like a pool shark si-dles into a saloon.

"I know this is weird," I continue. "But I want to thank you. For not taking advantage of her." I concentrate on the game, avoiding his eyes. Still, I swing and I miss. The ball rolls to a stop at the door to Roberto's secret bedroom. I grab it and return to the table.

"You're right," Malcolm says finally. "This *is* weird."

I try for an easy, relaxed laugh. "Probably better not to talk about it."

Of course it's better not to talk about it. What on earth am I thinking?

"Probably," he says. I put a spin on the ball, the only trick I know, and he expertly returns the shot.

Right now, at this moment, I miss Maureen. I miss the hours we spent dissecting the challenges of raising our children: How to get them out of diapers and how much television to let them watch, but also the thornier questions, such as how to raise good people and how to maintain our own identities amid the crush-ing tedium of motherhood. Maybe Ingrid is right; maybe Maureen wasn't always wholly attentive, maybe she was spiteful, maybe some of Malcolm's mistakes are because of her shortcomings as a mother, but she did it. She raised him. Diapers, television, tedium and all. Soon Malcolm will finish high school, even if it's at a special program for rich kids in trouble. And as his night with Clementine proved, he's a good kid who still makes some good choices among the very bad ones.

"I wanna play." It's Ivan. He has his little hand out and I can see that his thumb is slick with saliva. "Gimme." He wants my racket.

"You can have it when we're done."

"I want it now. I want to play."

"Here," Malcolm says, approaching him. "You can have my racket." Of course that is the right thing to do, to offer the five-year-old a chance to play this child's game.

"But I want to play with *you*. Not with *her*." He points at me. I surrender my racket and he snatches it from my hand. "Ding dong."

Malcolm pretends to wind up for a killer serve and then softly hits the ball right to Ivan's forehand. "Where are the parental units?"

"They're upstairs. In our room. Mommy is mad. She's mad at Daddy. She told me to go find *the others* so I came here and now we're playing Ping-Pong."

"Well," Malcolm says. "I'm glad you found me."

"Are you one of *the others*?" Ivan takes a hard swing and misses the ball.

Malcolm shrugs. "I guess I am."

I'm praying Malcolm will ask his brother what Solly and Ingrid are fighting about. Is there an appropriate way for *me* to ask what they are fighting about?

Malcolm looks at Ivan. "Play to twenty-one?"

"Yes," Ivan says. "But I only want to play if I get to win."

DINNER IS SPARSELY ATTENDED. It's just Solly, Peter, Malcolm and me.

We'd agreed that dinnertime was the one nonoptional activity, but this was back when all we knew of this villa was the website, and all we knew of Puerto Vallarta was in the guidebook. When our dream vacation was still a dream vacation.

Clem never did get dressed. *Mommy, bring me a grilled cheese*, she pleaded and took it to the room with the VCR and set herself up with *Charlotte's Web*, the old cartoon version, not the live-action remake. She closed the door, retreating further, crawling deeper into the recesses of her own childhood.

Peter thinks she's hiding out from him, and he's had it with her preciousness, so he was less than thrilled that I indulged her, following up that grilled cheese, which was really a grilled torta prepared by Luisa, with a pineapple smoothie, also prepared by Luisa.

Ingrid is supposedly looking after Ivan, who is supposedly not feeling well, but I know that neither of these things is true because of Ivan's Ping-Pong table confessional. I still don't know why Ingrid is mad at Solly but of course I can't help but wonder if Ingrid has discovered the truth about Gavriella.

Imagine being trapped in a house with your cheating husband and your best friends, who have all conspired to keep the same secret. How humiliating. What is Ingrid supposed to do? Put on a sundress and come to dinner? Sit down and unfold her napkin and praise the food? The flower arrangement? The view?

As promised, dinner is chicken. It doesn't reach the level of Luisa's earlier efforts. The margaritas, however, are stronger and I wonder if Roberto made them this way intentionally.

Solly doesn't let on about any marital unrest. He's upbeat and boisterous as usual, regaling Malcolm with a story about the time he was in Paris after his senior year of high school and found himself, unintentionally of course, in a brothel, and before he knew it he was hundreds of dollars into champagne he hadn't ordered, and when his credit card was declined and the three-hundred-pound bouncer blocked his exit he had to call his father in New York. Though his hands were shaking as he dialed the number, his father met the news with unbridled glee. He gave Solly an alternate credit card number to use. He said it would make quite a story, and why else do you travel the world but to collect stories?

"Sometimes, my boy," Solly finishes with a hand on Malcolm's shoulder, "it's okay if your stories are better in the retelling than they are in the moment you live them."

It is impossible for me to believe that Malcolm doesn't know about the brothel in Paris. I could have told him this story myself, with the very same dramatic pauses, the same Don Corleone voice Solly employs for his father, the same delivery of the life lesson at the end.

But Malcolm laughed in all the right places, as did Peter, who has heard this story more times than probably anybody else. They look at me. How can I sit here not reacting when Solly just played the consummate raconteur? Am I immune to his charm? Entirely without humor? Am I carved out of ice?

I should try to show kindness. Patience. I should use this chance to abdicate the throne of queen of unsubtlety. With all the allegiances fraying, why not shore up mine?

"What a story," I say.

THE SIRENS WAKE ME.

I bolt upright, heart racing. "Peter!"

"What?" He's groggy, not at all alarmed.

"Did you hear that?"

"Hear what?" He doesn't lift his head from his pillow.

But now I don't hear anything. Only a rustling of the palm trees in the night wind. Did I dream the sirens the way I used to dream Clementine's cries? I'd rush to her crib, ready to soothe her, only to find her sleeping, unperturbed. I'd stand still, watching the rise and fall of her tiny chest, waiting to see if she'd cry out again, questioning my postpartum sanity.

"Nothing," I say. "Sorry."

He doesn't hear me. He's snoring. He won't remember this tomorrow. I look at the clock.

Tomorrow is only two minutes away.

FRIDAY

There are voices down the hall.

I get out of bed. I grab the robe I failed to return to Clem and throw it on over my pajamas. I creak our door open slowly, not wanting to wake Peter again.

I tiptoe past Clem's bedroom down our wing to the front entryway, where I find an unlikely duo huddled together.

Roberto and Ingrid.

"What's going on?" I whisper.

"I heard a siren." Ingrid says.

"I heard it, too!" They look confused as to why I'd deliver this news with such enthusiasm. I lower my voice. "It sounded like it was close."

"Yes," Roberto says. "It is close. The police, they drive our road." He wears light blue cotton pajama pants and a white ribbed tank top, but he might as well be standing in a pair of briefs, it's equally jarring seeing him this way.

"We're on a dead end," I'm still whispering. "Why would they drive down our street?"

"I do not know," Roberto says. "But I go outside and I see nothing. They are gone now. It is okay."

It's then that I notice the nightstick in his hand. He sees me looking at it.

"It is for protection," he says. "Just for to be safe."

I don't remember reading about this on the villa's website. *For your safety our house manager carries a nightstick.*

"I tell Mrs. Solly it is okay. Police are getting control. The cartel, they agree to release the men they kidnap. This I hear on the radio. Can go back to sleep now. Tomorrow will be better. It is Good Friday."

Ingrid does not look mollified. In fact, she looks like a wreck. Gone is her effortless magazine-worthy beauty. All those months spent detoxing her system, undone by a single day of stressors.

"Listen to him," I tell Ingrid. "We're fine. We're safe."

Just then Luisa enters. Either she's thought better of coming upstairs in her pajamas or she sleeps in her clothes.

Come back to bed, Roberto, she says. *Put away that ridiculous nightstick. What are you going to do with it anyway? What are you, some kind of tough guy? Come on. Leave these crazy women with their paranoia about lead in our pottery and all their other nonsense and come back to bed.*

This is what I imagine she is saying to him in her rapid-fire Spanish.

"*Sí, querida,*" he replies. She takes him by the hand and leads him back to the secret bedroom.

Over his shoulder he calls, "Good night. Have good sleep. No more worry."

When they're out of sight, Ingrid collapses into my arms and lets loose a sob. I rub her back like I'm soothing a child, if I had a child who would let me hold her like this.

"I'm sorry," she cries. "I'm just . . . a bit of a mess."

I lead her over to the sofa and sit her down. She takes her oversize Boychick Bagels T-shirt and dabs at her eyes with it. I switch into my default mode for uncomfortable situations: I offer to be useful.

"Let me go get you some water."

Down in the kitchen I fill a large glass from the filter and then grab a half-empty bottle of tequila from the counter. I hold up both when I return.

"A little something for each of us."

She points to the bottle. "Actually . . . I think I'll take some of that."

I grin. "Hold on. I'll get you a glass."

"Don't bother." She grabs the tequila from me and takes a modest swig. She does the all-over body shake of an inexperienced drinker.

I sit down next to her. I slide the water glass closer.

"Thank you. I know I'm like a broken record, but you're a great friend."

"Well," I say. "It's unsettling to be woken by sirens."

"I wasn't sleeping."

"No?"

"Solly and I had a fight."

I try for a look of surprise. "You did?"

She holds the tequila bottle in her lap. I'm waiting for her to take another sip so that I can follow that up with a healthy slug, but she just spins it slowly around in her hands. Her eyes refill with tears.

"Oh, Ingrid. I'm so sorry."

Ingrid sniffles. "We don't really fight. I know that sounds weird, but it's true. I'm conflict averse and he's a people pleaser. And we're lucky enough not to have a third rail."

An affair, I imagine, would count as a pretty significant third rail. So clearly she hasn't found out about Solly's affair with Gavriella or else she wouldn't be describing him right now as a *people pleaser.*

"Surely you can still find things to fight over," I say.

"Do you know the top three reasons couples fight?"

"I'm not sure I do."

Ingrid takes a long pause. She picks at the label on the bottle of tequila, then holds up three fingers. "Sex. Money. Kids. We don't fight about sex—let's just say we have compatible drives and appetites. Money is something we have plenty of and I never cared much about anyway. And as for kids, Ivan is a joy and a pleasure, and by virtue of Solly's age and the fact that he's already raised one child, he's happy to take a backseat and let me be Ivan's primary parent. I know some women scoff at me, they think I'm failing to live up to the feminist ideals of my generation by taking on more than fifty percent of the child-rearing burden, but to me it's far from a burden, it's a privilege, and I enjoy being in control of that privilege. I wouldn't want it any other way."

She moves the tequila to her lips and then pauses.

For the love of God, I think. *Please take a sip and pass it on.*

She lowers the bottle back into her lap, untouched. "And then . . . there's Malcolm."

"So you *do* have a third rail," I say.

"No." She shakes her head. "I love Malcolm. He's Ivan's brother. He's Solly's son. I care deeply for him. He's never been a source of contention. I've always wanted to see more of him, to have him with us for more than what is set out in the custody agreement. I never thought Solly should have let Maureen take him to New York; I always believed she did it out of spite."

Ingrid removes her hands from the bottle and grips her bare knees. I seize this opportunity to snatch the bottle from her lap. Since I don't know when I'll get it back again, I take two long pulls, one after the other, before I pass it back.

"I don't live with guilt like Solly, so I can see clearly when it comes to Malcolm." She sinks a little deeper into the couch. "And what Malcolm did . . . well . . . it was just . . . unconscionable."

"He sold drugs?"

She looks at me, surprised. "You know?"

"Only that he sold pills to some kids at school."

"Did you know that one of the girls died of an overdose?"

I shake my head. I wonder if Peter knows and somehow managed to leave out this detail, but then I think that no matter how much snooping, prodding and interrogating I do, I'll never know what secrets Peter and Solly keep for each other.

"Solly and Maureen, they think *Malcolm* is a victim because he was kicked out of school. Malcolm is lucky! The only reason he didn't face criminal charges was because it couldn't be proven that she died from the drugs he sold her rather than drugs she bought elsewhere. But still, they say: *'Malcolm was targeted.' 'Malcolm was just doing what other kids do.' 'Malcolm was treated unfairly because he's biracial.'* They never, in my opinion, held him accountable for his actions. I know I'm younger. I'm newer to being a parent. But Jesus. What kind of message are they sending him?"

"I think sometimes it's hard to know who's really to blame for the terrible things that happen. Can't he bear some responsibility and also be a victim?"

"I don't know. Can he?"

"He's still a good kid," I say.

At long last, Ingrid takes another swig from the bottle. The shock is milder; she only wiggles a little in her seat.

She shrugs and then turns to face me, a sad smile on her flushed face. "It's so easy to forget here. The sun shines, most of the time. The water is warm. The house is spectacular. All our needs are met! And yet, right outside . . . right down the street . . . it's ground zero for the terrible chain of supply and demand that led to the death of that poor girl at Malcolm's school. And whether Solly and Maureen want to admit it or not, Malcolm, this boy of unfathomable privilege, this *good kid*, was a crucial link in that chain. This is what I'm struggling with. This is why Solly and I had a fight. He doesn't want to think about it. Doesn't want to talk about it."

"Who can blame him?"

"I can," she says. "After what happened last night, after the kidnapping, after all the sirens . . . I can't stop thinking about the connection between what's happening here and what happened at Malcolm's school and what's happening everywhere. Refusing to think or talk about these problems or to acknowledge our role in them is irresponsible. Did you know there are more deaths from opioid use in the United States than there are from car accidents?"

"I didn't." What I do know with a piercing clarity is that I'm an idiot for worrying about my daughter spending too much time staring at her phone or having sex with her boyfriend or puking on a friend's Turkish kilim from drinking too many wine coolers. I'm an idiot for worrying about half of what I worry about.

"Look," Ingrid says. "I know I'm violating the basic number one rule of vacation: Leave the tough stuff at home. Sit in the sun and forget." She lets loose a quick and not entirely genuine laugh. "*Sit in the sun and forget.* That's my mantra for tomorrow."

She takes another, longer, sip from the bottle and holds perfectly still as it goes down.

"Maybe you should take it easy," I say. "Last time I checked, tequila was not a complex carbohydrate."

She laughs, a real laugh, and puts a hand on my leg. We are compatriots, she is saying. Sisters-in-arms.

There are so many ways I misunderstood Ingrid. I saw her as self-involved in that way young attractive moms are, where they think all they do is give, give, give, and in fact all they really do is think about themselves as objects of desire and affection. I underestimated her as a friend, as a writer, as a woman of substance.

"I haven't forgotten your kindness, Jenna. I'm still feasting on every word you shared about my manuscript."

"Well, I meant what I said. And when we get back home, with your permission, I'd like to send it to my agent."

The tequila has made my face, my insides, warm. I am *el cabron suertudo*. I am a lucky bastard. I have a husband who loves me. I have a child who is not in terrible trouble. I have a book under contract that I will finish eventually. Why not help out a friend who is about to face tough times?

I feel expansive. I have power. I hold keys.

Ingrid slides even closer to me on the couch. "I don't know how to thank you."

The last lines of Ingrid's email that she sent with her manuscript come back to me: *Please, be brutally honest. No good will come from trying to protect my feelings.*

No good will come from lying. From keeping what I know to myself.

"You're an excellent writer," I say to Ingrid. "I mean it. And I think you have a big career ahead of you."

"Jenna—"

"Wait. There's something more. Something else I need to tell you."

"Okay." She smiles. Her hands clench the bottle in her lap. She is an eager listener. A rapt audience.

"It's about Solly."

"Solly? What about Solly?"

"I . . . I . . . think Solly may be having an affair with Peter's assistant."

Ingrid lifts the bottle from her lap and puts it down on the coffee table. She stands up slowly. She walks to the far side of the room; I think she's leaving, heading toward the master to rouse Solly from sleep, to drag his not insubstantial mass from the king-size bed and let him have it. But instead she walks the perimeter of the living room, past the balcony with its view of the moon over the Bay of Banderas, around the back of the couch, until she's come full circle. She sits down in the chair facing me.

"Jenna," she says, her voice calm. "Solly isn't having an affair."

"I don't want to hurt you," I say. "But as your friend, as a wife, I felt like I had to tell you. That you had the right to know. I'm sorry."

"Jenna," she says again. She is still calm, but more emphatic. "Solly isn't having an affair."

I reach for the bottle between us. I unscrew the cap. When did she put the cap back on the bottle? I take a long drink.

"I know it's hard to process. It's a big bomb I'm dropping in your lap, in your life. I hate to do it, but I also hate to sit by and watch you get hurt. I don't want him to do to you what he did to Maureen."

"Jenna."

"What?"

"Solly isn't having an affair."

And just like that the years between us open up again, a wide, yawning canyon. We are no longer compatriots. Sisters-in-arms. She is too young. Too naïve. Too nice to see the hard truth about the man she loves. The man everyone loves.

"Ingrid, I'm sorry." Like Roberto, I keep apologizing for something entirely out of my control.

"Jenna," she says. "Solly isn't having an affair with Gavriella." She reaches across the table for my hand. "Peter is. It's Peter."

.   .   .

THE AIRPORT IS STILL CLOSED. We are little more than twenty-four hours away from our scheduled flight back to Los Angeles and the fucking airport is still fucking closed.

This is what Roberto tells me. Roberto knows this from making a phone call on the mustard-yellow rotary phone mounted on the kitchen wall. Telmex still has not restored our service and I am on the verge of a Big Red–style tantrum about this.

There was an all-inclusive horse ranch near Solvang that made our final list of destinations. Why didn't we go to the fucking horse ranch? God, how I wish we'd gone that route, even though I've never much cared for horses. It would have been a far better place to gather for the birthdays if for no other reason than it's only a two-hour drive from Los Angeles. I could have hopped in the car and driven through the dark. I'd be in my house right now, sitting in my kitchen, staring out the window onto my backyard, instead of sitting here, in this foreign place, an incalculable distance from my life back home.

It is very early in the morning.

I spent hours watching minutes go by. Time collapsing. I stared at my iPhone, the clock its one remaining utility—I'll never take another picture in this place. When it turned 6:00, an hour I convinced myself was a justifiable hour to wake the caretaker of one's luxury vacation rental, I knocked on Roberto's secret bedroom door.

"*Que pasa?*" he mumbled. Clearly he'd been dead asleep. This made me feel even more embarrassed for appearing at his doorstep at this ungodly hour.

"What is happening?" he asked again, awake enough now to remember I don't speak Spanish, as if I don't know what *que pasa* means. "Everything is okay?"

"No," I said. "Everything is most definitely not okay."

"You wait," he said, closing the door.

I thought about opening it. Following him, uninvited, into his glorified closet of a room. Hiding out in there until he and Luisa would have to leave to cook breakfast, make beds, wash towels, arrange flowers, mix drinks, or any of the myriad magic tricks they perform each day to further the illusion of perfection vacationers seek and pay a pretty penny for when coming to Villa Azul Paraiso.

Would the others know where to look for me? Do the others even know about the secret door to the secret room?

I feel no compulsion to escape the children. They are not why I want to hide in Roberto's room and come out only when the taxi is idling, ready to drive me to the airport. I have no issue with Ivan and his neediness, or Malcolm and his recklessness, or even Clementine, whose secrecy is just part of the natural order of things. A mother need not know, and probably should not know, the intimate life of her child; the same is not true of a wife and her husband.

By the time Roberto reopened his door wearing his white faux doctor's coat, I was crying again. I thought I'd stopped. That I was through with tears. I was wrong.

"It is your daughter?" he asked.

Why else would a full-grown woman clearly not bleeding from an open wound demonstrate this sort of pain and anguish— it must have something to do with her child. Is this who we become when we become mothers? People who can feel deeply only on behalf of others, who have lost the right to cry for ourselves?

"No," I told Roberto. "She is fine. It's me. I need to go home."

"Is something wrong? Back in your home? Where you are from?"

"Yes," I said. "Something is wrong back in my home where I am from."

"I am sorry," he said. "How can I help?"

"There's still no wi-fi. I need to reach the airline. I know my flight is tomorrow, but I'm hoping to leave today."

"We go to the kitchen," he said. "I make for you the coffee. I call from there."

He moved toward the stairs but I didn't follow, so he pivoted and returned to where I stood, motionless.

"Should I get for you your husband?"

"No. Not my husband. I don't want to see my husband."

He rubbed some sleep from his eye. "Okay," he said. "I do not get him. You come with me. I make for you the coffee."

He took me by the elbow, and led me up the stairs. In the kitchen he sat me down at the table and then pushed the button on the coffeemaker he'd prepared last night as per usual.

"You do not sleep?" he asked.

"No."

"It is early for calling the airline. But first I find out if the airport is open."

I don't know who he dialed or what he said but somehow he managed, on the ancient rotary telephone, to discover that, no, the airport is not open. There are no flights landing or leaving Puerto Vallarta. This is what he tells me now.

I start to cry again.

"Is there any other way?" I ask him. "Any other way to get out of here?"

"No," he says. "I am sorry. There is no other airport close with flights to United States. And anyway, many roads, they are blocked. But it is okay. You are safe here."

I am not safe here.

I am anything but safe here.

Solly knew about Peter and Gavriella, and what is perhaps worse, even though I've known Solly longer, is that Ingrid, a woman, a wife, a mother—she knew about Peter and Gavriella, too.

Imagine being trapped in a house with your cheating husband and your best friends who have all conspired to keep the same secret.

Oh, the humiliation.

When I thought I knew Solly was cheating on Ingrid I worked up the courage to tell her. It took me a few days, and a few slugs of tequila, but I did it. Ingrid has known for months, and yes, she did finally tell me, but only in the face of what I'd said to her: my funhouse mirror version of the facts. We sat together, Ingrid and I, sharing the bottle, side by side on that couch, and I told her. I felt expansive. I felt lucky. I thought I was holding keys.

And then she reached for my hand and said: *It's Peter.*

For a brief flash I thought that it was Peter with whom Solly was having the affair. It even made sense to me. *That explains so much.* But then I saw her face, soft with pity.

I don't remember what happened next. Knowledge, slow at first and then picking up speed, like a hurricane, winds clocking in at 200 miles per hour and gusts approaching 250. I do not know the difference between winds and gusts, truth and lies.

Time collapses. I do not know how long we sat across from each other, the bottle between us on the table.

I know that I asked her, finally: "Why did you come on this vacation?"

I whisper-screamed this at her. The last thing I wanted was to wake Peter. Or Solly. Or Clementine, who does not need to know the intimate lives of her parents.

Why did you come on this vacation? How could you let me plan this trip? Why didn't you say: no, I won't go? Why didn't you say: I can't go along and pretend?

"Why are you so angry with *me*?" she answered in a true whisper, not a whisper-scream. A whisper of regret and remorse. A conflicted whisper, with a hint of self-righteousness. It was a prism of a whisper, refracting a rainbow of reactions to the moment in which she'd suddenly found herself. "Shouldn't you save your anger for Peter?"

My anger does not need saving. It does not need rationing. I have plenty of anger to spread around. My anger runneth over.

"He's the one who's been lying to you for all these months," she continued. "I told Solly . . . I *begged* him to fire Gavriella. But there are rules about that sort of thing. So I told him he had to make Peter stop. And Solly tried. He even threatened to dissolve their business partnership." She sighed. "It went on for too long. And when Peter finally did end it, well . . . Gavriella . . . she just won't accept it. She has abandonment issues *and* daddy issues, a lethal combination, really. It's been a nightmare. *She's* been a nightmare. Solly is trying to handle it. He's even consulted a lawyer. Look. Peter loves you. He never planned on leaving you for her. It's not like what happened with Solly and me. It really isn't. As cliché as it may be, I think you can chalk it up to a midlife crisis. Not that it's a reasonable excuse. But Peter never loved her. He loves you, Jenna."

Still not looking at Ingrid. Not looking at anything. I stared at the bottle on the table between us with an unfocused gaze. All I could see was blur.

"I'm so, so sorry." She took a deep, slow breath from her center. Something she likely learned in a meditation class. Something she paid an expert to teach her to get her through the tough times she doesn't have to face because she lives a perfectly charmed life. "I wanted to tell you. I really did. But I thought Peter should be the one to do so."

"So I'm the cuckquean."

"Sorry?"

"Please. Just . . . leave me alone," I said, speaking now in a controlled voice that did not match the hurricane within me. "Go back to your sleeping husband. Go back to your weird kid who still shares your bed. Just . . . go."

She stood, momentarily forgetting her perfect yogi posture. Back curved, shoulders slumped, head hanging.

"I'm sorry," she said.

Roberto slides a cup of coffee in front of me. "You drink," he says.

I stare at it.

"Please," he says.

I take a sip. It's warm and earthy.

Luisa enters. Her hair, usually up in a neat bun, is down at her shoulders. She's also given up on her uniform. She wears a gray sweatshirt with her white cotton pants. I hadn't noticed her natural beauty. Had barely noticed her looks at all. Luisa does not need a diet of complex carbohydrates eaten off of lead-free paper plates to attain her good looks. All she has to do is be seen, and this morning, I see her.

"Esta ella enferma?" she asks Roberto.

He shrugs. She comes and takes a seat next to me at the table and puts her hand on mine. I have to hold myself back from collapsing into her arms and sobbing into her loosened hair.

"Estas bien?" she asks me.

"No," I say. "I am not *bien*."

She pats my hand. Roberto brings her a cup of coffee. She holds it up, as if toasting me.

"My husband has been having an affair with his assistant," I tell her.

Luisa shakes her head at me.

"Everyone knew but me. I don't want to see him. I can't see him. God. I've got to get out of here."

I put my forehead down on the table. In this moment, I can't even stand to have on me the eyes of a woman who doesn't understand what I'm saying, who has no comprehension of my pathetic situation.

Luisa and Roberto have a long back-and-forth in hushed, tender tones.

Roberto taps my shoulder. "Luisa say you need sleep," he tells me. "She say women, they need sleep for to deal with this. So you do not do or say things you do not mean. Is not good for to talk with husband if too tired."

While I hate few things more than being told I'm tired when what I am is upset, I have to admit that she's right. I'm exhausted. I'm not thinking clearly. At this moment, Luisa is my best friend in the world—Roberto, too—and I should listen to my two best and only friends, and I should go get some sleep.

"You're right," I say. "I need to sleep. But where? There's nowhere for me to go."

Luisa says something to Roberto. He says something back. They look at me, then back at each other, then back at me, like in a Ping-Pong match.

There's a bench in the kitchen. I could lie down on that. It doesn't look comfortable, but I'm so very tired. "Maybe I'll just stay in here."

Luisa stands up from the table and puts her hands on my shoulders. She grabs them and lifts a little. *"Vienes conmigo."*

"You go with Luisa," Roberto tells me. "She will make for you the bed."

I'm too tired to argue. Too tired to talk. Too tired to do anything but follow.

I figure Luisa must be taking me to the living room with the TV in it, but instead she leads me back downstairs, to the secret door to the secret bedroom. She motions for me to stay, so I do, I stand there like an obedient dog while she darts around the corner and underneath the staircase, where the washer and dryer are hidden. She returns with clean sheets in her arms.

"No," I say to her. "I don't need you to change the bed. Please. You do enough. I don't mind. I'm just going to close my eyes for a little bit. I really don't need fresh sheets."

She stares at me while I speak but it's clear she doesn't understand or care about whatever it is I'm trying to say. She's going to do what she's set out to do and that is to change the sheets on their bed for me. It's then that I realize maybe she isn't doing it for me; she's doing it for them. I may not care about sleeping on their used sheets, but she may very well care about sleeping on mine.

She opens the door and turns on the exposed overhead lightbulb. She switches the sheets quickly, like a pro.

"*Aqui,*" she says, patting the bed. "*Para ti.*"

I want to hug her but that feels inappropriate so instead I end up bowing a little in her direction, which ends up feeling even more inappropriate. "*Gracias,*" I say as I crawl into the crisp, fresh sheets.

She turns to leave and switches off the light. Before she closes the door behind her I call out, "Luisa?"

"*Sí?*"

I sit up in the bed. "Please . . . no tell the people upstairs where I am?" I point to the ceiling. "No tell my husband? No tell anybody that I'm here. Please?"

She smiles at me. "*Sí.*"

I have no idea if she understands me. She closes the door behind her.

I'm cast into utter darkness.

.   .   .

I **WAKE UP** six hours later.

I check my phone. No wi-fi signal.

I lie still, listening for sounds. Splashing in the pool. Feet on the floor above me. I hear nothing. This secret bedroom is an impenetrable fortress.

By now everyone must be awake. By now they must be wondering where I am. By now Ingrid has told Solly who has told Peter. By now they know that I know.

The fact that nobody has come knocking on my door proves that either Luisa understood when I asked her not to tell anyone where I'd gone or nobody is ready to face me.

I get up. The darkness is deep. The room has no definition. I shuffle carefully to the wall that faces the foot of the bed and I make my way down it, palm over palm, until I find the switch by the front door. I flip it. The bulb buzzes to life and summons a group of moths. *An eclipse.* This is what a group of moths is called. I know this because Peter and I have made a habit over the years of collecting and then quizzing each other on the proper group names for various species. A shrewdness of apes. A mischief of mice. A cyclone of scorpions.

A trio of liars.

I crack open the door and peek outside. The midday light is blinding. The swimming pool is still and all six loungers lie empty. I push the door open a bit more until I can see the whole of the pool area and a large swath of the beach out front. No sign of life.

I close the door again and step into the tiny bathroom where

I splash my face with cold water and wipe away the black from yesterday's mascara with some scratchy toilet paper. I'm wearing what I wore to sleep before the sirens woke me: cropped draw-string pajama bottoms and a tank top. I could use a shower and I debate hopping into the one in the corner that has no curtain, but instead I grab from the sink the stick of deodorant that must belong to Luisa—the flowers on the label are a giveaway—and slather it on.

I'd like to cover up a bit more. My tank top is cut low in the armholes and I'm wearing no bra, something that didn't bother me this morning in the kitchen with Roberto and Luisa, but now, with six hours of sleep in the bank, I'm acutely aware of the copious amount of side boob I'm showing.

I pick up Luisa's white coat from a hook on the back of the door. It's short sleeved and has buttons instead of zippers. It's what she wears when she cooks in the kitchen with her hair done up in a bun. I slip it on, open the door and step outside.

Once I'm standing on the patio by the pool, underneath the overhang, I can hear that there's music playing above me. I can't place it either by artist or by genre. It's not party music. Not eighties pop. It's not one of the lugubrious folk singers Ingrid loves who Solly will, when he's feeling generous, put in the rota-tion. It's not jazz building to a resolution that will never come. I shake it off. What do I care what they're listening to?

I'm not sure of my next move. I'd like to go be with Clemen-tine, to ally myself with her against everybody else, but I know I can't draw her into my crisis; I can't force her to choose a side. It isn't fair.

But oh, to huddle up with her in her room, or on the couch

by the TV for an encore showing of *Charlotte's Web*. To retreat
back into the recesses of her childhood with her, back to when
she sang off-key in a tutu and wasn't having sex. Back when the
introduction of this child into our young marriage gave us what
the poet Donald Hall called *a third thing*, an essential something
two individuals can turn their collective gaze upon. A project, a
cause, a passion like a shared love of architecture. More often
than not, that third thing is a child. But unlike a shared love of
architecture, a child will eventually pack up and leave you. And
then what? Where do you turn your collective gaze?

If I walk toward the gate that leads out onto the beach I run
the risk of being seen by anyone who stands near either the
second- or the third-floor balcony. I do not want to be seen. Not
in my current state of distress, with my side boob and stolen
chef's coat. Instead I stay under the overhang. I go around and
behind the staircase and skirt the side of the villa where various
unsightly utilitarian units are kept—heating, water filtration,
power generators. These are guesses of course. What do I know
about what's needed to run a luxury villa in a foreign country?

I squeeze between two of these units. They're large, loud and
hot enough either from the sun or from doing their job that I
jump back as I brush one with my elbow. Beyond them is a
fence. It's only chest-high and I climb up and over it easily, even
without shoes. I land in a patch of dirt only a few yards from the
beach.

I could walk south. Nobody would see me if I walked toward
the rocks where Malcolm took Ivan searching for starfish. But I
don't know what's beyond those rocks, and I *have* walked the
beach to the north. I know what's around that bend. I know that

I'll pass the villas Shabby and Tacky as well as Villa Perfect. I know I'll reach the stretch of private beach where I sat with Clementine and Malcolm, where they later escaped the club to be alone, where Malcolm would ultimately decide not to have sex with my daughter and this would crush her in a way I don't fully understand because even if I try to inhabit that world through my fiction, it's been too long since I've been sixteen.

I go north. It feels better in this moment to walk toward something I know than toward something I do not.

I keep close to the gate that protects the house from outside intruders so I can't be spotted from the balconies. To be even more careful I drop to my hands and knees and I crawl the perimeter of the gate, staying in its shadow, catching my pajama pants a few times on the wood's errant splinters.

When I get a safe distance from the villa I stand up. I wipe the sand from my pajamas. I rub my knees, sore from the crawling. I know what Officer Delgado said. He told us to stay close to home, and that's what I intend to do. I'm not going to walk all the way to town. Not with no shoes, in a stolen chef's coat.

I round the bend to the other three villas. Like the other day, they look empty. It's too early for siesta. Maybe all the guests are gone. Maybe they got out before everything fell apart. Maybe they wrapped up their perfect vacations and headed to the airport, bags full of rainbow-colored blankets and chunky stone necklaces, to catch flights that were still leaving.

But where is Maria Josephina?

I see the hammock. It is not a U shape. It is not a smile beckoning me. It is flat, sagging and low to the ground with the weight of a seventeen-year-old boy.

Malcolm.

I try to sneak by him, tiptoeing up to the metal gate at Villa Perfect. There is a keypad. And a camera. I'm not sure what to do. This is a far more sophisticated security system than the splintery wooden gate with a latch that protects us at Villa Azul Paraiso.

"Hey, Jenna." I don't want to turn around. I don't want him to see me in my ridiculous getup. "What are you doing?"

"My friend lives here." I point at the house. Malcolm looks at me. A shadow from the palm trees falls on his handsome face.

He has climbed out of the hammock and it swings behind him. He catches the rope in his hand and steadies it. "Everyone is wondering where you've gone. They're, like, kind of freaking out, actually."

I pull Luisa's coat tighter around me. "I'm sorry. I was just . . ."

"It's okay," he says. "You don't need to explain."

"Thank you, Malcolm." He knows. Of course he knows. Everyone knows. And if they didn't already know, they know now. I wonder what Peter has said to Clementine. By disappearing I have left him with the unenviable task of explaining to his daughter why I needed to escape from our perfect vacation.

"So? What do you want me to tell everyone?" Malcolm asks. "You know, about where you are?"

I turn back to the keypad. I have no idea what button to push to ring the doorbell. How do I let Maria Josephina know that I am here? That I need a safe place to hide? Should I push 9-1-1?

"I'd rather you not say anything, if that's okay."

He shrugs. "Sure . . . I guess."

"Malcolm?"

"Yeah?"

I might have slept for six hours, but I'm as tired and lost and hollowed out as I was before locking myself into the secret bedroom. I'm fragile. A husk. The hurricane winds have subsided, but still there is the storm, the *tormenta*.

I want to ask him if his mother is happy. Does Maureen feel bitter and rudderless or does it feel like her life is *hers* again? Is she maybe even happier now than she was when she was married to Solly?

Right then a loud buzzing noise comes from the metal door. I look at the camera. Its lens is trained on me. From a speaker I hear Maria Josephina's voice.

"Would you like to come inside? Have something to drink?"

I could weep from the kindness of this invitation. I fear I might choke on my answer so instead I just reach for the door handle and push. It opens.

I turn back to Malcolm. "Never mind," I tell him. "I'm sorry."

"You really don't need to apologize," he says.

MARIA JOSEPHINA STANDS waiting for me. She is wearing that sheer black cover-up which hides a tiny black string bikini. I can't help but notice her taking in my bare feet, my pajama pants, my chef's coat.

I look around at the large deck with the infinity pool, a modern open living room and enormous kitchen with state-of-the-art stainless steel appliances.

When Peter and I first moved in together, combining our two modest incomes to rent the duplex in West Hollywood, I couldn't believe our good fortune. We had one and a half bathrooms! A guest room! When friends would come over we'd proudly give them a tour of our apartment that lasted all of a minute. But since I'd moved from a studio, and Peter had moved from a three-bedroom bungalow with four roommates, we felt flush. This was luxury living. Then we got married and starting thinking about having a kid and Peter started making more money and we bought our three-bedroom house with the backyard with fruit trees and it became hard to fathom how we ever coexisted happily in that tiny duplex.

This is how it feels seeing the inside of Maria Josephina's villa. I'd thought Villa Azul Paraiso was the apex of luxury living, but that is only because I hadn't yet stood on the deck of Villa Perfect.

She calls out something in Spanish to the woman in the kitchen who doesn't wear a white button-up coat; she wears all black, a T-shirt and cropped pants. At first I'm not sure who this woman is—a domestic worker, a friend, a sister—but then she responds with *"Sí, señora."*

We sit at a glass table under a canvas umbrella. The infinity pool makes a hypnotic lapping sound in the background. The woman from the kitchen appears with a bottle of sparkling water and a bottle of white wine on a tray. She pours both of us a glass of each.

"Jenna. Are you okay? Most people, they are not going outside of their homes since the events in town. Do you know about this?"

"Yes," I say. "My daughter was at the club the night of the kidnapping, but she left before it happened. And we don't know much about what's going on now because our villa is without internet connection."

"Ours, too," she says.

"I'm supposed to go home tomorrow. But I want to leave today. And the airport is still closed."

"Is it?"

"There's no other way for me to leave."

"Why do you need to go? Do you not feel safe? It is safe here. Where your villa is and mine. It is a safe place to be."

I reach for the sparkling water and take a long drink. My throat feels thick. "It is not a safe place for *me*."

"So this is not about the events in town."

"No. This is not."

"I see."

We sit in silence for a few minutes. The pool, the ocean, the glass table—everything reflects the punishing sun.

"Thank you, Maria Josephina, for inviting me in," I say. "You have provided me sanctuary with your kindness."

"It is my pleasure." She clinks her glass against mine. "*In vino veritas, in aqua sanitas*. It is an old Latin phrase. Do you know this? It means in wine there is truth, in water there is health."

I take a long drink of the wine. It is cold and crisp and wonderful. This old Latin phrase has it all wrong. In wine there is escape. In wine there is rewritten history. In wine I am enjoying a leisurely Good Friday with a new friend I've made on my perfect vacation, an infinity pool lapping hypnotically in the background. In wine my life isn't falling apart.

And in water there are just bubbles.

I want to know how she's done it. How she's made this life

for herself. Endless sunsets and bottomless glasses of sauvignon blanc. But she hasn't asked why I've shown up at her door in a chef's coat and no shoes, so perhaps I shouldn't ask how she manages to spend her days on perpetual vacation. Better that we behave like children, engaging in parallel play, side by side, drinking our wine.

Before the silence stretches on too long, a man appears.

Is he her Roberto? His hair is also slicked back. He also wears a uniform of sorts, all black like the woman in the kitchen. Across his chest: a thick black strap. Over his shoulder: the narrow black barrel of a machine gun.

I freeze.

They speak in a rapid back-and-forth. He is agitated. She is calm.

He hands her a cell phone. She speaks into it for only a minute. She finishes with *"Sí, mi amor."*

My head is spinning. Who is this alternate universe version of Roberto? Why is he carrying a machine gun? Who is the *amor* on the other end of the phone? Wait . . . *there's cell service here?*

Maria Josephina reads my questioning face. She takes a sip of her wine and then lights a cigarette. She offers me one. I haven't smoked a cigarette since college.

I take it.

"He has a . . ." I motion to my back. For some reason it is difficult for me to say the words *machine gun.*

"Yes," she says. "For safety."

"Has it gotten that bad? You said we were safe in these villas. I thought the danger is only for the men involved in the warring drug cartels."

She takes a slow drag of her cigarette. "Yes. This is true."

"But then why does he need a machine gun?"

I know the answer to this question as soon as I've asked it.

She watches me come to an understanding.

"So . . . were you there?" I ask her. "At the club that night?"

The girl in the street told me that the kidnappers took the men but left behind the women. If her *amor* was kidnapped, then Maria Josephina was likely one of the women left behind. If her *amor* was a kidnapper, she was likely home, safely ensconced in her perfect villa, sipping her wine.

"Me? No." She shakes her head. "I was not at the club."

I take a drag of my cigarette. I don't cough, which I worried I might do. Smoking a cigarette is like riding a bike, though I haven't ridden a bike since college either.

I take another drag. I go for the smoke ring and nail it. I watch my perfect circle drift up and blow apart. Why did I stop smoking? What's the point of making all the right decisions? Has my life been better because of all of the responsible, healthy, grown-up choices I've made?

My wineglass is empty. I pick up the bottle to refill it, but the bottle is empty, too.

"The *amor* on the phone. He is . . ."

"My lover."

"Oh."

"We are not married. He has a wife. She does not live here. When he is here in Puerto Vallarta we are together. When he is not I am on my own. Free. It is a good life. It is the life that is best for me."

"It sounds . . . complicated."

"No. It is very simple. Marriage," she says. "Now, *that* is complicated."

"*Very* complicated."

"And this is why you are here? Why you do not feel safe in your villa? This is because of your husband? Because of your marriage?"

"My husband is having an affair." This is now the second time I have said this sentence out loud and it still feels as if I were speaking a line of dialogue, saying something that someone else has written for me to say. Even my voice doesn't sound like my own as I say it.

"So he has a lover?"

"Yes. But it's different. We don't have an understanding. In fact, our understanding is that we're faithful to each other. Infidelity is for other people. Not for us."

"So you worry that your husband does not love you? That he loves this other woman only?"

"No. In fact, I think things are over between them. And I do believe Peter loves me. I do."

The bottle is empty but Maria Josephina reaches for it anyway and holds it upside down over her wineglass. A few drops pour out. She drinks them. We sit staring out at the ocean.

"I suppose it is hard for you to understand why I'd be so upset," I say.

"No," she says. "It is not. Like we agreed: marriage is complicated."

"Yes, it is."

"But I wonder if you are living a good life. If you are happy. If you are living the life that is best for you."

"I . . . don't know."

"JENNA?"

It's Peter. What is he doing here? Did Malcolm tell him where to find me? I thought Malcolm and I had an understanding. I thought we were friends.

"JENNA?"

He's walking up the beach in his shorts and a misbuttoned white shirt, hands to his mouth in an effort to amplify his voice, which grows more frantic with each repetition of my name.

"JENNA?"

He reminds me of Tom Hanks in *Castaway* with his scraggly beard and hair. His desperation is apparent even from this distance.

"Who is this?" asks Maria Josephina. "Is this your husband?"

I sit back a little farther in my chair. I wish I had her large sunglasses to hide behind.

He stops and stares up at Villa Perfect. He puts his hand to his eyes to shield them from the sun. He is trying to decide if it's me next to this glamorous woman in her sheer black cover-up on the deck by this infinity pool.

"JENNA?" he calls.

"JENNA!" He starts waving frantically.

I take a drag of my cigarette. He drops his hands to his sides and cocks his head. If he were in a cartoon, the word balloon above him would read:

> That can't be Jenna because that woman is smoking a cigarette.
>
> Jenna doesn't smoke.

And my word balloon would say:

> Fuck you, Peter. Maybe you don't know every single thing about me.
>
> Maybe I keep secrets, too.

"JENNA!"

I take another drag.

"Your husband," says Maria Josephina. "He is very excited to see you."

"My husband knows he is in trouble," I say.

"JENNA!"

"Is he a bad husband?" she asks.

"No. Not entirely."

"JENNA!" Peter shouts. "PLEASE COME DOWN HERE AND TALK TO ME!"

"And you? You are a good wife?"

"JENNA! PLEASE! I NEED TO TALK TO YOU!"

Am I a good wife? I have never cheated on Peter. When one is called upon to give an account of her role in a marriage, that fact matters. I have loved him—sometimes more, sometimes less—for nearly twenty years. I have never told him the big sorts of lies, only the small ones we all tell to make everything run more smoothly. I have faults; that's for certain. I can insist on things done my way. I am not always patient. I am sometimes petty. I have shunned enough embraces that he has grown cautious in how and when he reaches for me. I can be anxious, worried. I sense storms on calm horizons. But I have, above all else, believed in the certainty of our marriage.

Am I a good wife?

"I think so," I say. "I've tried to be."

"JENNA! PLEASE!"

"He must love you very much. Why else would he shout like this?"

"JENNA!"

"He's humiliated me. And maybe even worse, he's gaslighted me."

"*Gaslighted?* What does this mean?"

"JENNA!"

"He has let me think I'm crazy. That I imagine things."

"Do you imagine things?"

"JENNA! PLEASE!"

"Yes, but sometimes what I imagine is true."

"JENNA!"

Maria Josephina calls out something to the woman in the

kitchen. She brings a tray with another bottle of wine and fresh wineglasses, which are unnecessary because the bottle is the same vintage we've already been drinking.

"JENNA! PLEASE!"

I take the final, delicious drag of my cigarette. "He's been lying to me for months. He let me believe it was his best friend who was having the affair."

"It is not good to lie about these things. It is much better to live out in the open."

Peter drops to his knees in the sand. "JENNA! COME DOWN HERE AND TALK TO ME. PLEASE!"

Maria Josephina watches him, laughing a little to herself. "This is why I do not have a husband."

I look at Peter. Prostrating himself before me. Alone on the beach in his misery.

"JUST COME DOWN AND TALK TO ME."

"I'll be fifty soon," I say.

"Yes. You tell me this already. And I tell you that this is not the end of living. It is not too late to have the life you deserve. To keep climbing the ladder like in the statue on the Malecon. I am fifty-five. And still, I climb."

"JENNA!"

"Twenty years," I say. "It's a long time to be with one person."

"It is an accomplishment. Or is it more like a sentence? I do not know . . . perhaps it is both."

"I WON'T LEAVE UNTIL YOU COME DOWN HERE."

"Would you like some more?" she asks me, managing the bottle in one hand and the burned-down butt of her cigarette in the other.

"PLEASE!"

I look at the bottle and at my empty glass and then I look out at Peter. He's shifted to a sitting position. He's settling in. He isn't going anywhere.

"I don't know what to do."

She pours herself some wine. "These are big questions."

"JENNA!"

"I'll take some more. Thank you." She refills my glass. "And another cigarette."

She lights mine and then lights one for herself.

I am a planner. I do my research. I think long and hard about every choice, I examine every option. I like to have all the facts at my disposal. Even the hidden ones. I try to prepare for the unexpected. And yet, I have absolutely no idea what to do next.

"I love him," I say. "But . . . I don't know if I can forgive him for betraying me in this way."

"You do not decide today," she says. "You take your time. And when you are ready, you decide what is right for you. What it is that *you* want."

"JENNA!"

"He will apologize," she says. "Many times over and then again. This I can tell. And you will decide if this is enough. If you are getting what you need from this desperate man on the beach. If you are living the life that is best for you."

I look down at Peter. He sees me looking at him and he makes a move to stand, he is hopeful, but then I turn back to my friend. Back to my wineglass.

"PLEASE," he calls out, his voice weakening as he collapses back into the sand.

SATURDAY

I wake up on what is supposed to be my final morning in Puerto Vallarta not in Puerto Vallarta at all, but rather in Nuevo Vallarta, about twenty-five miles to the north. Nuevo Vallarta is a planned resort community, a made-up place, an ersatz Mexico for tourists who want no part of the real thing. It is a place I had no interest in going, until I found myself desperate for somewhere to go. I wake up to the news that the airport is still closed.

I am in a hotel that is one of five on a vast property of interconnected fake waterways, chain restaurants, golf courses designed by celebrities and twenty-seven pools that stretch out like strands of DNA.

My view is not of the Bay of Banderas but of this fake paradise.

Here in Nuevo Vallarta nobody knows about the kidnapping or the violence or the closed-off roads. Or if anyone knows, they do a fine job of acting as if nothing at all has happened. Nuevo Vallarta is in another state of mind as well as one of geographic boundary—it is not in the state of Jalisco, but in a state called Nayarit.

To get here took some planning. I do not mean tracking hurricane websites or watching for airfare sales or negotiating with a rental company that represents the property interests of an old couple in Wyoming. Because many of the roads were still blocked on Friday and because there were no taxis willing to find a creative way to reach this vacationers' paradise, Maria Josephina offered the services of her version of Roberto.

"Do not worry," she told me. "He will get you there safely."

Clementine didn't complain about leaving the villa. She loves our hotel. The wi-fi is stellar. She's been on FaceTime with Sean for most of the time we've been here. It even works down by the nearest chain of pools.

She has not asked any questions about why we made the change. She didn't even ask about our machine-gun-toting escort out of town. I'm not sure what Peter said to her during the hours I was gone, nor am I sure what she makes of the fact that we left her father behind with the Solomons. One thing I know about teenagers is that very little of their parents' lives seeps into their consciousness. They are first and foremost narcissists. This is okay. It's what it means to be sixteen. And for now, I'm grateful that she just seems content to have uninterrupted service and a room number to which she can charge a cheeseburger or a Cobb salad because she's *so over* Mexican food.

Last night, I asked her, from my bed on the opposite side of our shared room, if there was anything she wanted to talk about. If she had any questions.

"Nah. I'm good."

"Are you sure?"

"Yes, Mother. I'm sure," she said. And then: "I want to respect your privacy."

One thing Clementine was right about: My problem is that I don't know anything about anything. But telling her this, affirming her worst appraisal of me, I knew, was not what she needed to hear in this moment.

She went back to her phone. I opened my computer and pulled up the app that lets me read her texts, and then, with a swift click, I deleted it.

Then I opened the file for my book, the one with no title, the one in the middle of which I am desperately stuck. It sprang to life. I scrolled through pages and pages of writing I've spent the better part of the last two years on.

It may be that the book I've been struggling to finish is simply no good. I may have done it all wrong, made all the wrong choices. Perhaps, I finally realized, there is no way out of this thicket; perhaps the only way forward is to start over again from the very beginning.

AFTER FINISHING the second bottle of wine and a third cigarette on the deck with Maria Josephina I had gone down to the beach to talk to Peter. He rose from the sand when he saw me, at first reaching his arms out and then, realizing I was time zones away from allowing an embrace, he shoved his hands deep into his pockets.

"Jenna . . . I don't know what to say except that I love you and I'm sorry."

"I had fucking cancer."

"Jenna. Come on."

"Come on?"

"I know you had cancer. But it was stage one. You're fine now. Please don't make me out to be the guy who cheated on his sick wife."

"Are you really trying to tell me what to do? Or how to feel?"

"Jenna."

"Peter."

"I'm sorry."

"Stop saying that."

"But I *am* sorry. God, I am so, so sorry. This isn't who I am."

"So you *aren't* the guy who cheated on his sick wife?"

"Jenna. Please. It's far more complicated than that. I made a mistake. You know this isn't who I am. This isn't who *we* are."

"*We?* Please don't blame me, Peter."

"I'm not. I'm just . . . Come on, you know me, even if I can hardly recognize myself. It's one of the reasons I love and need you like I do."

A cloud passed in front of the sun and with it, a long silence. In this diffused light everything around and between us felt dialed down a half notch.

I walked to the water's edge. Peter followed. We stood side by side, letting our feet get wet.

"There's a billboard I pass every day on my way to the shop," he said finally. "On the corner of Pico and Sixteenth. For the Church of Scientology. It's black with white lettering and all it says is HOW WELL DO YOU KNOW YOURSELF?"

"I've driven by it, too. Because I also go into the shop. All the time."

"I know. Of course I know. I know the important role you play in my life, in the business, in our family, in everything. I don't question that. I really don't. But what I'm trying to say, Jen, is that when I've passed that sign these last few months I've looked up at it and thought: *I don't know myself very well at all.*"

"Huh. When I pass it I think: *What a bunch of fucking weirdos.*"

He moved his hand as if to touch my shoulder, then thought better of it and pulled it back again. "Jenna, this had nothing to do with love and everything to do with me being an idiot and an asshole."

"So you still love me?" I asked.

"Of course I love you."

"Then you will do what I'm about to ask you to do."

For the first time, he smiled. When they play, boys like to smash, crush and kill, and then they grow into men who want to fix things. To take action. To *do* something. "Anything at all," Peter said. "You name it."

"Go back to Villa Azul Paraiso. Pack my suitcase. Bring it here, to me, along with our daughter and her suitcase."

"Jenna."

"Do not pack yours. You will not be coming with us."

"Jenna. Please."

I looked back up to the deck of Maria Josephina's perfect villa. The table was empty.

"What can I do to make this right?"

I looked up to the infinity pool. To the floor of rooms above.

To the roof. To the tops of the palm trees. The clouds had passed and I looked up into the fierce, blazing sun.

"I don't know what you can do, Peter. Or if there's anything to be done. I don't know what I want. I don't know what happens next."

"Jenna."

"All I know is that I don't need to decide today."

I AM SITTING by the pool. In a new cover-up I purchased in one of the hotel's many gift shops. A margarita in my hand. It is not as good as Roberto's margarita, and it cost nearly fifteen dollars, but it will do. Clementine has gone back to our room. When I complained about her spending too much time indoors on her phone instead of soaking up what I pray will be our final day of sun she said, "Look at me. Look at my skin. Don't you think I've had enough sun? Haven't we all had enough sun already?"

"Mrs. Carlson?"

I open my eyes and push my sunglasses on top of my head. It's Diego, from the concierge desk. I have already asked him not to call me Mrs. Carlson.

"It's Jenna," I remind him.

"Jenna," he repeats. He is wearing a floral, short-sleeved button-down shirt. Tan and pale blue. If it wasn't the same shirt that every other person who works for this hotel is wearing you could mistake him for a fellow vacationer. "I have for you some pleasant news."

"I could use some pleasant news."

"The airport. It will be open tomorrow. Easter Sunday. You

are confirmed on a three o'clock flight to Los Angeles. You and your family."

"Thank you, Diego."

"Can I do for you anything else?"

"No, that's all. Thank you so much."

He stands by my chair. I take the last sip of my margarita. I put down the glass and settle back into my lounger. I lower my sunglasses and close my eyes. I can feel him still standing by my side. Is he so attentive because it was Maria Josephina who called to arrange our stay? Does her association with her lover wield power here in Nuevo Vallarta? He remains standing next to me for a few more seconds before he finally takes my empty glass and walks away.

A tip.

Dammit.

He was waiting for a tip. And I'm the stupid American who didn't think to give him one. I've spent all week having every need catered to, having the staff go so far as to invite me into the sanctuary of their temporary marital bed, and I never once tipped them because in a luxury villa rental, my research told me, it is customary to wait until the end of your stay. Fortunately, I know that before he leaves Villa Azul Paraiso, Solly will tip and tip generously, enough to cover all of us.

I pick up my phone. There are eleven missed calls and too many texts from Peter to count. I don't want to talk to him. I don't want to hear his voice or see his face or read the words he has typed with his thumbs. I want to sit out here alone in the abundant sunshine and enjoy the last day of a vacation I worked so hard to put together; a vacation that is ending in a way and in a location that, despite my careful planning and research, I could never have anticipated.

Or perhaps I could have anticipated this ending. Perhaps I *should* have anticipated this ending. How did I not see this coming? Wait . . . *didn't* I see this coming? Didn't I wonder about Gavriella? About the attention this young and beautiful woman paid to my husband? Didn't I ask him about his relationship with her? And didn't he tell me I worry too much? That I look in the wrong places?

I get up and rotate my lounger 180 degrees. I turn my back to the sun so that it will fall instead on my outstretched legs. I turn from the view of the pool and the pristine beach in the distance so that I am facing the chain of buildings in which there are thousands of soulless rooms occupied by thousands of people who have come to this fake paradise to escape the monotony of their regular lives, or to celebrate a special occasion, or perhaps to breathe new life into something that is dying.

I told Peter not to blame me, but I wonder how much of this really *is* my fault. What could I have done differently? Can I bear some responsibility and also be a victim?

I didn't plant the devil grass, neither of us did, but we let it spread untended.

What do I do now? What do we do next?

I do not know. I do not know if we can weather this *tormenta*.

All our minutes are high-value minutes. I have a keener sense now, since that first meeting with my doctor, that I do not want to waste them. I do not know if I want to spend them with a man who has betrayed me. I do not know if I want to spend them in the constant company of Solly and Ingrid, because being married to Peter means also being forever tied to his best friend. I do not know anything about anything.

My phone buzzes in my hand.

PETER: I just want to go home.

It buzzes again.

PETER: With you.

I want to go home, too. I am ready to go home. I don't know what will happen once we get there, but I believe that home is the only place we can discover if the pieces of our lives can be put back together; if everything still fits. If maybe there's a secret room we didn't know about. A room we have left untouched, waiting to be discovered. If our home holds within it an expansive space, an astonishing surprise.

ME: We leave tomorrow.

ME: 3:00 p.m.

PETER: I'll bring the Life Savers.

EASTER SUNDAY

It is an undeniable truth that there is nothing duller than someone else's travel mishaps. But when those mishaps are encountered in an effort to escape the worst vacation in the history of vacations, perhaps they deserve to be heard.

When I say *the worst vacation in the history of vacations,* I mean to say in *my* history of vacations because I am aware that there are things worse than finding out your husband has been cheating on you. And lying about it. And pinning the transgression on his best friend of thirty-two years. And I'm open to the possibility that these worse things happened to these other people while these other people were on other vacations.

But back to *my* vacation.

When I trusted the job of packing my suitcase to my husband, who, left to his own devices, would have never unpacked in the first place, I held out no hope for expert folding. That when he took my bag out from where I'd stashed it underneath the bed he'd put the shoes in first. Or that he'd place the nice dress, the one I'd brought along for his birthday, back into the plastic wrap from the dry cleaner's to minimize wrinkling.

What I did expect, however, is that Peter would remember to take my passport and Clementine's from the drawer in the table by my bedside.

I didn't catch his oversight until this morning. And just as I realized it, Peter—in a different state to the south, inside a luxury villa on a private beach—was realizing the very same thing.

So when my hotel room phone rang I knew it was him. On the morning of any international trip the first thing we both do when we wake is double-check that we have our passports. He figured that I wouldn't pick up the cell because of the exorbitant international fees, and because I hadn't yet picked up a call from him, and so he was calling from the mustard-yellow rotary phone in the kitchen at Villa Azul Paraiso. I could picture him standing there like Richard Nixon might have—hand in pocket, head heavy with shame.

"I'm an idiot. I could bring them to the airport, but maybe it's better if you come get me here and we all go together? I think it's better that way. You and Clem shouldn't be without your passports. You can wait in the taxi. You won't see Solly and Ingrid anyway. Their flight left late last night."

"They left last night? I thought the airport wasn't opening until today."

"I guess it opened earlier than expected and a few flights made it out. They got lucky."

Of course Solly made it out on the first flight. Of course he got lucky. There is nothing at all about this that I find surprising.

"Jenna . . . I'm sorry I forgot to pack your passports. That was stupid of me. I'm so sorry. For everything."

I'm not sure how long this sort of contrition will last. It's nice, but it's not real. It's the Nuevo to the Puerto. I can see how I'd grow tired of it.

Later, as we're packing up our things, Clementine says to me, "I had a really good time, Mom. Thank you."

I wonder if this is how she will remember this vacation. As a good time. If the night of the kidnapping and our retreat to this sprawling hotel in this northern state, if her embarrassment at the way things unfolded with Malcolm, her fights with her father about entitlement, with me about intrusions into her private life: if it will fade away and that all she'll remember are the sunlit images, the photos on her phone of the beach, the pool, the house, the views.

We bring our bags down to the open lobby. This fake paradise also eschews walls. We make our way across the vast, white marble floors. There are trees inside and birds in these trees that sing. Our flip-flops slap and echo and the wheels of our suitcases make noise, too, but we are silent. We move out toward the pickup zone side by side, not speaking a word.

We drive south. Through the gaps in the buildings and the trees I see the Bay of Banderas, the water dotted with the brightly colored sails of boats taking snorkelers out on expeditions, and up in the air the multihued parachutes of adventure seekers— everyone on the hunt for a different perspective.

Back near the heart of Puerto Vallarta we slow down. It is Easter Sunday. The streets are full. Our driver isn't shy about using his horn. We wind our way through the traffic that grows thicker the nearer we draw to the main square and the Church of Our Lady of Guadalupe.

We are on a street now that runs parallel to the water; beside us, a promenade. The Malecon. Throngs of people are heading to Mass to celebrate Jesus's resurrection. Families in fancy clothes. Young friends, arm in arm. Old ladies carrying black umbrellas to shield themselves from the sun. And there are equal numbers of people who have no intention of going to church—barely clad beachgoers with towels around their necks and day drinkers holding neon, frozen cocktails. The week that follows Easter Sunday is an even busier time in Puerto Vallarta than the week that precedes it. At least that's what Roberto told me.

Rising above the crowd I see the top rungs of a ladder cast in bronze. And two figures, one in front of the other, climbing up toward a windless, cloud-scattered sky. It is the sculpture Maria Josephina told me about.

En Busca de la Razón.

Searching for Reason.

Before I can get a closer look, before I can understand if they are climbing toward or away from something, before I can see what the artist carved into the bronze slabs of their faces, how he captured their expressions, whether they climbed with fear, joy, anticipation, desperation—it is already in our rearview mirror. I turn around in my seat. I look at their backs. They each hold the ladder with only one hand. With the other they grasp at air.

We leave the town and the traffic and drive up the empty road Peter and Solly and I walked home late Wednesday night in a dazed panic, desperate to locate our children, to chase from our imaginations the unthinkable scenarios.

We make the turn onto the patchy paved street that gives way to dirt and then surrenders to jungle. We pull up in front of the entrance to Villa Azul Paraiso with its large wooden doors and park behind a minivan. Our taxi driver keeps the engine running.

I see Roberto. He's helping unload bags. A few children run in and out of the open doors. Two men take suitcases from Roberto and then wheel them inside as the women confer. Perhaps they're debating who gets the room with the volcanic tub. Maybe they'll decide to switch halfway through—that would be the fair thing to do.

Peter steps outside with his suitcase. He shakes hands with Roberto. It takes me a minute to notice the change. He is clean shaven; his vacation beard is gone.

"*Daddy!*" Clementine calls out the window.

He waves at us shyly. He looks like a stranger to me.

The men who have just arrived step back outside; each puts an arm around one of the women. They look at the exterior of Villa Azul Paraiso, nodding with satisfaction, congratulating themselves on their expert vacation planning.

Peter makes his way toward the taxi. The radio is tuned to a news station. I don't know what they're saying, but they sound calm. Gone is the hysteria, the breathlessness.

Enrique steps outside in his white zip-up coat and his slicked-back hair. He holds a tray of margaritas. He offers them to the guests. They each take one and smile.

Everyone looks happy.

MAR -- 2019